Also by Mariah Fredericks

STANDALONE NOVELS
The Lindbergh Nanny

THE JANE PRESCOTT SERIES
A Death of No Importance
Death of a New American
Death of an American Beauty
Death of a Showman

YA NOVELS
The True Meaning of Cleavage
Head Games
Crunch Time
The Girl in the Park

The
WHARTON PLOT

The
WHARTON PLOT

A Novel

Mariah Fredericks

MINOTAUR BOOKS
NEW YORK

First published in the United States by Minotaur Books, an imprint of St. Martin's Publishing Group

THE WHARTON PLOT. Copyright © 2023 by Mariah Fredericks. All rights reserved. Printed in the United States of America. For information, address St. Martin's Publishing Group, 120 Broadway, New York, NY 10271.

www.minotaurbooks.com

Designed by Gabriel Guma

Library of Congress Cataloging-in-Publication Data

Names: Fredericks, Mariah, author.
Title: The Wharton plot : a novel / Mariah Fredericks.
Description: First edition. | New York : Minotaur Books, 2024.
Identifiers: LCCN 2023038041 | ISBN 9781250827425 (hardcover) |
    ISBN 9781250827432 (ebook)
Subjects: LCSH: Wharton, Edith, 1862-1937—Fiction. | Phillips, David
    Graham, 1867-1911—Fiction. | LCGFT: Biographical fiction. | Novels.
Classification: LCC PS3606.R435 W47 2024 | DDC 813/.6—dc23/eng/20230913
LC record available at https://lccn.loc.gov/2023038041

Our books may be purchased in bulk for promotional, educational, or business use. Please contact your local bookseller or the Macmillan Corporate and Premium Sales Department at 1-800-221-7945, extension 5442, or by email at MacmillanSpecialMarkets@macmillan.com.

First Edition: 2024

10 9 8 7 6 5 4 3 2 1

For Griffin
Who has his own splendid story to tell

CHAPTER ONE

B rownell paused in apprehension. In the afternoon quiet of the Palm Garden of the Belmont Hotel, his spirits were made uneasy by the sight of Mrs. Edith Wharton. As her editor for more than two decades, he had much to say to her, none of it what she wished to hear. Publishing was a genteel endeavor; but even in the sensitive realm of words, the brute reality of numbers could intrude. As it did in the matter of royalty payments, for example, which Mrs. Wharton wished to discuss. Also in deadlines, which he was keen to address. The number of books promised them: four. The years since her last novel: three. The sales for that novel, *The Fruit of the Tree* . . . well, being a gentleman, he would set that aside. For now.

Standing by the entrance, concealed by one of the extravagant palms that gave the tearoom its theme, he watched as Mrs. Wharton summoned a waiter to complain about the temperature of the water and the freshness of the linen. But she did so with none of her usual relish, and Brownell worried that she did not look well. She was a woman who collected maladies—asthma, nausea, flu, bronchitis, hay fever—as she collected small dogs. She was now nine-and-forty, and the features that one would have called moderately appealing in her youth were tense and strained. He took in the parched skin and hollowed eyes. The auburn hair, still piled proud and abundant atop her head, showed signs of graying and brittleness. There was nothing wrong with her face, he thought, save that there was too much of it for her small, unremarkable features. The jaw was heavy, the forehead prominent. As a man, she might have managed. He had seen pictures of her as a girl. As a child, she had resembled a pinched, sickly little boy with thin lips and miserable gaze—Oliver Twist. As a young woman, at her best, a handsome, sharp-eyed rogue.

Perhaps that was why she buried herself in clothes, barricading herself in a profusion of lace and furs, pearls roped like armor around her neck and wrists, her hands sunk deep in a muff of dark mink. Even her hats had a touch of the martial to them, giving the impression of a fine, plumed helmet.

In short, a woman you did not engage lightly in battle. One might have expected a woman of wealth to embrace the call of art for art's sake, eschewing all thought of commerce, certainly any hope of financial remuneration. Mrs. Wharton, however, did not merely hope to be paid. She expected it. She expected other things as well. With her very first book, she had written them, "I daresay I have already gone beyond the limits prescribed to a new author in the expression of opinion; but since you send me the title page, I shall consider myself justified in criticizing it." Another note read simply: "Gentlemen, am I not to receive any copies of my book?"

Brownell disliked meeting with authors face-to-face, preferring the cool distance of letters, where words could be considered at length. But Scribner's had been waiting for Mrs. Wharton's words for too long, and when they heard she was coming to New York in order to sell her house in the city, a meeting was proposed. He and the magazine editor, Burlingame, had tossed a coin as to who might have the pleasure of tea with Mrs. Wharton. Brownell had lost—and so here he was.

The waiter had returned, bearing a silk tasseled pillow of blue and gold. This he set down on the floor, and a Pekingese appeared, padding on tiny unseen feet to the pillow's edge, where it was lifted, then set down. Settled on its luxurious cushion, it seemed to lie down; at least it quivered and looked lower than before. This was new. Previously, Mrs. Wharton had favored long-haired Chihuahuas. If it were possible for a breed to more closely resemble vermin, Brownell was not aware of it. The Pekingese at least had the advantage of volume, although the bright black button eyes were the only sign that it was a living thing and not a footstool.

Just then, those eyes moved in his direction; the thing seemed to pant. With the exquisite sensitivity of all pampered creatures, it sensed it was being observed. As if on cue, his mistress also looked up. Her expression told him she was aware that he had assessed her—and she was now assessing the assessment.

Bravely, he advanced. "Mrs. Wharton, my deepest apologies for being late. To atone, I bring you a gift."

Sitting down at the small table, which was laden with china and silver, he slid a red book in front of her. "The first printing of *Tales of Men and Ghosts*. We do hope you like it."

Immediately, he worried that he had overstressed the *you*, alerting Mrs. Wharton that Scribner's was less than thrilled by a collection of short stories that, in terms of content and style, bore little resemblance to *The House of Mirth*, her raging success of five years ago. When it was serialized, readers had buzzed for months over the fate of Lily Bart. Would she marry for position, for money, or for love? The public shock when the beautiful Lily destroyed herself had rivaled the clamor over the death of Little Nell.

Now Lily's creator gazed at the book over her gilt-edged Minton teacup of deep rose. Laying her gloved fingertips on the edge of the book, she opened it to the frontispiece and frowned.

Setting the cup aside, she sat the book upright and raised the cover to peer at the spine. Then she split the volume in two and inspected the typeface.

"Words fail to express how completely I don't like it. The ellipses alone. You could drive a coach and four between these dots."

He had expected this and gave her a game smile. "I should have been disappointed if you approved."

It was meant as an affectionate reference to their earlier quarrels, but the pained twitch of her mouth indicated indifference to her happiness felt all too familiar. He had heard that her marriage was in difficulties. There were rumors of her husband cavorting with young actresses, of missing funds. Even madness. There, he had doubts. Teddy Wharton was the most conventional of men, of an old Boston family, partial to dogs and golf and not much else. "Far too dull to be unstable," said Burlingame, and he, Brownell, had agreed. True, Mrs. Wharton had written to him that her husband's health claimed much of her time and energies, leaving her less opportunity to write. But he took that as a delaying tactic, much like her headaches and hay fever.

A rumble beneath the thickly carpeted floor set the silverware tinkling. Taking advantage of the diversion, he joked, "I suppose that is what comes of building a hotel directly above the subway."

"That is what comes of letting August Belmont build a hotel," she said, referring indirectly to the fact that Mr. Belmont was also the founder of the Interborough Rapid Transit Company. "As a child, I once saw his mistress in a bright yellow brougham on Fifth Avenue. My mother told me to avert my eyes." She raised an eyebrow, letting Brownell know that it was up for debate whether the formidable Lucretia Jones had been more appalled by the scandalous lady or the gaudiness of the carriage. Mrs. Jones, née Rhinelander, whose ancestor had gone riding with General Washington, had been deeply concerned by her child's passion for stories. Mrs. Wharton had told him that when young, she had to beg old brown paper wrappers from the kitchen staff to write on, as it was inconceivable that she should need writing paper beyond the stationery required for invitations and thank-you notes.

Which brought him to his first point. "We are tremendously excited about *The Custom of the Country*. A beautiful young heiress makes her way in the glittering world of aristocrats and millionaires . . . a tale only Edith Wharton could tell."

She made a vaguely pleasant hum and fed the dog a macaron. Brownell waited as she inquired if the macaron was delicious, did the dog enjoy it, would it like some more, yes, yes, she thought it *would*.

She said, "I trust that means there will be a vigorous advertising campaign."

Queen threatens pawn, he thought. *Pawn moves to protect castle.* "Difficult to say until I've seen something of the book . . ."

"But you said you were so excited."

"Any work by you, Mrs. Wharton, is cause for excitement."

"Really?" She gazed at him, as if puzzled. "I can't say I was terribly excited by the promotion for *Fruit of the Tree*. My friends wrote to me, saying they couldn't find the book anywhere."

The Fruit of the Tree. A novel about textile mills. In New England.

Heroic middle managers. Spinal injuries. Euthanasia. Response, both in-house and without, had been anemic.

She persisted, saying, "The reviews were excellent. The *Times* called it 'a powerful study in modern life.'"

The *Times* had also said "Central Incident Repels." Taking up his tea, he said carefully, "I think the exploitation of labor is perhaps not your subject. *Your* readers adore your ability to reveal the secret lives of the wealthy. You are their guide inside homes they will never enter, clothes they will never wear. They love your wit, your perception, the satirical portrait of the joys and cruelties of New York . . ."

"And I believe with the right support from Scribner's, they would love my portrait of joy and cruelty in rural New England just as much. I have another story in mind, the tale of a marriage. A poor farmer whose wife is an invalid . . ."

Rural? Farmers and invalids? *Poor* farmers and invalids? It was time, Brownell decided, to take things in hand.

"Mrs. Wharton, I feel strongly that *The Custom of the Country* should be your next book."

"How strongly?" She looked directly at him, all pretense with the dog abandoned.

". . . How?"

"Five percent more strongly than you have felt about my work in the past?"

Breathing in deeply through the nose, Brownell contemplated the number of women he knew who were familiar with the word *negotiation*, much less its practice. Then he calculated the number of women he knew who were adept at figures, followed by those who would dare bandy percentages. He came up with a very small number. One, to be precise. Unfortunately for him, that one was seated across from him, in possession of a book he wanted very badly.

Lowering his voice, he said, "A twenty percent royalty is the top market rate."

She lowered hers to match his. "There are authors who get twenty-five percent."

He smiled. Broadly and at length until his face hurt. His mind groped for a decorous response but could not overcome the hurdle of outrage that Mrs. Wharton had asked for twenty-five percent. Twenty-five percent! What did one say to that? To a woman, in a public place where expletives were impossible? By letter, he fumed, this would have been far less aggravating.

Later, he would blame that aggravation for the error he was about to make. Had he been less riled by Mrs. Wharton's regal assumptions as to her worth, he would never have called out to that man. Never invited him to join their table. Indeed, had he not turned in his chair, frantically seeking someone—anyone—on whom to focus other than the percentage- and punctuation-obsessed Mrs. Wharton, he might not have noticed the gentleman at all.

Although it was hard not to notice David Graham Phillips. The writer wore a white suit in the city in late January and sported a large chrysanthemum in his lapel. As he moved through the tearoom, several people turned to look at him and whisper—whether in recognition, admiration, or approbation, it was hard to tell. Everything in his affect proclaimed him a man of higher purpose as he weaved in and around tables, arms swinging, legs leaping one after the other, eyes fixed upon the exit. And yet he pulled up short when Brownell said, "Why, here's David Graham Phillips, if I am not mistaken!"

CHAPTER TWO

✦

M rs. Wharton at once perceived that her editor, having no answer to her request for increased royalties, wished to change
the subject. She also perceived that the man before her in the blin-
dingly white suit was not to her taste. At all. His upper lip—brutish,
clean-shaven—appalled her; the gentleman's hairless perimeter was
positively aggressive. *Adorn myself?* it seemed to say. *Sport plumage?
Make an effort at style or elegance? For what? For* you?

There was vanity here; that ridiculous suit and the luxuriant
sheen of his black hair told her so. His gaze, blue eyes slightly narrowed, invited, nay, insisted on the adjectives *piercing* or *keen.* The
cleft in the pugnacious chin—obvious. The way he stood, restless,
hands tensing to suggest fists, imitative of boxers, whom he no doubt
affected to admire. As he gave her the briefest glance, then looked
back to Brownell, she sensed his resentment as you would an odor.

She gathered from the male chatter that at one time Mr. Brownell and Mr. Phillips had both worked for the *New York World*. And that Mr. Brownell admired Mr. Phillips's articles in *The Sun*. Even more, he admired Mr. Phillips's novels, which he called "courageous" and "uniquely American." Mr. Phillips claimed to regret that Mr. Brownell was no longer with *The Nation*.

Casting an expansive hand in her direction, Brownell said, "Ah, but at *The Nation*, I would never have had the chance to work with Mrs. Edith Wharton."

It was the cue for deference, and she waited. At her ankles, she felt the brush of fur; Choumai in search of food.

Mr. Phillips grunted, "Well, that's true enough."

From this, Edith understood the following: Mr. Phillips knew her work and did not admire it. She was a woman, which he also did not admire. Further still, an *old* woman, whose age demanded he make a show of manners he no doubt found insulting to his *authentic being*.

Peering at the gentleman's lapel, she remarked as if she had just noticed, "A chry-*san*-themum."

Knowing an opening salvo when he heard it, Brownell said hastily, "Mr. Phillips is considered one of America's leading novelists."

"The," Mr. Phillips corrected him.

Brows raised to her hairline, Edith marveled. *The? The* leading American writer. Not James, not Dreiser, not Twain—although Twain had just died—*certainly* not she. And to insist upon it. *No, no, not* one of, *old chap*—the.

The! She repeated the word to herself until it rang with absurdity. Phillips added, "By H. L. Mencken at any rate."

Sighing, she said, "Well, Mr. Mencken," and plucked a champagne wafer from Brownell's plate and dropped it to the dog below.

But she felt Brownell's anxiety. For whatever reason, the editor wished to further his acquaintance with Mr. Phillips and he wanted her help in doing it.

She gestured to the vacant chair. "Won't you join us, Mr. Phillips?"

From Brownell, a waft of gratitude; from Mr. Phillips, condescension. Even the way he pulled out his chair was grudging, and she longed to say, *Oh, please don't if it hurts you so.*

But decades ago, as a newly made matron, she had applied herself to the art of that particularly bland form of charm known as pleasantness. In parlor after parlor, dinner after dinner, she had murmured agreeably, asking only those questions that would allow the other person to flatter themselves. And while it had been many years, she could still discipline her features and voice in that style—blank yet ardently attentive—and she did so now, asking, "Are you also with Scribner's?"

"Appleton."

"An excellent house. And—forgive me, I've been abroad—I'm not familiar with your work."

Brownell said, "Perhaps you recall *The Great God Success . . .* ?"

Smiling serenely, she shook her head.

"*The Plum Tree? Old Wives for New? The Grain of Dust?*" And when again she shook her head, "Surely, *The Treason of the Senate.* In the words of President Roosevelt—'Here is the man who rakes the muck!'" Brownell swung his fist with a heartiness she found unconvincing.

"Oh, dear," she asked, "what did you do to displease King Theodore the First?"

She offered this light ridicule as she would insist that her guest take the last strawberry. The president was a personal friend; he had recently visited her in Paris. But she wished to show herself as someone who could laugh at those in her own caste.

Flinging one leg across the other, Mr. Phillips said, "I told the truth, Mrs. Wharton."

"The *truth*," she echoed as if amazed.

He heard the mockery and his expression hardened. "Yes, the truth, Mrs. Wharton. About how this nation's government is corrupted by money. About the hire and salary of the people's representatives by big business. Aristocracy has no place in a republic."

Edith was aware that many people had these views. She was also aware that these views did not interest her. At least not enough to be lectured by Mr. Phillips.

But he had more to say.

"I told the *truth*, Mrs. Wharton, about the stranglehold on our economy held by a parasitic class that does nothing, produces nothing except its own doodlewit descendants who will, like their forebears, simply *exist* on inherited wealth."

A great slam of his index finger on the end of the table to punctuate the point. Edith looked to Brownell; unless she was mistaken, she had just been called a doodlewit. Did he care to comment? Brownell, intent on splintering a meringue with his fork, did not.

She asked, "And these . . . parasites, are they the subject of your novels?"

"They're the subject of most novels these days, Mrs. Wharton." The legs unfurled and he turned to face her. "So many happy, silly stories about people tootling around in automobiles from one fussy house to the next, one showy entertainment after another. Dressing, chattering, playing at love. Those books are popular, I'll grant you that. But that kind of story doesn't make a bit of difference to the lives of real Americans."

He was so obtuse, she found it difficult to know: *Did* he understand that this could be construed as a criticism of her work? Her life and self? (She adored motorcars and could still remember the exhilarating stench of India rubber of her very first, a cream-colored Panhard et Levassor.)

She was pondering her response when Brownell stepped in, saying, "I actually feel Mr. Phillips's novels have something in common with yours, Mrs. Wharton, in the subject of the contemporary American woman, the, ah, perils of not knowing . . ."

Edith was about to disagree when Mr. Phillips laughed. "Mrs. Wharton hardly writes about the real American woman."

She paused. Gathered herself. "I don't?"

His head reared back in surprise. "A woman of your means? Who spends so much time abroad? What could you possibly know about the American woman of today?"

"But *you* understand," she said acidly. "You, Mr. Phillips, understand this singular creature, the American woman of today. The real American woman."

"I think so, yes."

"You understand her thoughts and feelings. The world in which she finds herself, the difficulties . . ."

"Well, I think you and I might define those *difficulties* differently, Mrs. Wharton. I can accept that in America, most novels are written about women, for women—"

"Magnanimous."

"—but so many of these novels fail to tell women the truth they so badly need to hear. They perpetuate falsehoods, build up their illusions. No woman on earth has been so ridiculously deceived as to herself and so spoiled as the American woman. The worst of it is, she's bringing the American man down with her. Did you know that the rate of divorce in America is now two times that of the rest of the Christian world?"

Like a prosecutor, he leaned forward, and for an ugly moment, Edith fancied he had read the gossip about her own marriage.

She said, "Perhaps American women have higher standards."

"Higher standards, Mrs. Wharton, or *appetite*?" The legs re-crossed. The fingers drummed upon the linen. "There is a certain kind of woman who toils not, neither does she spin. But she consumes, Mrs. Wharton, oh, does she. I tell you, a man is lost forever if he falls into the hands of a luxury-loving woman."

Folding a piece of candied lemon peel into her mouth, Edith nodded: *Go on.*

"While her husband labors, she spends. But not on the house that they share, not on the meals she provides him, not even on herself, at least not the part of her that a husband cares about. She grows fat. Slatternly. Rather than have children, she advances herself in society. She cultivates the art of leisure, drifting from one diversion to the next. Fashionable, ornamental, she seeks pleasure in New York, then pleasure in Europe. And lest anyone think her a mere sloth, she dignifies her indolence with nonstop fiddle-faddle about culture and *passion*. When what she really means is consumption."

What a joy you must be to live with, she thought. "Tell me, Mr. Phillips, does your wife enjoy your novels?"

She was pleased to see him retreat from the edge of the table. "I am unmarried. I work too much to have time for a wife."

"Yes," she said. "That *must* be the reason."

But it was a perfunctory sally; his spleen and determination to give offense had made her tired. She gave him her profile, her customary dismissal with bores.

Then she heard him say, "But you know this, Mrs. Wharton. Is not Lily Bart destroyed by her love of luxury? Are we not meant to feel that if she had given herself to Selden, a man of modest means, they might have been happy? I wish . . ."

Suddenly he seemed to be talking to her, rather than at her. Curious, she said, "Yes?"

"I wish you had given Lily courage. How much more powerful if she had made her choice—yes to love or yes to luxury—rather than drifting into self-destruction."

There was something wistful in his voice that, despite the criticism, drew her to ask, "And is that the *truth*, Mr. Phillips? Do you find that people are often courageous? Able to break the rules of their world and come through unscathed?"

For the first time, his eyes were open, free of scorn. "I admit, it's a rare thing to be able to burn one's spiritual bridges. But only love gives you the power to say farewell to your old existence and to take flight toward a new one."

Her first thought was *What absolute twaddle.* Her second was *Why did you not begin with this? I might have liked you better.*

Mr. Phillips, she wondered, *can it be you are in love?*

She felt Brownell was agitated. Well, he had brought this hideous man to her; let him suffer. Irritably, she turned to find the waiter; the table needed clearing. She listened as Brownell insisted they not keep Mr. Phillips any longer. Also that it had been a very great pleasure to see him again.

Then, almost shyly, Brownell said to Phillips, "One hears rumors that your next book is soon upon us. May I know the title?"

"It's called *Susan Lenox: Her Fall and Rise.* Taken me ten years to write, and almost as long to get the cowards at Appleton to publish. The public will not soon forgive me for this one." He grinned as if the prospect of popular loathing appealed to him.

"Explosive stuff, eh?" guessed Brownell.

"Let's just say if they're not scared now—they should be."

Pushing back the chair as if it were a dog that had gotten too familiar, he nodded curtly to Brownell and then to her, saying, "Mrs. Wharton, a pleasure."

She returned the pleasantry, matching his tone precisely. She and Brownell waited until Mr. Phillips had passed through the doors of the tearoom, staying silent as they imagined him racing through the vast Belmont lobby, shoving his way through its doors, and hurtling onto Park Avenue. Far below, the subway came and went, causing the table to tremble. Placing one hand gently on the surface, she took up the tongs and gave a sugar cube to Choumai.

"Forgive me," said Brownell.

". . . at some point. Perhaps next year. Around Easter."

"I didn't realize his views on women were so emphatic."

"And so *ignorant*!" She massaged her temples, then gave it up. What she needed was a cigarette.

She asked, "Are you trying to lure him to Scribner's?"

"He sells very well," said Brownell.

Rationally, she knew Brownell's talk of sales was not intended as an insult; she took it as one anyway. The ranting, successful, oh-so-American Mr. Phillips had left her with the feeling she often had in this country: of being profoundly inadequate and unfairly disdained, both abused and deserving of abuse. Looking at Brownell, she recalled his intense gaze upon her when he first entered the room, the way he examined her as if she were a manuscript. Was she to his liking? Perhaps she was too old-fashioned. Ridiculous, passé. Lacking the dash and energy—the *modernity*—of a David Graham Phillips.

Hearing shouting and the roar of falling stone, she glanced out the window to Forty-Second Street. It was an unlovely sight. Almost a decade earlier, it had been decided that old Cornelius Vanderbilt's Grand Central Depot no longer served. With twenty million passengers in a single year, the station was judged to be filthy, overcrowded, even dangerous. So the old depot would be destroyed even as the new terminal was raised in its place. No more steam—all must be electric! Ever since then, they had been tearing up the street, blasting into bedrock, slapping tracks here, there, and everywhere. For years, they had promised a marvel. From what Edith could see, they had achieved only mess.

Hating everything, she reached down for Choumai. But the traitorous creature had sensed her mood and retreated under Brownell's chair. The table was cleared; there was nothing left with which to find fault. Still, she observed, "I've had better food at a French provincial railway station."

"When do you return to Paris?" Brownell asked.

"We are awaiting my husband's physician, Dr. Kinnicutt. He arrives from Massachusetts tomorrow. Mr. Wharton is setting off on a world tour; he yearns to see California. But I would like his doctor to see him before he goes. Mr. Wharton has had health difficulties. I think I wrote you in my last letter."

Brownell murmured sympathetically. "What do the doctors say?"

She attempted a laugh. "Which one? I could write a Molière play on specialists. This one says neurasthenia. That one Riggs' disease. It's senile decay. No, it's gout of the head. Then again, perhaps it's toothache. But Mr. Wharton's sister places great faith in Dr. Kinnicutt, and so it is to him I must appeal." What she did not say was that Nannie Wharton, if asked, would say Teddy's only difficulty was Edith and her "extravagances." Nannie would probably enjoy Mr. Phillips's novels.

The fingers of her right hand ached; she realized that she had been crushing them within the dark cocoon of mink in her lap. She longed to say something banal. Or literary. Something to prove that she was in control of her faculties. But her mind was fogged with misery. That was just one of the awful things about her situation. It made her mute. Not even mute, for she had nothing to say. Her mind was empty. There were days when she opened her eyes in the morning and was not certain she even existed.

Briskly folding up her linen napkin, she revived herself with anger. How dare Brownell compare her to that repugnant man. How dare he say they had subjects in common. His skittish half-reference to the "perils of not knowing." How coy. How insufferably—

Another memory came, sinuous and unstoppable: the warmth of breath in her coiled hair as he whispered, "*That's* something you know nothing about."

Words spoken by a very different man under very different circumstances. Oddly, David Graham Phillips looked a bit like him. The commanding blue eyes. The flower in his buttonhole. The certainty and vigor as he demanded, "What could you possibly know about the American woman of today?"

To console herself, she seized on the most obviously ridiculous thing about Mr. Phillips: a *chrysanthemum*. In winter, for heaven's sake. Did he know its symbolism? A heart left in desolation.

She highly doubted it.

CHAPTER THREE

As he gave Mrs. Wharton time to collect herself, Brownell was reminded of the most astonishing rumor he had heard concerning the Whartons: that Mrs. Wharton had taken a lover.

It seemed unlikely. The woman was nearly half a century old and had never seemed in any way inclined toward that sort of thing, preferring to surround herself with men who for various and discreet reasons had never married. True, she had seemed moved by Phillips's earnest talk of love and breaking free. But now, looking at her creased, careworn face, Brownell could not credit it. This was a woman drained, not fulfilled.

He felt a soft, rustling presence; the Pekingese was nuzzling his ankle. Withdrawing his feet with as much tact as possible, Brownell said, "This little fellow is a change."

"I am in the mood for change," she said quietly.

"Yes, but . . . *das Kind mit dem Bade ausschütten.*"

He had spoken quickly, and her German was rusty.

"Babies and bathwater," he explained. "Don't throw them out together."

"I am not ending my life in America," she assured him. "Merely selling a house in New York."

"But don't abandon New York as your subject," he said. "If people want stories of Americans abroad"—*or in the wilds of Massachusetts*, he thought—"let them read Henry James."

"I do detest it when people call me the female Henry James."

"Better surely than when they called you the male Henry James," he said and was pleased when it raised a faint smile.

The train clattered below them, this time at high speed, causing the lid of the porcelain teapot to rattle. The sugar shifted in its Meissen bowl like sand. The silverware jumped. Moving gingerly in her chair, Edith wondered how anyone lived in this appalling city. How were their nerves not severed and jangling like violin strings pulled to the breaking point? How were their brains not scrambled, their bodies exhausted? The *noise* alone. In the streets, people, horses, cars, trucks, so many and so crammed, one was left to pick one's way through fearfully on foot, praying not to be in the way should something suddenly lurch forward without reason.

The city of her childhood had been balanced. So many homes, so many people, room enough that everyone might occupy their own small space in peace. But the number of people in New York had exploded since then from a sedate million or so to five million. All pace and proportion had been destroyed. Instead *growth*, rampant and indiscriminate. You saw it in the multitude of redbrick buildings, cheaply built and already decaying. The steel, vast brute girders slammed every which way—horizontal, perpendicular—the dripping skeletal supports for elevated trains and the first stark outlines of ever taller, ever uglier buildings. It made one feel as if one were living in a factory, not a city.

And the *wires*, everywhere wires—electric wires, telegraph wires, flung across the city like black spittle. *Oh, we must all be connected*, insisted the great minds. Leaving her to ask, *Truly, must we? Does it bring happiness, being shoved in all together, connection without discernment? Connection without choice?*

The busy, busy Mr. Phillips might say this was progress. But was it progress, she wondered, a city so chaotic anything might happen to anyone and no one would take the slightest notice?

"Do New York," Henry James had commanded. But this had never been a place where she heard her own mind, for all that her mind conjured visions of it that people took for truth. She couldn't bear to tell the excellent Mr. Brownell that she feared writing about New York because she had lost the feel of it. It had grown beyond her.

She had, in her fragile chair of the Palm Garden, worked herself into a fury. Her anger sluggishly churned in her stomach like a heavy meal, until she felt disgusted with herself. She was old and, worse than old, ridiculous.

"Forgive me, Mr. Brownell. I seem to be impossible these days. You shall have your book, I promise."

"And shall it be a story of New York?"

His tone was gentle, cajoling, and she smiled, even as she thought, *What on earth would that* be? It was impossible now to see New York as anything other than something always becoming something else. The train hurtled through once again, its rumble seeming to say, *This is the city now, but soon we will be bigger, noisier, more crowded. Love nothing, attach your affections to no street, no building nor park, for we will knock it over in an instant and rebuild.* Brutality masked as dynamism. *Why*, she wanted to ask the most patient Brownell, *would you want a story about that?*

At her feet, Choumai was restless. Gathering him on to her lap, she said she would try.

Appeased, Brownell inquired as to her plans. Three works of Millet were on view at the American Art Galleries—did that interest her? At Carnegie Hall, the violinist Mischa Elman was giving a recital—that could be charming. Grace Vanderbilt was giving a dinner dance—no doubt she would attend.

"No doubt I shall *not* attend," she corrected. "Grace Vanderbilt's house is a Thermopylae of bad taste." In a gentler vein, she added, "But I am going to Alice Vanderbilt's musicale this evening. Caruso and Miss Emmy Destinn are to perform. Tomorrow is my birthday." She waved off his congratulations. "It is a well-worn tradition, it requires no great celebration."

"Nonetheless, I wish you many happy returns," said Brownell.

He was pleased at having rounded off a difficult meeting with emollient pleasantries and was preparing his farewell when Mrs. Wharton said suddenly, "As a matter of fact, I shall be seeing Mr. James during my stay."

". . . Oh?"

"As well as Walter Berry and Morton Fullerton. I wrote you about Mr. Fullerton—he's a journalist, very good on Paris. I've asked them to dine with me here at the Belmont."

Brownell kept his face composed, even as he remembered that Walter Berry was an old friend of Mrs. Wharton's—and one of the names whispered by those who accused her of having a lover. "Quite the gathering of minds."

"The best minds I know. I . . ." Abstracted, she patted the little dog on her lap. "I have a question I wish to put to them."

"Matter of life and death, eh?"

He spoke in jest, expecting levity in return. But Mrs. Wharton's expression remained serious.

"Perhaps."

As Mrs. Wharton described her dinner plans, David Graham Phillips was charging down Park Avenue. He had stayed at the hotel longer than he meant to, and now he was late. Not for any particular person or event; he was simply not where he wanted to be and had not done all that he wanted to do that day. Leaving the Belmont, he had considered taking the subway for the sake of speed. But it was only just over a mile to his apartment near Gramercy Park, and whenever possible, he preferred to walk. Once you became dependent on motorized transport, you lost all memory of the body's capabilities. Then you lost the capabilities themselves. You became an inert . . . thing to be carted around, pushed whatever way they wanted you to go.

Slowing, he reviewed that last thought. It was limp; why? *Thing* was wrong. Sloppy. He tried it again.

You became one of the idle . . .

No, still not right.

Freedom, you lost your freedom. Yes. As this assertion came to him, he envisioned it on a piece of paper, in bold black ink, anticipated the physical release of setting it down.

As he swung onto Thirty-Fourth Street, he imagined throwing off the furred, bejeweled weight of Mrs. Wharton. The conversation had been aggravating. Worse than aggravating—pointless. And yet even now he could not *leave* it. There were things he should have said, better ways to say what he did. He should have challenged the silly woman more; if he couldn't change her mind—there wasn't much to change with that old New York type—he should have at least made her feel her limitations more keenly. Made her see that yes, she could live her life such as it was, but for God's sake, have the decency to shut up about it. His point about Lily Bart had ended up sounding like praise. Which had not been his intention.

Two people, a couple with a dog, came his way. The dog's leash and their bodies spread the length of the block, forcing Phillips to choose: He could take himself to either edge of the street, sidling along the margins, or he could hold to his path and push through, no matter if he yanked the dog off its feet or shoved the girl sideways. The girl was a noddle-head, wittering on about the sweetest little pair of court shoes, pale blue with rhinestones . . .

On *rhinestones*, he increased his speed. Alarmed, the couple shuffled right. As he passed, the dog yapped. The young lady cried, "Rude!" *The American Girl*, he thought in disgust. Her chin angled demurely into her velvet collar, her gaze lowered so she could peek up at opportune times. Not yet a "Gone to Pieces" woman, but a Parasite most certainly . . .

Then he thought of another young girl, her head low, her eyes lowered, not in flirtation but in misery, and shame curled through him. There was nothing so wrong with this girl. She was only doing what she'd been told to: bartering herself.

As always, when he got too heated, he made a mental list: everything he needed to do in the time he had left. He thought of the proofs for his next book, just delivered from the publisher. It was his masterpiece—he was certain of that. The new ending was the best thing he'd ever done.

He had written many fine books. But none of them belonged so purely to her. It was his gift—her struggle as it should be told, without all the foolish morality myths a lesser writer might impose on it. He envisioned her turning the pages, her delicate fingers on her lips as she realized . . .

He hoped he was there to see it.

As he neared home, he felt calmer. The day had not been wasted after all. He became aware that he had been walking with his fists raised, swinging his arms for greater momentum. Perhaps he had gotten a bit worked up. In the sharp, frigid air, his hands were cold stone, and he put them into his coat pockets. As he did, he felt the crumple of paper.

He had received the note that morning. It had been pushed through the letter slot. Really, he decided, it was impressive he hadn't given it a thought until now.

It read, *Tomorrow Is Your Last Day*.

It was signed David Graham Phillips.

He thought that rather funny.

CHAPTER FOUR

E dith, you've returned to us! We thought we'd lost you to the gardens of France."

As Edith offered her cheek to her hostess, Alice Vanderbilt, she tried to think if there was anything she would less rather do than dine at the Vanderbilt mansion on One West Fifty-Seventh Street. Walk on broken glass—stark naked? Reread *The Wings of the Dove*? She shivered. Alice and her late husband, Cornelius II, had built this 137-room monstrosity to outshine her sister-in-law Alva Vanderbilt's château on 660 Fifth Avenue. The vast stone entry hall offered all the warmth and comfort of a mausoleum.

Tiny, imperious Alice Vanderbilt was dressed as she had been for the last twelve years: in black velvet and ropes of pearls that reached to her knees. The former Sunday school teacher had spent her life battling women bolder in their enjoyment of wealth and privilege than she. Now sixty-five, she did not often entertain on a grand scale, but when she did, you were *expected*.

Alice tilted her head to address Edith's husband. "*Teddy*. You must stop Edith whipping you all over the globe like this."

"So I keep telling her!" said Teddy, who could still play the part of a bluff old soul when required. Earlier that evening, as he dressed, Edith had seen from the set of his jaw, the way he moved fitfully from one room to the next, growing fretful over a missing hand-kerchief—he did not want the one in Irish linen, the linen was too rough; cotton from Turnbull & Asser, *that* was the one he needed. A mood was coming on. She could only hope they would survive the evening without incident.

She said, "Actually, Teddy is off on a world tour soon. I'm wildly envious." Then, to distract from Teddy's glower, she cried, "These flowers, Alice, I'm ravished!"

As she proceeded into the crowded salon, nodding here, smiling there, Edith understood that Alice's question to Teddy had been more than a pleasantry; it was an inquiry: Why did he not have control of his wife? Had the Vanderbilt matriarch heard the gossip? Recently, *Town Topics* had made a sly reference to Walter's visit to The Mount, Edith's home in Lenox: "Edith Wharton and Walter Berry are the most *devoted* of friends. Selden, the hero in *The House of Mirth*, is said to be an accurate picture of him." Alice would certainly hear the sneer behind *devoted*.

Which was why Edith had felt it necessary that she and Teddy make a public appearance. Now she imagined her reception if she had arrived alone. No longer Mrs. Edith Wharton, but the woman who left poor Teddy flat. The things people would say—never to her face, of course. The hostesses who would tut before striking her from the list. In every room she entered, the hum of surprise and slither of whispers—*My dear, you invited her?* The greetings seemingly the same, pressed hands, the brush of cheek on cheek. But then the escape, planned well in advance. *Must have a word with . . . we'll talk later.* Over and over until she stood alone, smiling reassuringly at all those who longed to talk to her but somehow couldn't get free.

Everyone knew: She had suffered. Everyone also knew: The blame was not Teddy's alone. *Well, it must be said*, she imagined them saying, *she is a selfish woman.*

Imperious, cold, demanding—the adjectives would flow, washing away Teddy's every fault until people wondered how on earth he had put up with her all these years.

As a couple, she and Teddy were often invited by the Vanderbilts as specimens of old New York or else "bohemians," to show the host had a dash of culture. Somehow, it always ended in disaster. She would never forget the night Cornelius had banged on the door of her guest room at the old Breakers in Newport to say there was a "small" fire. An hour later, they were standing in the snow, watching flames leap from the Newport cottage until it collapsed to charred wood and ash. Then there was the summer when she had been a lunch guest of Alva's when that gorgon was trying to ensnare the Duke of Marlborough for her hapless daughter, Consuelo—a union so ill-omened, Edith felt she had witnessed an event every bit as catastrophic as the Breakers fire. Once, in Newport, Alice's useless son Reginald had taken her and Teddy for a spin in his new Renault, and someone had thrown a rock at them. "Some of them," drawled Reggie, "don't like us round here."

But now she was pleased to see one of her favorite Vanderbilts, George, examining the atrocious family portraits that lined the wall. Taking her husband by the arm, she called, "George—will they never finish renovating poor Grand Central Station? Your brother must be beside himself."

Slender with large, heavy-lidded eyes and a resplendent dark mustache, George was one of the more handsome members of the family. Amused, he said, "I don't know how much running of the railroad Willie does these days. It might interfere with the Grand Prix or America's Cup. The poor fellow barely has time to tell the newspapers that money doesn't make you happy."

He nodded to a vivacious redhead who was chattering away to a tall, stone-faced young man. "But tonight you witness a miracle. Alice has permitted her much loathed daughter-in-law into her home."

Years ago, Alice and Cornelius had furiously opposed the match between their son Neily and the socially ambitious Grace, formerly of the "marrying Wilsons." Their presence here tonight was, indeed, miraculous, and Edith was about to say so when she was interrupted by a man speaking quite loudly to alert people to his presence. Edith examined him with distaste. There was no hair on his smooth, gleaming dome, but the snow-white mutton chops were resplendent. His keen blue eyes were topped with brows that resembled eagle's wings.

He seemed vaguely familiar, and she said so to George. "That's our senator, Chauncey Depew," he told her. "You met him at Biltmore that Christmas years ago. Shall I reacquaint you?"

Edith's first instinct was to say no. She remembered the gathering fondly enough; it had been 1905, her year of triumph with *The House of Mirth*. But she remembered the senator as the sort who squeezed one's hands too hard and looked over one's shoulder as he spoke to you.

Then she saw that Teddy was gazing at the ceiling as if wondering what it was doing all the way up there.

"That would be delightful. Teddy?"

As they approached, Alice said, "Ah, here are the Whartons returned from their travels."

"How do you find the city, after so long away?" the senator demanded of Teddy.

"Much changed," said Edith smoothly. "But I suppose New York is too young a city to settle."

"Too young," he boomed, snatching the subject of the city and its evolution from her. "Too vital. Too dynamic! No, you mustn't ever expect to leave New York and find it the same when you return."

"Mrs. Wharton writes novels," said Alice to explain Edith's strange propensity for opinions.

George said to the senator, "On the subject of change, I understand from the newspapers that you are considering retirement."

Edith saw the slightest crack in the bright veneer before the senator answered, "Yes, like an old gladiator, I shall quit the arena someday."

Alice put a fond hand on the old retainer's arm. "We shan't let you."

Eyes twinkling on cue, the senator said, "Well, we shall see. The workings of politics can be strange indeed. Especially in Albany!"

Then he indicated the ungainly dark-haired gentleman who had been held captive by Grace. "May I present my son, Chauncey Depew Jr."

The junior Depew sidled over. He had his father's bushy brows, but none of his panache. His height gave him a sad Gulliver look, making him seem a monstrosity among the normally sized. He seemed to know it, standing with his shoulders hunched, his head lowered as if he hoped to take up less space.

"Fine fellow," said the senator. "In my dotage, I rely on him more and more." He clapped his progeny on the shoulder. The young man cringed.

A butler, in powdered wig and maroon velvet knee breeches, announced that dinner was served. As they followed Alice and the senator in, Edith whispered to George, "Do you know this new scent? Hair oil and halitosis, they call it *l'air Depew.*" He laughed.

The dining room had been changed since she was last here. The stained glass ceiling had been removed, and the room was now smaller. Edith vividly remembered an endless dinner of seven courses where she and Walter sought to identify the most egregiously awful picture in the room. Edith had given the prize to a painting of a leering cow, while Walter argued in favor of a tree that looked like nothing in nature. Over dessert of flambéed peaches, they had proposed a Bad Art Show, for which Alice would be asked to loan much of her collection.

Now she noticed that Alice had placed Teddy close to her at the head of the table, whereas she, Edith, was much lower down with the morose younger Depew and Reggie, who was regaling guests with stories of his latest racing triumph. When the footman set consommé en tasse before her, Edith thought the little cup of broth might be her most diverting companion of the evening.

Then she rallied. Perhaps she had been put with the dullards to spice up the conversation. When the footman whisked away the first course, replacing it with filet de boeuf jardinier, she took a small bite, then said to the glowering Depew Jr., "The beef is very good, don't you think? They haven't overdone it. I find that so *often* these days, beef is overcooked."

This got a grunt. The beef gambit having failed, Edith tried a different approach.

Neatly slicing up her asparagus, she said, "I met *such* an irritating man this afternoon. A writer. The prophet type. Harangue, harangue. Apparently, he sells well, but if his work is *anything* like his conversation . . ."

She sighed merrily, inviting young Depew to join in her dislike of writers with faddy politics. He gazed at her, unmoved.

"David Graham Phillips," she tried. "Very black hair, intense eyes that *bore* into you. I felt like a sinner in the front pew of some hideously strict church."

A flicker of something in the eye. "David Graham Phillips," he repeated. "The writer."

"Yes!" Relieved to have some reaction, she said, "Apparently, he's about to publish some huge novel. Been working on it for ages. Explosive, explosive! Will expose the hypocrisy and evils of . . . well, everything, I suppose, those novels usually do."

Clutching her knife in her fist, she pronounced, "He means to tell the truth!"

"Are you making a joke?"

If he were smiling, it would be a return of conversational serve. But he was not smiling.

"I beg your pardon?"

"I said: Are you making a joke?"

It was not a question, she realized, but a sort of . . . threat. As she tried to figure out why on earth this awkward person she had known for half an hour would threaten her, she became aware of the tinkling sound of a glass being tapped; a toast was underway. Distracted, she looked up the length of the table. The senator was speaking—how ironic, she thought, to be relieved by that. But the private joke didn't help. Unnerved, she kept her eyes firmly fixed on the senior Depew, determined not to face the younger man again.

When the senator had finished, she heard Reggie ask the young Depew if it were true that it cost $100,000 to join the state legislature and half a million to become a senator. There was no malice in Reggie's slack walrus face; he hadn't the wit to know his question might offend. Edith waited. Would Depew demand to know if he was making a joke, in that monotonous voice?

But no. He had turned in his chair and was now stammering his way through an answer. Politicians were not *bought*, he explained, but public service cost money. Reggie, he assured his host, would be astonished by the expenses: travel, mail, staff. And that was only a few of the difficulties. Even for someone as admired as his father, there were always . . . unforeseen obstacles to be dealt with.

As he spoke, the younger Depew's manner was earnest, even humble, and Edith realized: He was not particularly terrifying. Just an awkward man caught in the hell of dinner conversation. He was an oaf, she decided. That was all. Oafs were always unnerving.

It was also possible he had heard her joke about his name. And not found it funny. Which was fair enough.

Turning to Grace Vanderbilt, she asked which brand of cigarettes her guests favored and could she recommend a florist—the suite at Belmont was desperately dreary. Then she looked at the clock and thought, *Dear God, how much longer?*

CHAPTER FIVE

W hy must it always be Rossini?" Edith complained as she and
Teddy rode back to the hotel. "All that simpering comedy.
Does Alice think we'll faint at the sight of drama?"

"I don't want to go to California."

Teddy spoke just as her nerves were beginning to settle. They had
pulled it off—for the most part. Teddy had become argumentative
when Reggie praised the new Packard motor, his voice rising sharply
and his manner becoming agitated. Edith had stepped in to say, *Must
go, so lovely, simply exhausted.*

Now she said, "I thought Emmy Destinn was in marvelous voice."

"I don't want to go to California."

Noting Teddy's fists, planted on his knees, she reminded herself:
It was difficult to be ill. Angelic invalids existed only in the works of
Mr. Dickens.

Dr. Kinnicutt had advised that when a tantrum loomed, she simply take no notice. In a bright voice, she asked, "How was the menagerie? You went today, didn't you? White tells me you saw a buffalo."

He turned to meet her eye; what she saw made her stomach flutter. "I don't want to go to California."

Facing front so she could feel reassured by the presence of the driver, she said, "Nonsense, of course you want to go. You said so yourself. Mr. Roosevelt tells me the thing one must *not* miss in California is the redwoods."

Teddy slammed his fist onto his leg. "I don't want to go and I shouldn't have to go. Alice is right, you whip me here and there . . ."

Edith felt pain bloom just below her ear. It spread along the line of her skull. Extraordinary, she thought, that a sixty-year-old man could sound so much like a six-year-old child.

"I know," she said, her voice low and soothing. "You've had such a trying time. With your teeth and . . ."

"I've had a trying time because you don't care for me. Nannie says . . ."

Yes, Nannie says. Edith was well aware of Nannie's views. In Nannie's view, there was nothing wrong with Teddy. Any treatment that went beyond Edith being a "better wife" was rejected with the full force of old Boston ignorance and self-righteousness. The doctors suggest a sanitarium. Nannie says no. A spa in Arkansas. Nannie says no. A rest cure in Neuilly. Nannie says no. Because to Nannie, any solution that did not rest with Edith giving her life over entirely to her brother was a veiled rebuke to her own sad, thwarted existence. There were times when Edith thought she and Teddy might manage, were it not for the endless litany of *Nannie says*.

Frustration made her sharp. "I certainly should have been more attentive when you spent fifty thousand dollars of my money on actresses and bad investments."

Immediately, the fight went out of him. He raised a shaking hand to his mouth, as if he'd been sick. "Yes. Yes, I know. You've been noble, Puss. The way you've forgiven me."

The word *noble* depressed her. For one thing, it was not true. She had demanded he repay the money out of his inheritance. And she had removed him from management of her financial affairs, a step his family thought humiliating. She did not want to be noble. Nobility required too much silence, sacrifices that meant nothing to her anymore. Moreover, they did nothing to help Teddy.

"I want to be with you," he said miserably. "I'm unhappy when we're apart. Just let me stay with you. Please. I can forget if you can."

His hand tried to cover hers; she pulled it away.

The car stopped in front of the Belmont. Edith waited as Teddy paid the fare. They smiled good evening to the doorman, then proceeded through the crowded lobby.

Groping her way back to a place they shared, she said, "I was thinking, perhaps we might visit the Society for the Prevention of Cruelty to Animals. Have a look at our water bowls. Show Choumai." She and Teddy were founding members of the organization; together, they had campaigned for water bowls to be placed on streets throughout the city so that dogs could be refreshed on warm summer days. The hot concrete was so brutal on their poor paws. Then she realized it was winter. The bowls would not be out.

Teddy said, "I am not talking of an afternoon or water bowls. I am talking . . . or trying to . . . about us."

They had reached the elevators. Looking left, then right, she whispered, "I cannot help but feel we are easier when we have some time apart."

"It is easier for you because you can be with him."

Even in this crowded, public space, he had not lowered his voice.

Glaring, she considered reminding him of their original understanding. Words were her domain. He must never expect to best her in argument. Already, she had her answer. Quiet and cutting, it would begin with real estate—that apartment in Boston. A gentle inquiry about the girl; how was she faring? Did Teddy mean to call on her on his way West? Had there truly been five others, as he once claimed, or was that rather a fantasy? Really, *five*, when he could not even manage one wife . . .

The elevator arrived. Getting on, they bid good evening to the operator. Waited, faces front, as they rose to the top floor.

Leaving the elevator, she moved a little ahead of Teddy. All she had to do, she thought, was get inside the suite. Then a swift kiss on the cheek, a *we'll discuss it tomorrow*, and she could retreat to her room. Throughout their marriage, they kept separate rooms, even when traveling.

Later, she would scold herself: She had been hasty. No sooner had she heard the door shut than she turned and said, "I'm exhausted . . ."

He had a small crystal bowl in his hand. It had sat on a little table in the hall, a place for keys and coins and such. His jaw was thrust forward, his eyes afire. His arm shaking, he hurled the bowl past her head—just—and it smashed against the wall. Then he stared at her as if to say, *Look what you made me do.*

She answered his look: *Is that such an achievement?*

Then, in the steadiest voice she could manage, she called, "White."

Teddy's valet appeared at the door to his room. She understood that he had been standing there since they came in.

"Mr. Wharton is ill," she told him.

"No," said Teddy, instantly and jarringly contrite. He took a step toward her, and she flinched.

"Forgive me, Edith. I didn't mean to . . ."

She said to White, "The green bottle."

"Yes, ma'am."

It was a hideously familiar scene. Hearing her instructions, Teddy dropped to his knees and hobbled toward her, liver-spotted hands outstretched. In her mind, the words *Oh, for God's sake* clashed with *Teddy, don't, for your own dignity.* It hurt her, having remembered him jolly, long arms swinging, to see him so shriveled. His hair was gone, his teeth irregular, the eyes confused and broken veined. Old. He was old.

Whining, he pawed at her legs, as if desperate to crawl into her lap. Putting her hand between them, she turned her head. She stayed thus as White pulled Teddy's hands from her and lifted him to his feet. She waited until she heard the door shut and the sound of his voice had faded into the other room.

CHAPTER SIX

It was David Graham Phillips's custom to work through the night. He wore a light gray overcoat, the sort a craftsman might use to protect his street clothes, and he wrote standing at a drafting table, what one friend called "his old black pulpit." It was possible, he supposed, he did look like some sort of preacher. Certainly, he felt inspired of late. With his last book, he had experienced a glorious flow, the right words spilling onto the page without any conscious effort at all.

He fell into bed just before dawn and was awakened at eleven by the brilliant winter sun streaming through the window. Almost immediately, he heard the thud of the icebox door, the crack of an egg. The smell of coffee was already in the air. Incredible, he thought—and yet he should not be surprised by her knowledge of his habits. She had her own intelligence, he mused. Not the brittle kind that some called wit, nor the vicious kind that was only self-interest. Hers was tempered and gentled by the most important asset a woman could have: the capacity to truly love.

Emerging from his room, he came up behind her. She was a fine cook, but she had a habit of overfrying the eggs.

Raising a hand to hold him off, she said, "I know. Eggs not too hard. Now sit."

"Yes, ma'am," he said obediently and sat down at the kitchen table. In a few minutes, she set out two plates—eggs, bacon, toast, just as they had eaten as children in Indiana.

He said, "I told you, no bacon. Animal fat clogs you up."

"I'm sorry." She removed it from his plate and hers, then returned to the table with a smile. "What are your plans for the day?"

He stretched. ". . . Stop by the club, pick up my mail."

At the word *mail*, she frowned.

"It's just a crank," he reminded her.

He had made it clear to her several times: The notes meant nothing. He'd received too many in his career to let such things bother him. The thieves must be drawn into the light and destroyed. Writing about them—truthfully—was the only way to do that. Of course they were angry. Of course they made threats. If they didn't, he wasn't doing his job.

But she was sensitive. And this time, there had been phone calls. Late at night, the shrill, invasive ring shattered her sleep and his concentration. Once, she had come out in her robe. Hand at her throat, she had whispered, "Perhaps you should take care not to make so many enemies."

"Some enemies are worth having, don't you think? What's the worst that can happen?"

"They've threatened to *kill* you."

For a long moment, they had stood in the dark hallway. He had wrestled with his disappointment in her; she, of all people, was supposed to understand. His mind had gone to that reassuring stack of pages in the other room; briefly, he wondered how his enemies had learned of the book's existence. No one had read it except himself and his editor. Supposedly.

"Let them try," he told her. "If I were to die tomorrow, I would be six years ahead of the game."

The next day, he had shown her one of the notes as they left the house, laughing as he held it out so she would know to laugh as well. This was nothing to be feared, he told her. And she had laughed—a little.

Now he forked up the rest of his breakfast. "The pages go back to the publisher today."

"When will it be out in the world?"

"A matter of months. Once it's in print, there's not much anyone can do about it."

They both knew there was much that could be done, by certain people.

"I'm proud of you," she told him.

He felt the tickle of a blush on his cheeks, said gruffly, "Well, when you read it, I hope you like it."

He had already bathed once, but he bathed again before leaving the house, just to be sure. Their apartment was at the National Arts Club Studio, which had been built five years earlier as a space where artists could work and live. For a man who made no distinction between the two, it was ideal, and he had been one of its very first residents. Located on Nineteenth Street off Park Avenue, the building was only a block away from Gramercy Park and a few blocks from his destination, the Princeton Club. Her faith, an excellent breakfast, and the prospect of sending the book to his editor had put Phillips in a jovial mood.

It had snowed during the night. On the street, the snow had been trampled to dark slush, but the trees and pathways of Gramercy Park retained the perfect pale softness of winter's blanket. Every point of the wrought iron fence that protected the two-acre garden was topped by a frosty white cap. The benches were lined with snow, giving them the look of stout dowagers in ermine. Every so often, the wind shook the trees, causing flurries to fly through the air. The paths were smooth and pristine. No footsteps pocked the surface; no eager hands had raked the drifts to fashion snowballs. Few children were allowed here and certainly no dogs. In fact, most people were not allowed inside this paradise. Only the residents of the thirty-nine buildings that ringed the park were given the keys to its gates. David Graham Phillips had never been inside. And he did not regret that.

It was a short walk. The Princeton Club was on the corner of Twenty-First Street and Lexington Avenue. The building had a notorious history, and as he approached, Phillips relished its fall from grace. The brownstone had once been the home of Stanford White. Virtually no surface—floors, ceilings, walls—was left unadorned by looted wealth. Some might say the house was unlucky; certainly it was not paid for. White was in serious financial difficulty when the rabid Harry K. Thaw put three bullets into the rapacious architect. No sooner had the plaster dried on White's death mask than his widow auctioned off his possessions to pay his debts. The house and all its luxurious contents—the lions and lutes, Delft tiles and marble fountains—went on the block. The house itself, the first item sold, was bought by Princeton University.

As Phillips crossed at the corner, he dodged an automobile as it rattled down the street. He felt a flash of outrage. Here was another way for the wealthy to separate themselves, leaving the mass of humanity to walk while they sped recklessly ahead on energy they had not generated but bought.

Now within sight of the club, he saw two fellow members coming out. He knew them vaguely and raised his hand in greeting. They drew up short, as if alarmed by the gesture. He searched his mind, unable to recall any argument he had had with these gentlemen. Then thought, oh, yes, he did remember a quarrel. Last week. The one with the moon face had it entirely wrong about the effects of an income tax . . .

Someone darted in front of him, blocking his view. A fleeting comprehension: *But I know you.* Then the first shot, which he understood as both a sound—firecrackers in January?—and a shove that left him stumbling. The firecrackers continued, recalling summers in Indiana, the smell of gunpowder. Also, snowball fights, being pelted over and over, and it hurt because they'd packed it hard, into ice, so it didn't explode and dissolve harmlessly when it hit.

His legs useless, he staggered, found the iron gate that surrounded the club and clung on to it. Vaguely aware of people behind him shouting, running. It occurred to him that he must present a pathetic image—cringing, unable to stand. And yet another snowball. No . . . baseball. To the belly. Hard. Hurting. Knocking the breath from him.

As the two men who had left the club helped him to the pavement, he looked up at the gentleman with the moon face and was pleased to recall, Davis, *Frank* Davis. Pleasant fellow. Too pleasant really. Easy to back him down in an argument. Thinking he looked distraught, Phillips thought to say he held no grudge over the quarrel—truly. But when he tried to speak, he found no air, just the taste of copper, for some reason.

It was now very hard to breathe. And his wrist was in agony. Looking down, he saw blood on the concrete. He let his eyes dart over his body, laid out before him. More blood. Below the trouser line. That was bad. He knew that was bad. He looked up at the house that had once been Stanford White's. How funny that they should finally get him here.

"Graham," said Davis. "What's happened?"

"I've been shot," he managed, desperately hoping the pleasant, anxious face of Frank Davis, a man who never knew what was happening and needed men like himself to tell him, would not be the last he saw.

CHAPTER SEVEN

It was Edith's habit to work in the morning. She rose early but stayed in bed, where she wrote until noon, using blue paper and black ink because she found it easier to read. She wrote in her favorite silk gown and cap, trimmed in lace, her writing board balanced on her legs, the inkpot poised on top. Finished pages were tossed on the floor, where her secretary would retrieve them, typing them up so Edith could review and revise as necessary.

Two days after the Vanderbilt musicale, she woke at her normal hour and began to write. She delighted in order. Simply because she was in a hotel did not mean she had to alter her routine; the smallest change in her day left her scattered. It was only when she dropped a completed page to the carpet that she remembered: Her secretary was not here to pick it up. Her secretary was in Paris because Edith had expected herself to be in Paris far sooner than it now seemed she would be.

Infuriatingly, the doctor was ill. Yesterday, news had come that the illustrious Dr. Francis Parker Kinnicutt, whose clients so valued his advice, they sent private railway cars to Lenox, Massachusetts, to fetch him, had come down with influenza and would be unable to travel for days. Teddy's family would not tolerate his being sent off without official sanction from his physician. And so Edith was stranded in New York until the doctor arrived. She had spent her birthday fuming.

The dinner had humiliated her; the fight with Teddy had exhausted her. And she was still feeling bruised from her encounter with David Graham Phillips. But she told herself, if the Vanderbilts made her feel conspicuous and gossiped about, if Phillips made her feel feckless and passé, and her birthday, ancient, there was only one thing for it, and that was work. Her whole life, she had been able to summon that mystical state where she knew nothing of the world but the story she was telling. It was a glorious realm, one where she was at once all-powerful and consumed in the wonder of what she called making up.

But this morning, it was all . . . sticky. Every word felt dredged up as if she were snorting phlegm from her sinuses. Looking over yesterday's work, she saw writing that merely pretended to wit, much like Undine Spragg, the heroine of *The Custom of the Country*. The name for the hotel, the Stentorian—she had thought it so clever when she first brought it into being. Now it seemed like the clumsiest of satire, the sort that reveals the defects of the author more than her target.

From the other room of the suite, she could hear White inviting Teddy to put on his overcoat. She had assigned them a visit to the Museum of Natural History; Carl Akeley would show Teddy the plans for his proposed Hall of African Mammals. Science interested

Teddy not at all, but animals did, and it was the best she could manage. Yesterday, they had avoided each other entirely, slipping in and out of doors only when they were certain the space was unoccupied. But, last night, as they put him to bed, she had promised that she would go with him to the New York Society for the Prevention of Cruelty to Animals later in the week.

Now, hearing footsteps, she went still. She could feel Teddy's remorse through the oak door. Then White murmured, "If you're ready, Mr. Wharton," and she heard the soft sigh of dashed hope, the door of their hotel suite as it opened and closed.

Squaring her shoulders against the headboard, she confronted the page. She couldn't improve on what didn't exist. Brownell wanted *Custom*; she would work on *Custom*. Willing herself into the mind of Undine Spragg, she wrote, "'Friday's the stylish night, and that new tenor's going to sing again in Cavaleeria.'"

She read the line over. Did it sound false because the character was putting on airs? Or because her creator was reaching for the voice of an ambitious young woman from the Midwest . . . and failing?

What could you possibly know about the American woman of today?

Odious Mr. Phillips. It would be long past Easter before she forgave Brownell. She guessed there were only a few years between herself and Phillips, but if he died tomorrow, people would call him "young." Whereas people never stopped marveling that she had written her first novel at the decrepit age of forty-three.

Unable to concentrate, she considered what else she might do. There were letters to answer, phone calls, invitations to this and that. She wasn't even supposed to be here, and yet people had found her. Alice Vanderbilt summoning her to that Fifth Avenue mausoleum. Elsie Goelet asking, would she like tea? Yes, but not with

Elsie Goelet. Even darling Minnie in Washington Square. She didn't want to see any of them. They would all have their questions and she couldn't face it.

Dissatisfaction rising, she felt the need to reject something and set aside the only thing to hand: her writing desk. Intrigued by the motion, hopeful for attention, Choumai leapt up from the floor and attempted to scale the bed. She lifted him up and placed him in the center of the yellow satin coverlet. For a little while, she watched as he explored, making heroic efforts to clear the hurdle of her legs to get to a small plate trimmed in green, which bore the last of her breakfast, a smear of egg and some toast crumbs. This he lapped up and, with renewed energy, went stomping across *The New York Times*.

Laughing, she said, "Shall we read the news?" She held up the front page, enchanted by the way his curious little gaze followed.

She enjoyed the mania of American newspapers, their cheerful obsession with crime, always announcing horrific events in the boldest and brassiest of terms as if assault and murder were spectacles on par with a baseball game or balloon races. Now she read to Choumai: "'Boy kills playmate.' One wonders what the playmate did. 'Murdered in berth of a sleeping car.' Well, that was in Chicago, and we shan't go there. 'New York Senator Chauncey Depew wishes to run again.' Dear God, and no thank you. Oh! Choumai—Prince Fürstenberg's been stranded overnight at a train station in Le Landeron without his valet. They had to lend him a *blanket*. Do you think they'd lend me a blanket? I would give it to you. Yes, I would."

Then she turned the page again, and instantly, her good humor vanished. In the top right corner of the page was an enormous, eye-catching advertisement. It was bordered in black like a mourning notice for royalty, and it blared to the public:

The publisher had even paid for the cover to be featured, and it was quite the cover. A beautiful drawing of a louche brunette in a splendid hat, picking daintily at her purse, placed cunningly at the intersection of her thighs. Only the awareness that it would frighten Choumai prevented her from tearing the newspaper to shreds. *This*— she wrung the paper as if it were Charles Scribner's neck—*this* was precisely the sort of advertising she had wanted for *Fruit of the Tree.* How dare they blame her for poor sales—how dare they? She had labored over it, finished it, delivered it to excellent reviews, all so the laggards of Scribner's could drop it into a few bookstores in Outer Mongolia and other far-flung, sparsely populated regions, settle back into their leather armchairs, and say with a yawn, *The public just wasn't interested, I'm afraid.*

The shrill command of the telephone interrupted her mental tirade. Snatching it off the table, she said, "Yes?"

"Mrs. Wharton? I am dreadfully sorry to telephone, I know it's your writing time."

"Mr. Brownell," she said, surprised.

"I wanted to tell you before you read it in the papers."

She went still. Teddy had done something. Been strange in public. The newspapers had gotten hold of it . . .

"It's David Graham Phillips." In his agitation, Brownell overexplained. "The writer who joined us when we had tea. He was rude, you didn't like him . . ."

He had written something about her, she thought. Wealthy women who ride in motorcars and divorce their husbands because they think too much and love too little. The ridiculous bombastic advertisement caught her eye; yes, she could see it: *His Agony*, the story of a good man ruined by an ambitious woman. For a moment, she contemplated the unspeakable pleasure it would give her to club Mr. Phillips over the head with the telephone in her hand.

Then she heard Brownell say, "I'm afraid he's dead."

"What?" Brownell must be speaking in metaphor.

"He was shot yesterday," he told her. "Outside the Princeton Club."

Bewildered, she called to mind the full arrogant figure of the man: dark hair, cleft chin, blazing eyes. *That* person, dead? He seemed entirely unkillable.

"The Princeton Club?" she echoed. "Isn't that Stanford White's old house."

". . . I believe so."

She was being idiotic—she did realize that. Focusing on the things that could not matter less because the word *shot* left a gaping, ragged hole in her understanding of things and it was difficult to see anything clearly except tiny, irrelevant fragments. She struggled to put the matter squarely before her: David Graham Phillips, yes, she saw him clearly now drumming his middle finger on the tearoom table. That deeply unpleasant man was dead. And it wasn't disease or a motor accident.

Someone had killed him. His life had ended. On her birthday, of all days.

Finally, an intelligent question came to her. "Who shot him?"

"What?" Brownell was still a bit lost. "Oh! They don't know. The fellow ran off."

"And *no one* stopped him?" At last certain of the rightness of her reaction, she let her voice rise. "Have we truly reached the point where one man might shoot another outside the Princeton Club in New York City and just walk away?"

Alarmed, Choumai skittered to the end of the bed.

"I . . . I don't know," said Brownell. "In any event, I wanted you to hear it from me. I understand the funeral will be held tomorrow."

"Really?"

"Yes, why?"

Tomorrow, she had promised to spend the day with Teddy. A thing she wished very much not to do. She could not admit to herself that the funeral of Mr. Phillips provided an excuse for postponing their journey and that the prospect of not being with Teddy unleashed a feeling of relief so intense it bordered on the physical. But she was aware that she would rather spend the afternoon with the corpse of a man she detested rather than her living, breathing husband.

She asked, "Will it be open to the public?"

"I should think so. He was well regarded, with many friends within the literary community."

"So it wouldn't be awkward if I attended."

She felt the astonishment over the line. Then Brownell said, "Forgive me, I thought you despised the man."

"*Despise*," she said airily, implying he was overstating things.

"You said you wouldn't forgive me until next year."

"Well, I forgive you now," she said promptly. "And I want to attend the funeral."

When she had hung up the phone, she smoothed Choumai's fur

and apologized for her loss of temper. She thought of calling White to take him for a stroll. Then remembered White had taken Teddy for a stroll and would not be back for some time. She thought of tomorrow's funeral. Had she brought anything suitable? Yes—thank God it was winter. Her wardrobe for the trip was mostly dark and somber.

There was, however, something else she needed. Someone else. She couldn't attend the funeral on her own. She needed someone to go with her.

No. She had written badly enough for one day. *Be truthful*, she told herself. *Be precise.*

She needed him.

There were others she could ask. But Henry had had enough of funerals lately, and Walter would only ask why she wanted to go and then tell her that she shouldn't.

Which brought her to Morton Fullerton. The man for whom the desire to do something was reason enough to do it; in fact, the best reason of all.

She smoked two cigarettes before calling. She lifted the receiver, then set it down again. Several times, causing the hotel operator to become sharp with her. Did Mrs. Wharton wish to make a call? Mrs. Wharton, Edith answered, would make such calls *as* she wished *in* the time she wished to make them.

She smoked another cigarette. Asked Choumai if he thought she was making a mistake. The dog regarded her gravely, which she thought meant yes.

Rapidly, she stubbed out the cigarette, took up the phone, and informed the snipe at the switchboard that she wished to be connected. Giving the number, she waited.

As she so often did with him, she considered her voice. She should sound . . . light. But not overly so. She should give the impression that there was a purpose to the call. And he would hear the falseness of overt gaiety. She knew that much from past failures. It struck her, how carefully she chose her words now with the man she had once considered a twin soul. But so much depended on the right words.

At one point, she had believed all you had to do was express need and the other person would respond—in honor of what *had* been shared, if nothing else. And when the response was silence, you were forced into the dreadful, grinding cycle of *But he said he loved me. If he loves me at all, he must care that I am unhappy. I will ask this way. I will ask that way. I will withdraw. I will be candid. I shall be distant. I shall be passionate. Something, something I do or say, will bring him to me.* You gathered the courage to say things you had spent a lifetime not saying. But still, he did not answer. Which brought the terror that you had been wrong to say those things or said the wrong things. Been difficult and blaming. Small wonder he stayed away! And so, the apologies, the begging, the demonstrations that you knew you were impossible, not lovable, how tremendous of him to even *try* to love you. The subversive, selfish hope that self-abasement would bring him back . . .

A woman's voice. "Yes, hello?"

She felt it as a blow, just above her sternum, slightly to the left; the heart, of course. From there, the misery worked a slow, tortuous path down her middle, digging deep into her belly and collapsing her until she was unable to breathe.

She cut the connection.

CHAPTER EIGHT

The service was held at Calvary Episcopal Church, not far from where David Graham Phillips had lived and died. The church had sanctified the arrivals, couplings, and departures of many of the city's most celebrated residents. Eleanor Roosevelt had been baptized there, her famous uncle standing as godfather. William K. Vanderbilt had married Alva Smith at Calvary. J. P. Morgan worshiped there—indeed it was known as Morgan's church—but so did Mrs. Margaret Sanger. In short, it served both the affluent and the earnest, the first being encouraged to financially enlarge the second, the latter encouraged to spiritually enlarge the former.

Edith had attended the church as a girl. It was an unlovely building of brown sandstone with a dingy circular stained glass window above the entry. George Templeton Strong had called it a "miracle of ugliness," and he had been right to do so. But the sight of it brought back strong memories: the sun burning the back of her neck, the wondrous smell of old books, the feeling of hard wood beneath her thighs, and the voice, vigor, and splendid hair of Reverend Washburn. Oh, how she had adored the Reverend Washburn. He had a daughter Emelyn, six years older than she, and he let the girls spend hours reading Dante in the church library.

Now she said, "'Midway upon the journey of our life, I found myself within a forest dark, for the straightforward pathway had been lost.'"

"Why," wondered Walter, standing slim and self-assured beside her, "would anyone murder a novelist?"

There were those who thought Walter Van Rensselaer Berry a snob, and it was true that he liked to say he only associated with those in "your front row in the Four Hundred." Many of her friends did not care for him, thinking him cold, pretentious, a gossip—worse, an unfriendly gossip, one who could not be relied on to share other people's follies yet keep one's own secrets. Those he liked, he liked. Those he did not, he made no effort with.

But what Walter's grumbling associates failed to understand was that Edith found his elitism liberating. Most of life was spent pretending one liked someone one loathed, lavishly praising a mediocre effort, or remaining silent, tacitly agreeing that one's point of view had no right to exist. Walter gave himself permission to be right, and he extended that permission to her as well. As a pair, she had noticed, they charmed and excited with their banter. Simply, there was no one else on earth with whom she felt as much herself.

Which was why, after the frustrating call to Mr. Fullerton, she had decided to defy the snide rumormongers of *Town Topics* and turn to the man she had known for more than a quarter of a century, a man equally at home in Paris, Egypt, or this, one of the most hallowed spots of old New York. Now past the half-century mark, Walter stood with his elegant, long-fingered hands folded on a walking

stick and surveyed the crowd outside the church with the studied distaste of someone who had always held himself apart—and above. His
gray hair was shot through with the old gold, his large eyes still so
absurdly blue, they had caught the heart of Proust. His button shoes
shone in the dim winter-afternoon light, his dark frock coat perfectly
cut, his frame lithe and long; one would not be surprised to learn that
he was very nearly the US tennis champion in 1885.

From the corner of the street, they moved to join the masses of
people waiting to enter the church, Walter swinging his stick ever
so slightly to clear space around them. There was a hum and hurried
shuffle in the crowd as a woman dressed in black arrived on the arm
of a man who bore a strong resemblance to David Graham Phillips.
She leaned heavily on him, her free hand fitfully touching her lips
beneath the lace veil. At the sight of the church, she let out a cry and
began to sink to the ground. Others rushed to hold her up. One, a
ravishing dark-haired woman, moved with admirable speed and purpose to put her arm around the veiled lady. After a long embrace and
sympathetic murmurings in English and French—"You took such
good care of Graham, Carolyn," "He took such good care of *me*"—
the group bustled into the church.

"The widow?" asked Walter.

"He wasn't married."

Up the block, Edith saw the hearse. The crowd, sensing its arrival, flowed toward it, among them a willowy young man with long
pale hair and a girl with a distinct underbite whose bright, avid expression showed nothing of grief. An older woman used her bulk to
work her way closer to the front, and a shabbily dressed man took the
cigar from his mouth as he craned to get a better look. Sightseers,
Edith thought with distaste. Gawkers drawn by the sensationalism
of the murder of a celebrated individual.

As they battled their way to the entrance, Walter wondered, "Will they even let us in?"

"Mr. Brownell has arranged it with Mr. Phillips's publisher."

"And who's that? Drudge, Scullery, and Wastrel?"

She gave him the mildest of glares. "It's Appleton, and you can stop playing the part of the martyred aristocrat."

Inside, it was packed. Every pew was filled with people embracing, sharing stories and handkerchiefs. They stood out, Walter so tall, she so elaborately furred and feathered, and Edith suggested they sit at the back. She was intensely curious to see Mr. Phillips's loved ones, but she was shy about explaining her connection to the murdered man. That morning, she had rehearsed a lofty reply, "I come as a fellow writer." Now she understood that claims to the universal kinship of artists would not pass muster with this austere, anguished group. And perhaps they shouldn't. Why was she here? Because she did not care to spend time with her husband. Overdressed, perspiring, Edith suddenly felt herself false. She had sneered at the scandalmongers outside the church, but wasn't she also indulging in another person's tragedy for distraction? She was about to urge Walter to stand so they could make a swift escape when the organ sounded and the mourners rose as one. The casket had arrived.

Eight men carried the coffin, which was adorned with violets. The choice of that small, demure flower—symbolizing modesty, of all things—surprised her. She kept her head lowered as the coffin passed, taking in bursts of sobbing that broke through the mournful wheeze of the organ and the choir's trills of "Nearer, My God, to Thee." Then, like a child, she peeked. And, like a child, was discomfited to think that Mr. Phillips was in that box. She imagined him, eyes closed, hands folded across his chest, hair too neatly combed and slicked as funeral parlors always seemed to do. The unreality of death struck her. People should not be in boxes, she thought. They should not be put whole into the ground, the earth patted down, a stone marking the space, then left to . . .

The casket was at the altar. The pallbearers withdrew and the mourners sat. The archdeacon took his place and began to read the service. She heard Walter yawn and nudged him sharply; now was not the time for a display of sophisticated ennui.

At the same time, her attention was less on the well-worn words of solace than on the other mourners. That mystery woman who put such a sad, wistful look in Phillips's eyes, was she here? Out of habit, Edith began to spin a tale: "The Writer in Love." She imagined a beautiful woman grieving alone and unacknowledged. But looking around the church, she found no one quite right for the part. There was the veiled, black-clad woman. But her immediate welcome from his friends argued against her being a secret inamorata. Who was she then? Edith looked next at the gentleman who had escorted her into the church. He had the same stern mouth and lowering brow as David Graham Phillips. Almost certainly his brother. Which meant the woman was probably Mr. Phillips's sister. Edith peered at the people around the siblings but saw nothing resembling a spouse. Was no one in the Phillips family married?

She did find the beauty who had taken charge on the church steps seated a few rows back from the family. Now *she* fit the bill of hidden beloved nicely, but beside her was a blandly handsome gentleman with a long face and prominent ears, a type Edith knew well from the croquet lawns of Newport. The cut of his suit indicated affluence, as did the gloss of his slightly receding hair. The way he and the lady managed their proximity suggested a connection, yet they seemed from different worlds: she bohemian, he patrician.

"That is William English Walling," murmured Walter, noting

her interest and glad of the chance to gossip. "Old Kentucky family. Inherited wealth and promptly became a socialist. Went to Russia several years ago and brought that back with him." He nodded to the dark woman.

Edith was always amazed by Walter's ability to absorb rumor like mist from the air. She was about to ask if he knew anything about the Phillips family when they were shushed from behind by a lady gorgon. Dutifully, Edith gave her attention to the eulogy. The speaker was a tall man with an impressive sweep of white hair and a flowing mustache.

He began: "Without question, David Graham Phillips was the greatest writer of novels in English of our time—and he was one of the best of men." He bowed his head and his voice became choked. "Even now, I cannot believe he is dead. Just this morning, I looked for him, that tall boyish man, striding down Fifth Avenue, so full of life."

From the family pew, an agonized wail from Mr. Phillips's sister. Edith watched as the beauteous Mrs. Walling lifted a gloved hand to her eye. Then, as if sensing Edith's gaze, she looked in her direction. Caught, Edith hastily turned back to the speaker.

"I have lived in many lands. I have known many men. I never knew a finer man than David Graham Phillips. His was a knightly mind, a paladin character. Men liked him. Women liked him when he liked them." A ripple of appreciative laughter broke the grief.

"But Truth was his goddess," thundered the eulogist. "He wrought honestly and *only* for her. The princes of corruption may believe David Graham Phillips has been silenced, but his truth shall be heard forever throughout this great land!"

The organ boomed and the mourners rose for the hymn. The archdeacon gave the final prayer. "Abide with Me" was sung. The eight pallbearers rose again to take the coffin. Obliged to wait until the Phillips family had left, Edith and Walter watched row after row depart. The church was almost empty when she saw the dark-haired lady with the fine eyes—*la Russe*, she thought—approach with a quizzical smile. Her lashes were damp from tears, her eyes glassy.

"Mrs. Wharton?"

"Yes?"

"I recognized you from your author portrait."

"Oh, dear," said Edith. "Scribner's always tells me those photos look nothing like me."

"They don't do you justice. But of course they wish to show you as the grand society matron. From your work, I suspect you are more than that." She held out her hand. "Anna Strunsky Walling."

It was terrible manners, but Edith could not help wondering why a woman would call herself Strunsky when she had the name Walling. "A pleasure, Mrs. Walling."

Catching the slight pause, the other woman said, "This taking of the husband's name by a woman when she marries merges her individuality into his. In my work I desire the use of the name that means me." She turned her luminous eyes on Walter. "I hope my views cause no offense, Mr. Wharton."

"This is Mr. Walter Berry," Edith explained. "A very old friend. My husband was unable to come."

She braced for censure, but Mrs. Walling seemed charmed by the unorthodoxy. Gesturing to the doors where William Walling stood, she said, "Shall we?"

Edith was not generally inclined to walk with people she didn't know, much less women who insisted on their maiden name, an affectation she found tiresome. But there was something good-humored, even mischievous, about Mrs. Walling. Of course she was a radical; radicals did not tend to like Edith's work, and in turn, she did not like them. But she had given Edith the first note of welcome since she'd arrived.

William Walling she liked no better on close inspection. He had that blend of feebleness and self-importance that confirmed her suspicion that his natural habitat was a croquet pitch. He responded to her condolences with a stiff nod, clearly feeling a woman of her means had no place at a celebration of a man of the people. Edith had met his sort before, a man who could think of no better way to show disdain for his own class than by treating other members of it with contempt.

As they emerged from the church, the men following, Anna Walling said to Edith, "I am curious as to how you knew Graham."

Noting the use of Mr. Phillips's middle name, Edith said, "I argued with him two days ago in a tearoom. That was the sum of our acquaintance."

Anna Walling laughed. "He once rebuked me for riding in a motorcar. He feared I was becoming an aristocrat."

The hearse was still parked by the church, its back door now open to receive the casket. A small group stood nearby, most prominently the woman in black and the man who resembled Mr. Phillips. "Members of the family?" Edith asked Mrs. Walling.

"His sister, Mrs. Carolyn Frevert, and their brother. Harrison, I believe. He arrived yesterday."

The gawkers were still present. They had stood in the cold throughout the service, just for the chance to encounter the key players of the drama one last time. The young man with long hair had procured a lily. Now he dashed up to the family and presented it to Mrs. Frevert. Startled, but not displeased, she took it, asking did he know her brother? No, but he was a writer himself . . . At this, a balding, round-bellied gentleman stepped forward and gently removed the young man from the family's orbit.

"And is that *Mr.* Frevert?" asked Edith, noting the plump man's protective attitude. He put her in mind of a penguin, which disposed her favorably toward him.

"No, that is Graham's editor," said Mrs. Walling. "Rutger Bleecker Jewett."

Edith recalled the large advertisement. "From Appleton?"

Mrs. Walling nodded. "Mrs. Frevert has asked some of us back to the apartment. I'm sure it would mean something to the family. The presence of . . ." A graceful gesture to indicate Edith's stature.

Edith was not overly interested in an introduction to Mrs. Frevert, who might expect effusive tributes to her brother she would find hard to produce. But an editor who showed his devotion to his author in ways both personal and material—that man she did wish to meet. And so, ignoring Walter's agitation behind her, she said it would be an honor.

CHAPTER NINE

Almost immediately, she regretted it. The Phillips apartment was small—to her eye, at least—*certainly* too small for the multitudes of Mr. Phillips's friends and admirers. She could feel Walter mutinous beside her; in this crush, it would be hard to quietly slip away. It was a motley group, spartan in their dress and aggressive in their speech. Two men, a veritable Tweedledee and Tweedledum, stood in the corner. One wept; the other stared glumly at the funeral repast, as if wanting to partake, but worried hunger would betray a lack of grief. They looked out of place and Edith said so. "They are from the Princeton Club," whispered Mrs. Walling. "They were there when it happened."

Determined to prove herself not the fussy society matron, Edith praised the apartment. So cunning of Mrs. Frevert to achieve graciousness in these rooms. Not to mention the feat of caring for both brother and husband in such . . . quickly, she discarded the words *tiny, cramped, crowded*, finally arriving at "the same household."

Impulsively, she asked Mrs. Walling, "Or is Mrs. Frevert widowed?"

A fraction of hesitation. "No. Henry Frevert is very much alive, but he no longer lives here. I believe he resides downtown somewhere."

And yet he had not come to the funeral. Edith was about to inquire further when Anna Walling turned to accept greetings. At that moment, a hefty gentleman stepped into Edith's path and someone went through with a bottle, causing the crowd to shift. Mrs. Walling vanished, Walter was carried off, and Edith found herself suddenly separated and alone. She felt the stirrings of panic. She was not used to crowds; every function she attended was carefully paced, with a specific number of guests and servants to move them gently through the event as though through a minuet. This was a scrum. Frantically, she searched for the Appleton editor, but he was nowhere in sight. On the opposite side of the room, she saw Walter towering yet cowering as he was besieged by a broad-shouldered man demanding to know his views on Taft. Nearby, a man wept extravagantly into a handkerchief, saying, "I knew it, I knew it would happen one day." Those around him muttered somberly in agreement. One woman cried, "I say we march to the senator's house!" There were murmurs of agreement, muttered accusations against the rich, the powerful, the enemies of truth. "It is the fault of society!" pronounced William Walling to general acclaim. *Well, yes*, thought Edith crossly, *society ought not to let madmen wander about with pistols.*

Oh, God, now even Walter had disappeared. Edith found herself turning this way and that. It would amaze those who did not know her well, but for much of her life, she had a terror of speaking. Assertions were unthinkable, requests impossible. Even conversation was a vast expanse of quicksand. A wrong step and you could plunge into suffocating depths of mortification. The wrong word to the wrong person could easily mean social death. Or a tantrum. Screaming. Threats. Breakage.

This was, in part, like a weak limb after a childhood illness. She dreaded the possibility that she might march up to someone, fully prepared to unleash *Mrs. Edith Wharton*, only to snap back into gulping, sad-eyed Puss Jones. She was better now, braver. But there were times when it still required courage to open her mouth and say what she meant. Sometimes, she resented that the other person had not made it easier. When she saw their disapproval of her sharpness, she grew sharper still. When the discussion was over and the other person had slunk away grumbling, she did not feel victorious, only that she might have handled it better.

So, yes, she was imperious because she had discovered that the internal dithering and stammering attempts at tact were not only unbearable but pointless; if she was going to be thought awful no matter what, better to just say it.

Awful made her think of David Graham Phillips, sideways in his chair, legs crossed, talking not in paragraphs but pages. Well, in honor of the murdered man, she too would assume everyone wished to hear what she had to say. Thus resolved, she made her way to the most harmless-looking guests, the Tweedledee men from the Princeton Club.

It seemed they had also gone unwelcomed because they responded to her overture with pathetic gratitude. They were Mr. Frank Davis and Mr. Newton Jarvis. When Edith introduced herself, Mr. Davis pointed to her, beaming.

"... *Mirth*!"

"Yes, I did write *The House of Mirth*," she said, pleased.

"Poor Lily Bart!" he said. "I was shocked by the ending. Never saw that coming."

"Who's Lily?" Mr. Jarvis wanted to know.

"A character in my novel," she told him. "I understand you were with Mr. Phillips at the last. That must have been some comfort for him."

"Don't know about that," said Davis dolefully. "Went his own way, Graham. Wasn't the chummy sort. Most fellows, you chat over a few brandies. He didn't care for drink, and the last time we spoke, we argued."

"I thought he was going to thump you over that income tax argument," said Jarvis.

Mr. Jarvis, she felt, was failing to strike the right note. Giving her attention solely to Davis, she said, "To witness such a thing! I cannot fathom."

She actually couldn't fathom it. What would it be like to see a man killed right in front of you? "Did you see the killer? Or did you hear the shots first?"

"Heard," said Davis as Jarvis said, "Saw."

"What did you see, Mr. Jarvis?" Edith inquired, even as she wished the more voluble Davis were the one with the visual memory.

"A man," he said as if it were obvious. "With a gun." He waved his finger in the air.

"Well-dressed, would you say?"

It was a tactful way, she felt, to inquire if the shooter was poor. But neither man seemed sure.

"He wore a scarf," said Jarvis. "Hung halfway down his back. I noticed that because I thought, 'Hello! That's a long scarf.' Striped," he added triumphantly.

Edith smiled even as she thought, *Striped—how useless.* Was it Breton? Chevron? Why did men not notice important things like height or hair color? Although, now she thought about it, most gentlemen wore their scarves tucked within their overcoats. A loose scarf indicated a student or a radical, hardly the wealthy "prince of corruption" the eulogist had accused.

"And you just let him run away?" she asked.

"He had a *gun*," Jarvis reminded her.

Davis shook his head. "After it happened, all I could think to do was look after poor old Graham. It was hard to see him down on the ground like that."

"Did he say anything?" asked Edith. "What were his last words?"

Davis frowned, trying to remember. "Oh, yes, he said, 'Davis, I've been shot.'"

Suddenly, Mrs. Walling was back with her. Quickly detaching Edith from the Princeton men, she said, "Mrs. Wharton, I should like to introduce you to Graham's sister, Mrs. Carolyn Frevert."

Mrs. Frevert was dark like her brother, but small and plaintive, with no brightness or ferocity to her, a wren to his eagle. She was, Edith guessed, five to ten years older. But rather than sniff at Edith's work as her brother had, she pronounced herself an ardent admirer of Edith's short stories. Mortified that she had prepared no corresponding praise, Edith said, "My encounter with your brother was so stimulating, I yearn to read his work."

Mrs. Frevert went still. "Do you mean that?"

Caught out, Edith stammered, ". . . Of course."

"Would you like to see Graham's study?"

An intake of breath from Anna Walling indicated that this was a great honor. Seeing no possible way to decline, Edith said, "*Very* much."

As she was guided out of the parlor, she caught sight of Walter, who glared. He wished to go. *Now.* She widened her eyes to show helplessness. Despite being petite, Mrs. Frevert was strong. And determined.

Mr. Phillips's study was down a short, narrow corridor. It was not a large room; in her own home, it might have been allocated to one of the junior kitchen maids. There was very little in it, save for a tall desk of battered oak—no stool or chair—and an astonishing amount of paper. No, pages. From what she could see, every scrap was covered in ink, stroke after stroke, line after line, words piling and tumbling across the page. There were piles of foolscap at least as high as her knee, tidier shorter bundles representing finished work, stray sheets half filled and allowed to fall to the floor, crumpled balls of discarded thought. She felt as if she were drowning in the words of David Graham Phillips. An old gray coat hung on a peg, arms limp, quietly human.

"Extraordinary. Are these all finished work?"

"No." Energized by the chance to explain, Mrs. Frevert darted to the center of the room. "No, these—" She extended her arm to the wall opposite the desk where some rough shelves of bare planks had been built. Pointing to the bottom shelf, she said, "These are ideas he felt were not working. These"—the top shelf—"showed promise, but he couldn't decide how to proceed. *These*"—she ran a hand over the four piles on the easily reached middle shelf—"were current works in progress. All plays. My brother felt his future was on the stage. And *this* . . ."

With one step, she moved to the desk, which Edith now saw, bore a single towering manuscript.

"This was his masterpiece. He was to send it back to the publisher that afternoon."

Carolyn Frevert laid both hands on the stack, as a mother would on a child's shoulders. Then her features creased with tears and she clapped her hands over her eyes. Offering a handkerchief, Edith begged her to sit and gestured to the window seat.

As Mrs. Frevert composed herself, Edith glanced at the "master-piece," *Susan Lenox: Her Fall and Rise*. The pages had been typeset, meaning it had already been edited and approved. Lifting the title page, she saw that Mr. Phillips had chosen to introduce his own work. One bold sentence stood apart from the blocks of text.

There are three ways of dealing with the sex relations of men and women—two wrong and one right.

A small sound—mirth or shock—escaped her. To cover it, she asked, "What is the subject of the book, Mrs. Frevert?"

"It is the story of a woman who escapes an unhappy marriage to become . . ." Mrs. Frevert hesitated. "A woman of business."

So, a prostitute, thought Edith; it was one of those stories. Also on the desk, a notebook where the dead man had jotted ideas, fresh phrasing, possible titles, notes to self. Scrawled in large letters: "Work is the only permanently interesting thing in life."

Touched in spite of herself, she said, "I do hope they catch the man who killed him. Do the police have any idea who did it?"

"I know who did it," said Mrs. Frevert listlessly. "The police don't believe me."

Remembering the fevered pronouncements in the other room, Edith suspected she wouldn't either. Not wanting to argue, she asked, "What will you do now? Is there someone to help you?" She glanced around the room. "This is a great deal to manage."

"It is. But it will give me something to do."

"Is there anything I might do for you?"

The hands leapt from the lap to claim hers; for an instant, she saw the woman's resemblance to her fierce sibling. "Not for me. But for *Susan*."

It took her a moment to realize Mrs. Frevert meant the novel. "When does it come out?"

"This is my fear, Mrs. Wharton: It may never come out. There are people who do not want this book to be published and I am terrified they will find a way to stop it."

Seeing Edith's disbelief, she said, "They *murdered* my brother, Mrs. Wharton. Do you understand? They killed him because they thought without him, the book would have no champion. No one to fight when they challenge it, which they certainly will now that he's gone."

This was why radicals were so irritating. To persuade themselves of their importance, they insisted the entire world was involved in a vast intrigue to thwart them. When in reality, no one gave a toss. Still, the woman was suffering. In the kind voice she used with Teddy, Edith said, "I am sure Appleton will stand firm."

"Publishers are businesses, Mrs. Wharton. They're slaves to common opinion and the market. You know that. They resisted publishing *Susan Lenox* for years because they were afraid of the storm it will cause. Now that my brother is dead, they may hold it back altogether. Or else they will cut it, make it tame and inoffensive." She pulled at Edith's hand. "Will you help?"

Edith liked to help. She prided herself on it. But she couldn't imagine how she could and said so.

"Be the champion *Susan Lenox* needs. Fight for her." Anticipating Edith's next point, she shook her head. "I can't do it. Not as you could. Everyone will be very kind, but in the end, they'll say, 'Poor lady, mad with grief,' and protect themselves."

Edith, who was also thinking *Poor lady*, said, "My editor tells me your brother's books sell well. His tragic death will only increase interest. Appleton has much to gain by publishing now."

"They have more to lose," insisted Mrs. Frevert. "*They* will threaten them as they threatened my brother."

Edith didn't want to expose the woman's delusions by asking the identity of the mysterious "they." The answer would no doubt be vague and all-encompassing. She was about to offer to speak with Mr. Jewett—which she wished to do anyway—when Mrs. Frevert smiled.

"Graham spoke of you, you know."

"Did he."

"Yes. You irked him quite a bit. He never liked to lose an argument. I thought what a formidable woman Mrs. Wharton must be to get the best of my brother."

"This is shameless flattery, Mrs. Frevert."

"Is it working? Will you help us?"

Us—as if she and Susan Lenox were a pair. "I don't publish with Appleton, I have no sway with them."

"But you are Edith Wharton."

Edith knew the woman's awestruck tone was only meant to spur effort on her brother's behalf. Still—she did like the feel of a pedestal beneath her feet.

"I would have to read it," she hedged. Unhappy, she looked at the manuscript. The thing looked a foot high, and she suspected it was all single-spaced. "And I can't take it with me. It's far too heavy."

"I wouldn't let you take it. It's returning to the publisher tomorrow."

This was better news, giving Edith an excellent excuse to visit the Appleton offices. And, she realized with relief, another postponement of her day with Teddy.

"In that case, I shall speak with Mr. Jewett tomorrow."

"Thank you. Thank you, Mrs. Wharton."

She looked back at the title page. "What is in this book that terrifies people so, Mrs. Frevert?"

"The truth, Mrs. Wharton."

Biting her tongue on *Ah, yes, the truth!* she said, "You are a very good sister."

"Graham was a far better brother."

As they emerged from Mr. Phillips's sanctum, she saw Walter regaling the beauteous Mrs. Walling with tales of Egypt, where he had just been stationed. Edith knew Walter's taste. He enjoyed tiny pretty women who adorned themselves with great skill, dubbing them "fairies." Mrs. Walling wasn't a fairy, but she was extremely attractive. Edith also noticed that across the room, William Walling was watching as his captivating spouse ran rings around yet another man.

Why yet? she questioned herself. Why did she assume this scene had played out before?

Oh, because Mrs. Walling had bold eyes and a bewitching figure and Mr. Walling a weak chin and no spark. It wasn't any more complicated than that. The heady whiff of conspiracy was affecting her. Working her way through the crush, Edith intervened, saying she regretted ending what was clearly a fascinating conversation, but they *must* go.

Taking her by the elbow, Anna Walling asked, "What did you think of Graham's study, Mrs. Wharton?"

"Impressive. Tragic."

"Did you and Mrs. Frevert discuss anything else?"

Edith realized: Anna Walling had known the purpose of the study visit all along. Had, in fact, invited her back to the house for that very reason.

"We did. I will read the book, advocate for it if I can do so sincerely. But I'm sure it won't be necessary. Mrs. Frevert's fears for the manuscript are groundless . . ."

"They're not."

Annoyed by the interruption, Edith said, "You seem an intelligent woman, Mrs. Walling. Please don't encourage his sister's fantasies of dark forces who want to block *Susan Lenox*. The worst any book has to fear is neglect from the publisher and indifference from the public."

They were at the door. Edith prepared her farewells, but Anna Walling followed her out of the apartment, closing the door behind her to say, "Even when its author has been murdered?"

"I highly doubt the lunatic who murdered Mr. Phillips has read his work. Most likely, he didn't even know who he was."

Mrs. Walling grew agitated, as if it were heresy to cast doubt on the dead man's renown. "I hope you are right, Mrs. Wharton. I hope Graham was not murdered by anyone who knew him."

She glanced at the closed door, worried she might be overheard as she added, "Or his work."

Feeling that marked the end of the discussion, Edith took a step toward the stairs.

But Mrs. Walling was not finished. "In the unlikely event that you are wrong, and I am right, I beg you to take care. They have already killed one writer. I should be very sad if the author of *The House of Mirth* were the second."

CHAPTER TEN

Walter was not familiar with the newest feature of the city, the taxicab, and he proved singularly inept at hailing one. First he stood. Then he raised an elegant finger. Next his walking stick. Every car passed them by. Stunned, he stooped to the vulgarity of waving his gloved hand, perhaps an inch from side to side.

Watching him, helpless on the street corner, Edith felt the wild impatience that came to her when she was kept still by other people. She had never expected to be in New York this long, or else she would have brought one of her own motors from Lenox. More for the chance to move than anything else, she suggested they try closer to Gramercy Park.

Just as they were about to turn off Nineteenth Street, Edith saw the Wallings emerge from the building. She lingered, wanting to see if they were any more skilled at taxi catching. The pair stood for a long moment. Then Mr. Walling grasped his wife's hand. Her head lowered, her eyes closed, Anna Walling's whole aspect was one of resistance. He murmured something, but it failed to please. Anna Walling abruptly pulled her hand out of his and walked away. He watched her, shoulders slumped, hands loose at his side, before walking in the opposite direction.

"What on earth was that comedy?" Walter whispered. Edith shushed him, nudging him around the corner before they were seen.

Walter took up position on the northwest corner of Gramercy Park. Unwilling to watch him flail, Edith drew closer to the iron gate. Between the bars, she watched a young nurse, not much older than her two charges, play blindman's bluff, a scarf tied over her eyes. She wandered, arms outstretched, hands reaching, her steps tentative in heavy skirts, as she called out to the playmates she could not see. The children, a boy and a girl, capered around her, drawing close, then leaping away when her stiff arms swung suddenly their way. Their laughter echoed over the chill air, gleeful and imperial.

Happy, thought Edith. She had been allowed inside the park once or twice when she was a child. It was a pokey little place. One would walk right through it and not think twice if not for the fence that made it feel so inaccessible.

The nurse had managed to capture the boy, throwing her arms around his chest and swinging him side to side. The boy's eyes were closed, his head lolled against the young woman's body. The little girl hopped up and down, proud that she was still at liberty but envious; the nurse and the boy were now a pair and she left out.

Suddenly tired of waiting, Edith advanced to the curb. Lifting her arm, she turned the full majesty of her form in the direction of an oncoming car. It stopped immediately. Walter, stony and silent, opened the door and they climbed in.

All the way back to the hotel, he rebuked her for wasting his day by dragging him to a funeral of a writer he had never heard of, and she herself thought talentless.

She said, "You seemed partly consoled by Mrs. Walling. That was in poor taste, Walter. No wonder she and her husband quarreled."

"I was making myself pleasant. The woman's an anarchist. No doubt she would have thrown a bomb at me directly afterwards."

A thing she loved in Walter, he never addressed her as a child, assuming she knew what he meant by *afterwards* and chuckling when she said perhaps it would depend on the quality of the before.

"*Do* you think she has lovers?" she asked.

"One heard rumors about Jack London. Why?"

"I find myself curious as to the women in David Graham Phillips's life. He was an attractive man, successful. And yet he wasn't married."

"I am not married," Walter pointed out.

She smiled to reassure him: yes, he was also attractive and successful. "His sister wished to show me his work. She has concerns."

"About?"

"She thinks Mr. Phillips was murdered to stop his next book." Ignoring Walter's derisive bark, she added, "She worries there will be efforts to block its publication."

"What does she expect you to do?"

". . . Advocate for it? I said I would have to read it first."

"Simple enough to say, 'Oh, dear, no time, I'm afraid.'"

"I suppose so. But if I can be helpful . . ." Aware of his disapproval, she cast about for justification. Memories of Dante returned and she said, "'The hottest places in hell are reserved for those who, in time of great moral crisis, maintain their neutrality.'"

"Neutrality? Despite the lofty talk of paladins and princes of corruption, the death of Mr. Phillips sounds like an everyday robbery gone wrong. Hardly a great moral crisis."

"Isn't it? Doesn't it disturb you, Walter, that a man can be shot in broad daylight in New York City and we all just go about our business? I mean, *guns*. This isn't the Wild West."

"New York City is in America," said Walter. "In America, we have guns. From the musket of the Revolution and Custer's rifle to Booth's pistol and little Johnny's Daisy repeater, firearms are part of our history. Who we are. I believe someone just shot the mayor this August. In New Jersey, of all places."

He smiled, inviting her to join his amusement over New Jersey. On a short angry sigh, she said, "It is possible to care too little, Walter."

His answer was silence. Edith prepared a retraction. But what she had said was true. And perhaps something Walter needed to hear from her. Still. Overly harsh and she was about to say so when he put a firm hand on hers and said, "Leave it. Tell me what you mean to do about Teddy."

His hand had trembled slightly as he reached for her. Looking at it over her gloved fingers, she said, "Tell *me* what I mean to do about Teddy."

"You mean to leave him," he said. "And you should."

There was a bass note in his tone that would have surprised those who dismissed Walter Berry as an effete dilettante, a thrumming insistence that took her back to that moment when she first saw him and knew she had never seen such a beautiful man. Silver blond, slim and precise as a rapier, he seemed created rather than born. She had asked him to look at some of her stories. He had laughed appreciatively with the very first page and she was thrilled. Even more thrilled when he said, "Come, let's see what can be done."

Hand twisting in his, she said, "You didn't use to say so."

"He didn't use to be so ill."

It was what she wanted to hear, and yet she fought. "He is mostly harmless . . ."

"On the contrary, he is doing you considerable harm. You are in *rags*. Insisting Henry, Fullerton, and I fly to your side, begging our advice—why? To tell you what you already know. How many books do you owe Scribner's?"

Feeling accused, she said, "I give them a book a year. I just published a collection of stories."

"Ghost tales. Where is the novel?"

If she blamed Teddy for the delay, that would only prove his point. She could not admit her fear that she no longer understood New York. And there were other reasons the work had been put off, other terrors to which she could not admit.

They retreated to their separate sides of the cab, each looking out the window at their own view. Worried the journey would end before they were friends again, she tried to think of common ground and found it in Henry—so melancholy after the death of his brother and despondent over the failure of the *New York Edition*, a much-heralded collection of his life's work that had been greeted with a vast shrug from the public.

"You and I must discuss what to do for Henry."

"His heart is broken, Edith. Don't make it worse by shoving."

"His bank account is broken," she said crisply. "That, we can do something about."

A wave of the hand rejected her plan to plan. Edith fumed. She detested when things were not as they should be, especially when people said, *Ah, well, nothing to be done*. She thought of Carolyn Frevert darting here and there in her brother's study, her hand clutching Edith's as she begged her to fight for his last work. Her fears were ridiculous, blown up by grief, as Anna Walling's were by radical grievance. But in both women, there was a feeling of purpose that drew her.

"Come with me to the opera next week," Walter said. "Opening night gala for *Natoma*. Alice will be there. The Harrimans and Goelets."

"I saw Alice last night. That was enough." She recalled that awful young man: *Are you making a joke?* How strange that they had been talking of David Graham Phillips, of all things . . .

The cab arrived at the hotel. Giving Walter a gentle kiss on the cheek, she got out of the taxi and proceeded to the lobby.

"This is only running away," he called after her.

She looked back.

"Your fretting about Mr. Phillips and who killed him. You're miserable and want to get free of an intolerable situation. If we were abroad, you'd get in your car and drive somewhere until you could think clearly about your future. As that's not possible, you're toodling off in your mind. But to the wrong destination. The murder of David Graham Phillips isn't a sublime garden or majestic ruin. It's a squalid back alley in a small provincial town."

In the long moment it took her to answer, she watched a pigeon with filthy, tattered wings make its way along the sidewalk. It strutted to the curb, then, surprisingly, took flight. She smelled the fetid water that had gathered in the gutter, felt the inexorable, dull-witted tremors of the subway. Looking across the street, she saw they had torn down the lovely old Baxter house, thrown up a twelve-story monstrosity in its place. Her view of it was obscured by wires, of course. Crisscrossing, dangling, tangled wires.

"New York is a small provincial town," she told Walter. "One of those places where we all know one another. Where we must keep secrets. And secrets are just stories. As for what people do in back alleys, well . . ."

She looked at her old friend. "Secrets and stories, Walter. What writer would not seek that out?"

CHAPTER ELEVEN

Edith awoke the next morning feeling bold and defiant. She ate a grand breakfast, then filled several pages with a speed and bravura befitting a master swordsman. Normally when she wrote that well, she felt a pleasant exhaustion. Deserving of tea or a long, slow walk in the garden. Today, her appetite for work was boundless. In a fit of good will, she told White she and Teddy would visit the Society for the Prevention of Cruelty to Animals that afternoon. Then she called the bellboy to give Choumai a trot around the block. "Mind, he picks up things from the street. You must pull them from his mouth. He may bite, but his teeth are minuscule, you'll barely feel it."

After that, she set her mind on what to wear to the Appleton offices.

She had, she told herself, ample reason to visit Mr. Jewett at Appleton. She had promised—hadn't she?—Mrs. Frevert. That lady's eccentric fears about her brother's murder could not be helped. But

Edith could certainly advocate that Mr. Phillips's last work be published as he had written it, not censored nor bowdlerized. Also—was it not her duty to make sure that the overwhelmed and underworldly Mrs. Frevert had her interests protected? Edith had never heard that Appleton actively cheated their authors. Of course publishers did so little *actively*, conducting their, which was to say *her*, business with a delicacy that bordered on languor, if not outright neglect . . .

She paused to remind herself that her frustrations with Scribner's were not the point.

But if the Bible instructed one to protect the widows and orphans . . . well, Mrs. Frevert seemed to be both and so doubly in need of aid. It was the right thing to do, Edith instructed herself. As a woman and an author.

Before leaving her suite, she telephoned Henry James in his rooms on the twelfth floor. "I'm going to pay a visit to Rutger Bleecker Jewett at Appleton. I thought you might like to come with me. Venture to new pastures to see if, perchance, they really are greener."

HJ was never not expressive, even in silence. His pause was a low chord on the piano, full of foreboding.

"Come," she insisted. "Mr. Jewett will be impressed."

A deep rumbling sigh. "Not by me. Not anymore. You go. When you return on the whirlwind of your determination, come and tell me how it went."

"If I have time," she said, tetchy. This was an evasion. Trapped in New York, awaiting Teddy's doctor, she had nothing but time.

One thing she already liked about Appleton: They spent money. Lavishly. Too lavishly, some might say. The company had been placed into receivership ten years ago. They had recently moved to handsome new offices on Fifth Avenue and Thirty-Ninth Street, only a few blocks from the Belmont. To buck up her confidence before meeting a new editor, Edith perused the window of a bookshop, hoping to see *Tales of Men and Ghosts* prominently displayed. Instead, piled high and triumphant, was the latest Mary Roberts Rinehart mystery, *The Window at the White Cat*. Crowded around that book was Mrs. Rinehart's huge success of a few years ago, *The Circular Staircase*.

Of Edith's books, there was no sign. Scribner's, she thought darkly, should be held to account. It would do them good to have a rival for her affections.

But her hopes of a grand welcome were quickly dashed. The juvenile at the reception desk struck her as too young to be able to read, much less work in publishing. Also apparently too young to know or care who she was. He made it clear: Edith was neither expected nor planned for, and so she was a problem and would have to sit until he could decide what to do with her. It had been many years since her name failed to gain entrance, and while she knew very well she should have made an appointment, Edith was miffed. She took a seat but planned revenge. An offer from Appleton moved down several places on her list of things she wanted; then moved several places back up, if only so she might dismiss them as she now felt dismissed. The chairs were offensive, built to accommodate a man's slim trousers, rather than a lady's skirts. The infant at the front desk was insufferable. Surveying the bookshelves on the nearby wall, where the pride of the house was displayed, she noted *The Red Badge of Courage*, by Mr. Crane. Works by Mr. Kipling and Mr. Darwin. Both sides of the Civil War were represented in books by Jefferson Davis and General Sherman. The sole female on the shelf was Mr. Carroll's invention, Alice.

There was a chance this visit had been a mistake.

In fairness, there did seem to be some sort of meeting taking place. From beyond the glass-paned door, she could hear voices, one vague and mollifying, the other barking and agitated. She tried to pick out words, but every time the barker got up speed, the murmurer was able to break his momentum. Shouting was not the usual thing at publishing houses, and she leaned forward, intrigued. But there were doors and walls between her and the argument, and to her annoyance, she couldn't make it out. She looked to the young gentleman, now neatly folding letters into envelopes. He raised his brows to acknowledge the discord but said nothing.

Edith looked at the clock. She had now been kept waiting for six minutes. As she pondered the effect of rising without explanation versus a gentle but pointed inquiry as to when she might be seen, her thoughts were interrupted as the barker broke through with, "You can't mean to publish!"

The murmurer went even lower, but she could detect from the brevity and the rhythm of speech that yes, they did mean to publish.

"But not now! Publish now and it ruins me!" shrilled the other man.

The voices grew suddenly louder—she realized a door had been opened. She could now hear the murmurer clearly as he said, "Oh, now . . ." She knew that *Oh, now*. She had heard it in various forms from Brownell and Burlingame. It never meant your complaint was wrong. It meant your complaint was pointless; they weren't going to do as you asked, and they felt it was high time you realized it. Before, she had disliked the barker on principle. Now, she recognized him as a fellow author and her sympathy changed in his favor.

But it disappeared altogether as he burst into the waiting room. Attuned to proportion, Edith found his face simply . . . wrong. His head bulged at the top and all but disappeared at the bottom in a dab of a chin. The eyes were so prominent, they suggested a vitamin deficiency; the nose was delicate to the point of insignificance. The ears were large and flapping; a few strands of dishwater-brown hair lay in a desultory way across his scalp. The rest of him was no better: small and thin with a paunchy belly.

He stalked past the desk where the secretary was resolutely focused on his envelopes. Suddenly aware that Edith was his only audience, the little man advanced on her and hissed, "Ruined!" Then he gave the desk a vicious kick and tore out of the Appleton offices.

"Oh, dear," said Edith.

The secretary did not deign to respond. Instead, he set aside the envelope, rose, and went through the door to the back. After a few moments, she heard, "*Really?*" A moment later, Rutger Bleecker Jewett sailed through the door, arms outstretched in welcome.

Once again, she was enchanted by his resemblance to a penguin. In some ways, it was an unremarkable face: egg-shaped, smooth except for a tidily trimmed ruff of gray around the back. His belly was expansive, his shape soft, the muscles of youth having given way long ago and with good grace. But he was a tall man and carried the excess of fifty-some-odd years on this earth well. His ears were largish, eyes warm and humorous with lively brows. He seemed to find life a cheerful business, endlessly fascinating. But he approached with the humility of a man peeking around the door at a wedding to which he was not invited but must linger because the bride is so beautiful, and the flowers smell so wonderful.

"Mrs. Wharton!" he exclaimed. "They told me you were here and I did not believe them. Come, come . . . and tell me why I am so fortunate."

"I should have made an appointment," she said.

Gravely, he gave the right answer. "The author of *The House of Mirth* does not need an appointment. She graces us if she chooses and when she will." A smile allowed for the possibility that he was not quite so deferential and she not really in need of such deference. They were, actually, two old pros. "Come."

As they made their way down the hall, she said, "You've had an exciting morning."

Glancing back to the door through which the misshapen gentleman had exited, he sighed, "Disgruntled author, I'm afraid."

"Are there gruntled ones?"

"An author's state of gruntledness matters not," he said, opening the door to his office. "Only her talent."

She liked Mr. Jewett and she liked his office, large with high ceilings and expansive windows, the space crowded solely by books. An oriental rug in reds, browns, and orange showed some wit. A small Tiffany desk lamp, the glass shaped like a pale gold tulip, a willingness to indulge good taste. The chairs were broad, well cushioned, but not so hard and slippery as some leather armchairs were. When he had resumed his place behind his desk, she announced, "I come on behalf of another writer."

Steepling his fingers, he said, "Mr. James?"

"No. David Graham Phillips. I saw you at his funeral yesterday."

He shook his head, amazed. "I had no idea you were acquainted."

"We met briefly at the Belmont Hotel. I spoke with his sister after the service. The poor woman is convinced there is a conspiracy against her brother and his work."

The bulk of Mr. Jewett's upper body rose and fell on a heavy sigh. "Yes. I urged Graham for months to go to the police."

Startled, she said, "The police? Why?"

He was equally startled she should ask; she watched him debate how much to disclose.

Finally, he said, "Prior to the shooting, David Graham Phillips received several death threats."

"*Death* threats?"

"By mail and by telephone."

Chagrined, Edith sat back in her chair. She had been wrong, a thing she hated to be. But she also found herself strangely exhilarated. David Graham Phillips's death had not been a random incident or a robbery. His killer knew who he was and meant to take his life. Threats meant notes, notes meant writing, writing meant narrative.

"But then you must have some idea who did it," she said.

"Alas, the notes were unsigned."

"All the same, the style of writing should tell you something about the person who wrote them." Suddenly eager, she said, "You don't have one I might look at?"

Jewett glanced about his desk, then leaned toward a drawer. "I do. Graham refused to take it seriously. He said he'd always been troubled by cranks and this was no different. He was going to throw it away, but I took it, thinking perhaps . . ."

"You would go to the police yourself."

"Then of course I felt foolish and didn't. Here it is." He held up a folded piece of paper. "I suppose it's evidence now. Perhaps we shouldn't . . ."

"It has been in your drawer for some time. And I am wearing gloves." She showed her hands to prove it.

Carefully, he unfolded the paper on his leather blotter, holding it down at the edges.

"It's good stock," she observed.

"I beg your pardon?"

"The paper it's written on, it's good quality. Is it watermarked?"

Turning toward the window, Mr. Jewett held it up to the light. They both squinted, murmuring "Yes" and "I think so."

"Crane's," she said. "That's unusual, surely."

"Is it? What sort of paper do assassins generally use?"

She had no idea. Until now, she had imagined Mr. Phillips's killer to be . . . well, not the sort of person able to purchase or even be aware of fine-grain paper. The handwriting was excellent as well, the letters beautifully formed in strong black ink.

It read:

You are a vampire and must die.

"*Vampire*—that's an odd term."

"What do you mean?" asked Jewett.

She wasn't sure and had to think. "Mr. Phillips's sister believes that he was killed by someone who wished to silence him. But 'You are a vampire' is hardly political language. You'd expect something more along the lines of *Sic semper tyrannis*. Or 'Stop writing these awful things about Senator Click-and-Cluck.' How did the messages come to him?"

"Some came to his house, I believe. One or two to his club."

"And of course you'd never give out an author's home address." Mr. Jewett looked inquiring. "I only wonder how the assailant knew where Mr. Phillips lived. Was he listed?"

The editor shook his head, gesturing to the note. "Due to this sort of thing."

"Precisely. In fact, how did the killer even know who he was? I am certain I don't know what—"

Casting about for the name of a writer she might wish ill, she remembered the mystery novels piled high in the shop window.

"—what Mary Roberts Rinehart looks like well enough to shoot her."

Mr. Jewett pointed to the wall where several framed author photos hung. "David Graham Phillips *was* a singular figure."

Looking at the scowling face, Edith remembered the white suit. The chrysanthemum. The dark hair and dynamic movement. Maybe it wouldn't be difficult to identify David Graham Phillips in a crowd. But the question remained: How did the letter writer know where to send his threats?

"You don't think it possible that his killer knew him personally?"

Mr. Jewett took his time. "As brash as Mr. Phillips was, as little concerned with the sensitivities of some, he was truly loved by those who knew him, Mrs. Wharton."

There was the gentlest hint of rebuke; she had been cavalier about his colleague's death, treating it as a parlor game rather than a loss. Straightening in her chair, she said, "Yes. You remind me of the purpose of my visit. You may have heard, I like to be helpful to writers."

He nodded gravely.

"They do not always welcome my assistance, and I feel certain that were Mr. Phillips still with us, he would tell me to go hang. But he is not here to defend himself—against me or others—and his sister has asked for my help. Mrs. Frevert confided in me her worries about her brother's final work. I gather the subject matter is provocative."

"It is."

"She is concerned there will be pressure to make it less so."

"I shall resist, you need not fear."

"I am sure you will. But she thinks it would help if other writers gave their support. If there is anything I can do to bring *Susan Lenox* to light whole and . . . unmucked with, I should like to do it."

She was surprised to find herself sincere. She had come with the purpose of charming Mr. Jewett. But people could be arrogant and destructive about a writer's words, thinking because they read them, they could cut, twist, and classify them as they liked. Of course a reader had the right to dislike a book; she herself disliked hundreds, some of them written by dear friends. But there were those who wanted to control what they had not created. To say a thing should never have been written. People for whom a book was not merely bad but wicked. Remembering Brownell's anxious, clammy attempts to steer her to the subject he thought she should be writing about, she felt indignant. Writers should not be told what to write, and they should not have their words altered by those who had no idea what it cost to put them on the page.

To Jewett, she said, "But I cannot speak for a book I have not read."

Now that they were at the point, he hesitated, his gaze sliding off. "Difficult . . ."

"Is it?" She smiled. "I have been able to read since I was a very small child."

"It is a manuscript of great interest, as you can appreciate. I can't let it out of the office."

"Oh, that's no difficulty. I'm staying at the Belmont, which is close. I would be glad to read it here."

It was a long book. That meant at least three, four days away from Teddy. More than enough time for the malingering Dr. Kinnicutt to come.

"If you can read it on the premises, and you promise not to divulge its contents . . ." He struggled. "I warn you, Mrs. Wharton. Mrs. Frevert is right when she says people will oppose this book. Powerful people, with considerable influence."

"Well, let the battle be joined," she said lightly. "We are unafraid."

He asked when she would like to read the manuscript. She said whatever time served him. He suggested tomorrow and she answered with, "Then it shall be tomorrow."

Looking at the vampire note still on his desk, she said, "It's odd how we respond to shock. When my mother died, I thought how she would have detested the shoes I wore to the service. With Mr. Phillips, I become fixated on writing paper."

"It is excellent paper," he said kindly. "I use it myself."

It occurred to her to say that of course he would never have killed so successful an author. Then it occurred to her that it would be a joke in very poor taste. Still, the quality of the paper, the sort of person who used it, its presence at the publishing house, writers and their jealousies stayed stubbornly on her mind.

Mr. Jewett escorted her to the lobby, informing the youth at the desk that she would return tomorrow and that he should find a space for her. Then, opening the front door for her, he said, "If it is not presumptuous to say . . ."

She raised an eyebrow.

"I very much look forward to reading your next book, Mrs. Wharton."

She gave him her hand. "You are kind."

He waited with her at the elevator bank just outside the office doors. She raised her hand to thank him for his gallantry, saying, "I've taken up so much of your time. Don't wait on my account." With a last smile, he returned to his desk.

Once he was gone, Edith hurried back inside the Appleton waiting room, where the bored secretary was still at his desk. Advancing swiftly before he could say her name out loud, she whispered, "I wonder if you could tell me the name of the writer who stormed out earlier."

He peered at her, suspicious. Information was his sole currency, but disdain his sole pleasure, and so he said, "Algernon Okrent," in a tone that suggested anyone who named their child such a thing should be flogged.

"Does he by any chance write novels with strong social themes?"

"He writes novels that don't sell," said the youth, still annoyed over the kick to his desk. Then, realizing this was not the line to take with an author, he said mechanically, "He has an upcoming novel that we're all tremendously excited about."

"What is the title? I'll look for it."

He met her gaze, holding it just long to express disbelief. "*No Shame but Ours*. Regrettably, it's been postponed."

Pointedly, he looked toward the back office to indicate that had been the cause of the fight. But not the sole cause, Edith remembered. Mr. Okrent had been shouting about another book. By another author. One he felt should not be published because it would "ruin" his.

She had a very strong feeling that the other author was David Graham Phillips. And the other book was *Susan Lenox*.

CHAPTER TWELVE

S he would tell no one.

On her walk back to the Belmont, Edith resolved to keep her suspicion that Algernon Okrent had killed David Graham Phillips to herself. It wasn't as if she'd witnessed the crime or even knew the murdered man well. It was none of her business. She was a writer, not a detective. Really, she was relying entirely on her instinct.

Although her instincts were excellent. And only a writer could appreciate the lethal desperation of another writer.

No, the matter would sort itself out. Mr. Phillips was well-known, with ardent friends and supporters. They would ensure justice was done.

However . . . Mrs. Frevert might be unaware of Algernon Okrent's existence, much less that his book had been postponed so that her brother's could have the best spot in the bookstore window.

But Mr. Jewett was certainly aware. And he seemed a sensible, intelligent man. If she was right (she was right, but one must add the humble *if*) then Mr. Jewett would take the appropriate action.

Then she remembered her fundamental belief that publishers had a deep aversion to action. At least where it concerned the interests of their writers.

No, she decided as she entered the Belmont lobby, she must tell *someone*; Algernon Okrent was unhinged. It was possible he would kill again—poor Mr. Jewett and the smirky youth! Not to mention the peace Okrent's arrest would bring Carolyn Frevert. Who was, now that she thought about it, probably right that the police would not find her brother's killer; what did police know about writers? That made it even more imperative that she, Edith, alert the authorities. At least warn Mr. Jewett and press him to act.

But in the elevator, as she imagined warning Mr. Jewett, she discovered her thoughts were not in order. The last thing she wanted was to present a poorly told story to an editor. How to persuade him that Okrent was the author of the vampire note—and therefore, the assassin of David Graham Phillips?

Returning to the suite, she found it empty. Teddy was off somewhere—she prayed White was with him. She asked Choumai: *Had Mr. Wharton been gone long? Would he be back soon?* She hoped not. Once Teddy came back, she would have to stop thinking about Algernon Okrent and the murder of David Graham Phillips. She would have to listen to Teddy's complaints, talk of pleasant, empty things, guard her every word lest a tantrum erupt.

She did not wish to.

Then she remembered Henry on the twelfth floor. The English language had no greater master than Henry James. If anyone could parse the meaning of the vampire note, it would be him. And how could Rutger Bleecker Jewett fail to respect the word of such an august author? Gathering up Choumai, she left the suite and instructed the elevator operator to take her back down to the twelfth floor.

As the elevator descended, Edith reflected that she had become somewhat addicted to confiding in HJ. In the madness of the past few years, this man who so avoided life had become the one person before whom she could strew her most chaotic emotions so that he might pick through them calmly, discerning valid concern from destructive hysteria. To him, she poured out her miseries about Teddy. In that, he was not unique; she wrote to many people about Teddy.

But only HJ knew about Morton Fullerton.

In fact, HJ had introduced them. When she and Fullerton went on excursions, he sometimes traveled with them so they could maintain the appearance of innocent friends. And so it was to HJ she had turned for advice on her affair. Back and forth, the letters had flown: This wild show of devotion—could she trust it? What did it mean, this endless silence? Was she being gullible? Had she been cruel? "Live in the day," he had told her. "Don't borrow trouble and remember that nothing happens as we forecast it—but always with interesting and, as it were, refreshing differences."

But even the most avid gobbler of human emotion could tire of your story, no matter how well you told it. Edith knew: Henry was sick to death of her love affair. When she knocked, he took his time in opening the door. When he did, his gaze was wary, a bear roused from slumber. "Is it Teddy?" he asked.

She assured him it was not.

"The other thing?"

"It is the murder of a writer. The one who was shot near Stanford White's old house."

He let her in, keeping a distrustful eye on Choumai. As she outlined her thoughts on the shooting of David Graham Phillips, he sat, sunk into the gold-and-pink chair by the window, a rack of toast and a pot of tea on the table beside him.

Finishing her account up to the point of her encounter with Algernon Okrent, Edith sat back and waited expectantly.

Eyes closed, hands clasped over his belly, HJ murmured, "Why?"

Baffled by his lack of excitement, she repeated, "Why?"

"Why would Okrent shoot Phillips?"

"Jealousy, Henry! Envy, resentment, rage, fear. What on earth do you mean—*why?*"

HJ opened his eyes. "All writers are jealous, Edith. We are weak, fanciful, arrogant, and insecure. Envious, hateful, miserable beings. And yet . . ." He spread his arms wide as if to say: *We are still here. We have not shot each other. Why this is so, I am not always certain, but the fact remains.*

"Who fears and detests a writer more than another writer, Henry? Especially a writer who has succeeded where they have struggled?"

She was sensitive enough not to remind him of his trouncing by Oscar Wilde on the stage, where Wilde's *An Ideal Husband* had triumphed almost as spectacularly as James's *Guy Domville* had failed. HJ had been unusually incensed, calling Wilde an "unclean beast" and a "fatuous cad."

Instead, she said, "Algernon Okrent clearly felt that Mr. Phillips's work posed a threat to his novel. 'Publish now and it ruins me!' His exact words."

"How can one book *threaten* another?"

"They are both novels about women who fall into a life of degradation. If *Susan Lenox* comes out first, readers may be less eager to read *No Shame but Ours*. At the very least, they will see it as an imitation."

Henry shook his head, bewildered.

Counting off points on her fingers, she said, "Carolyn Frevert thinks her brother was shot to stop the publication of *Susan Lenox*. I gather Mr. Okrent's book was ready first, yet they've delayed publication in favor of Mr. Phillips's novel. So Okrent either killed him in a moment of vengeful frenzy *or* because he thought without Mr. Phillips, *No Shame but Ours* could come out first and take all the acclaim. Phillips's books sell well. Mr. Okrent's do not. Mr. Phillips was a handsome man. Mr. Okrent certainly is not."

"You *cannot* accuse a man of murder because he is unattractive. Both you and the family are dramatizing what was probably a simple robbery. A thief demanded his wallet. Mr. Phillips refused and got himself killed." HJ waved a swollen hand. "Sad, random—and banal."

"Ah, but not so random. The murderer sent David Graham Phillips death threats. Mr. Jewett showed me one."

HJ shuffled upward. "Really? What did it say?"

"'You are a vampire and must die.'" She leaned forward. "It's an interesting choice of words, don't you think? *Vampire*. Poetic. Literary. Strangely personal."

"As if the murderer were the victim's victim," he mused.

"You wrote a novel about vampires," she reminded him. "*The Sacred Fount*." In the tale, an anonymous narrator attended a weekend gathering at a stately home. He wandered the rooms, attempting to discern which of his fellow guests were having relations with one another. Edith had read the book with trepidation, unsure if she were the inspiration for a woman who remained vital and blooming while her husband grew ever more feeble or another woman, once brilliant, now "voided and scraped of everything, her shell was merely crushable."

HJ shifted irritably. "It was not about *vampires*. It was about passion. What we take in relations, what we give."

"But what is a vampire, Henry? Think."

"An individual who feeds off people, draining them . . ."

"*Or* is nourished by them," she parried. "Is it so wrong to take sustenance from our fellow human beings?"

HJ said pointedly, "To the point where you deprive them of life?"

"Precisely." She clapped her hands to emphasize the point. "Mr. Okrent must have felt that *Susan Lenox* would steal the place that rightfully belonged to *No Shame but Ours*. Deprive a writer of attention for his work and you kill the thing he loves best."

She ended on a note of triumph. But Henry looked stricken. Edith realized: Her pronouncement that literary obscurity and death were one and the same had hit too close. Flailing to make amends, she thought, *We all fail, Henry. Look at* Fruit of the Tree. But that had been a single novel; the *New York Edition* had been his life's work.

Choumai emerged from behind HJ's armchair, waddling toward her with studied nonchalance. It occurred to her there was an odor in the room. From the tightening of HJ's nostrils, she could see the same thought had occurred to him. A glance behind the chair confirmed her suspicions. There being no staff to hand, she cleared it away herself. When she returned from the bathroom, she answered HJ's accusatory stare with, "You need another dog. It's been too long since Max passed."

"No more pets," he said. "Too many graves already." Like her, he had a small plot near his home where his beloved dogs were buried.

"That's why we bring in new life, to balance it out," she said. Then, wanting him to think of the future, she added, "You should have come with me to Appleton. You'd like Mr. Jewett."

"I like Mr. Brownell and I like Mr. Scribner."

She struggled not to say it, then found she couldn't not say it. "How *can* you feel loyalty to Scribner's after they botched the *New York Edition*?"

HJ's shoulders rolled in a sort of shrug. Frowning, mouth puckered, he looked for the toast. As he strained to lean forward, he appeared to Edith as an assemblage of boiled eggs—head, belly, hands—each part soft, wobbling, and distended. The plate was beyond his reach; picking it up, she presented it to him, along with the reminder, "You said the royalties were shocking."

"I did not say shocking. I said they left me 'rather flat.'"

"It was your entire body of work."

"I withheld some of the fiction," he said, sighing. "And the permissions were costly. Macmillan was particularly usurious. It all took so much time. In the end, I had to leave it to poor old Brownell. I was *spent.*"

Spent, she thought, and with nothing to show for it. She knew that he felt the public's rejection more keenly than the financial loss. On one of their jaunts, he had wondered aloud if she felt as he did, that they were among the few survivors of a past world few recalled and fewer still cared about. At the time, in love and enraptured by a self she had never imagined, she had believed in the possibility of endless rebirths. Boldly, she had proclaimed that people would care because their books would make them care.

Now she recalled David Graham Phillips's scornful challenge— *What could you possibly know about the American woman of today?*—and felt old all over again. It was hard, she thought, simply to . . . keep up.

But necessary, she decided, mentally slapping away the glooms. "Scribner's and the excellent Mr. Brownell aside, I shall return to Appleton tomorrow and make my case to Mr. Jewett."

Henry intoned, "I hear the flap of eagle's wings, the majestic bird of prey ready to take flight, her talons poised . . ."

Hearing his disapproval, she said, "Okrent said *Susan Lenox* would ruin him. Its author is now dead. Mr. Phillips received death threats which were literary in tone. The term *vampire* suggests some-one who believes Mr. Phillips was sucking him dry, taking the life that rightfully belonged to him . . ."

"You don't know that," he objected. "And you do not *need* to know. Dispense with your schemes, forgo your passion for plots. Why not amuse yourself with Walter or"—the turtle eyes widened—"the elusive Mr. Fullerton?"

She plucked at a tassel hanging from the arm of the chair. She didn't want to talk about Fullerton. She had no discipline on the subject; if they stayed on it, she would tell Henry about the disastrous phone call, and he had chided her enough for one evening. HJ was funny that way; he greatly enjoyed the melodrama of his friends, but then he would grumble about how it exhausted him, rather like a guest who devours the dessert, then scolds his hostess for serving it, it's so bad for his health.

"He is, as you say, elusive." Picking up Choumai, she stood. "I suspect it's best if he stays that way. Good night, Henry."

In the elevator, she found herself still restless and said to the oper-ator, "Lobby, please." Taking Choumai out on the street, she set him down on the curb and waited. Then remembered the dog had done his business in Henry's room and no longer needed a walk. The dog made that very point by scurrying back to the hotel. She informed him he was impossible. But that she loved him, nonetheless.

Denied a stroll, Edith stopped at the front desk to ask for mes-sages. As the desk clerk searched the mailbox—an array of cub-byholes in good stout walnut, richly varnished, the room numbers marked in cheerful brass—she made a list in her mind like a child of all the things she wanted: Mr. Jewett begging her to bring her new work the next time she came to the office. Or Brownell, calling her to

Scribner's to see the newly created advertisement for *Men and Ghosts*. Dr. Kinnicutt announcing he had recovered and would be with them in the morning.

"Just this." The clerk laid a white envelope on the desk. Inside was a single sheet of paper, neatly folded in two. Raising the top half, she saw a single line. No signature. Big bold, swooping letters, all capitals.

DO NOT WRITE THIS

Her first thought was of the children gamboling in the park with their nurse. It had that feel, notes passed between playmates, secret messages, dire warnings. A code made up of matching numbers and letters; *a* for 1, *z* for 26, or the reverse if you were feeling clever. *How extraordinary*, she thought. *I've been invited to play.*

Then she realized. It was exactly like the note Mr. Jewett had shown her in his office. It was *that* note. Her mind still groggy from shock, she struggled to be clear: a note from *that man*. The man who had killed David Graham Phillips.

Rapidly, she made an inventory: everywhere she had been since the murder. Calvary Church. Phillips's sister's home. Appleton. The murderer had seen her in one of those places. He knew she had taken an interest. And now he was warning her: "Do not write this." In his view, she was stealing his story. *Oh, Mr. Okrent*, she thought gleefully, *how presumptuous you are.*

"May I speak to the man who was on duty when this was delivered?"

"He has gone home. Is there something I might assist you with?"

She shook her head. She did not feel in need of assistance. In fact, she felt wonderfully clear on what she had to do, as well as the fact that she was the one to do it. *Do not write this.* What words could be more provocative to a writer? What clearer sign that there was a story here to write? This awful man wished to be the only author of the story of the murder of David Graham Phillips. Well, from what she had seen of his work thus far, he was a poor storyteller, trampling his subject with a brutal, overwrought approach. He had no style. No insight. No humanity.

He did not deserve the last word.

CHAPTER THIRTEEN

⊰⊱

Teddy had not slept.

Edith was still in bed when she heard a knock at the door and a slight cough she knew to be Alfred White's. White had been in Teddy's employ for nearly twenty-five years. He knew she was not to be disturbed in the morning. Nerves on edge, she called, "Yes?"

The door opened, White slid through it, closing it behind him. "I apologize for the interruption." His voice was miraculously pitched: audible, pleasantly baritone, yet never rising above a whisper. "But Mr. Wharton is sitting on the floor. Facing the wall. He has been in that position all night."

"I see." Teddy's nerve fits were often followed by exhaustion and melancholy.

"Did something in particular agitate him?"

"He spoke of plans to visit the Society for the Prevention of Cruelty to Animals."

A slash of guilt. Her promise to meet Teddy yesterday afternoon—
she had forgotten. Teddy would have returned from the morning's
outing, no doubt pressing White to hurry, expecting to find her waiting and finding empty rooms instead. Because she had been at Appleton with Mr. Jewett and then with Henry.

The proper words came to her. *Very well, I'll go in to see him. Poor
dear, let's see if we can't get him into bed.*

". . . Unfortunately, I have an appointment this morning."

"Yes, ma'am."

"On the whole, best not to disturb him?"

"I think so, ma'am."

She was intensely grateful. Had White simply echoed his earlier *yes, ma'am*, as was correct, she would have felt his disapproval.
Instead, he had used informal language—the shocking *I think*—to
pointedly agree with her. Whether he did or no.

She made a note: something for White.

When White had withdrawn, she flung herself out of bed. She
would find something splendid to wear. Then, with her note as proof,
she would go to Appleton and warn Mr. Jewett about Algernon Okrent.

Oh, and read *Susan Lenox*, of course.

Regrettably, the youth informed her, Mr. Jewett was unavailable.

"Unavailable?" Edith repeated the word as if it were a mala-
propism.

"Regrettably," stressed the youth.

"When will he be available?"

"When he is no longer unavailable," said the assistant.

"But I need to speak with him," she insisted. "It's extremely important."

The youth gazed at her with thinly veiled pity. So young in publishing, she thought, but already he had learned: Nothing that concerned writers was *extremely important*.

"Mr. Jewett did leave instructions that you were to be given a spare office where you could read the manuscript." His face bright, he held up a key, as if to say, *What more could you possibly desire?*

But this was not at all what she desired. She had not left poor Teddy to wade through a lengthy tome about the "authentic" American woman written by a shouty American man. She had come because lives were in danger. She had *come*, she fumed, following the youth down the hall, to protect him and the unavailable Mr. Jewett from further assault. Yet here he was dumping her in a spare office—a veritable garret only large enough for one desk and an old armchair someone was too lazy to throw out.

But she would not complain. She had shocking news to impart, and she didn't want to prejudice the men at Appleton by seeming hysterical. Theatrically, she smiled and remained smiling until the assistant had closed the door.

Leaving her alone with the work of several years by a man not given to brevity. Taking up the first hundred pages, she settled herself into the battered leather chair and confronted the title page: *Susan Lenox: Her Fall and Rise*, by David Graham Phillips.

For some reason, she felt reluctant to begin. Peeking at the introduction, she saw again, "There are three ways of dealing with the sex relations of men and women—two wrong and one right." As Phillips went on to rail against wishy-washy literature and perverted palates, Edith felt irritated, as if the dead man were sitting opposite with his ridiculous chrysanthemum, hurling pronouncements at her.

Skipping the pompous introduction, she turned to the first page. But the anxiety was still with her.

This was preposterous, she scolded herself. She had read countless scandalous books; this one was no different.

Except, of course, that its author was dead.

And there was another cause for worry.

What if *Susan Lenox* was *good*? Not just adequate, but fine enough to justify the dead man's arrogance? What if it was truly a masterpiece about the American woman—her subject? It was bad enough to read excellent work written by friends. But to be impressed by a book written by a man who had nothing but contempt for her work—that would be unbearable.

You are Edith Wharton, she reminded herself. *He is not.*

Whipping the page away, she confronted the first lines.

> **"The child is dead," said Nora the nurse.**
> **The young man did not rouse from his reverie.**
> **"Dead? What's that? Merely another name for ignorance."**

Oh, this was positively bad. She began to read eagerly, feeling the deep relief of all writers when reading a rival's work: *It was not good.* The baby declared dead at the outset was, in fact, not dead. She was Susan Lenox, born illegitimate, raised in an obscure Midwestern town by small-minded relatives. Edith was captivated by the manic use of adverbs; all was gently or abruptly, wickedly or drearily. Brows were stormy. Eyes snapped. Passion was indicated by saying things three times.

> **Love—love love! She was a woman and she loved!**
> **"Go—go!" she begged. "Please go.**
> **I'm a bad girl—bad—bad! Go!"**

This then was the authentic American woman, she thought scornfully. Young Susan fell into an unsuitable love affair, shocking her guardians, who promptly married her off to a crusty old farmer named Zeke or Jeb—Edith forgot which. The wedding night was entirely grisly, a wrestling match of shrieks and slobber that left poor Susan catatonic.

Disgusted, she slapped down the page. How could Mr. Jewett think this book *dangerous*? Or Mrs. Frevert imagine it a bold exposé of the dark forces of society? So far, the only things Edith had learned were: Don't live on farms, and don't marry men named Jeb or Zeke. Both of which she already knew, as did any sensible human being. So poor Susan was unaware of the facts of married life. That might be revelatory to Mr. Phillips, but it would come as no surprise to most women—including herself. Just before her own wedding, she had asked her mother what would happen *after*. Airily, her mother replied that, having seen statues of men and women, she should be able to put it together. Thinking of those cold, smooth marble forms, Edith had compared them with her own soft, ungainly body with its peculiar, changeable openings and thought, *No, I cannot put it together. And if we cannot even speak of it, how horrible must it be?*

Quite horrible, as she discovered. Something so strained and futile, she and Teddy had agreed: There were things they did very well together. Things they enjoyed. Best to stay with those. In fact, it had become something of a joke between them, how ill-matched they were. "Like a podgy St. Bernard and a skittish whippet," Teddy had said. "The mechanics—ludicrous!" She had laughed and loved him very much then.

She became aware of a shuffling sound; someone was at the door. Puzzled, she called out "Yes?" but the shuffling just grew more frantic. She stood up and cracked the door. It was the youth, nearly buckling at the knees with the weight of several more books. She let him in, and he staggered to the desk, where he deposited them with a thud.

"Mr. Jewett's suggestion," he explained. "In case you wanted to read Mr. Phillips's other novels."

His gaze fell on the massive stack of unread pages. "Have you . . . formed any opinion?"

She meant to be professional. *Bold. Stimulating. Like nothing I've read before.* But then she spotted the line "Some likes the yeggs biled" and pressed her fingers to her mouth to stop from laughing.

"Yes," he said. "I've heard it's terrible."

Then they *knew.* They knew it was bad. Amazed, she asked, "How can they publish it in this state?" A horrible thought came to her: This was the edited manuscript. How much worse had it been?

He shrugged. "They say it will create a sensation."

"Oh, but not in the right way," she said, her voice low and certain.

"Well, perhaps you could tell Mr. Jewett. He's available now. If you're so inclined."

Excited, she took up her reticule. "Yes, I am very much inclined. Thank you—"

Embarrassed, she realized she didn't know his name; it was always difficult with people who were not actually important enough for introductions. Waving her hand, she mumbled "Mister" and hurried down the hall to Mr. Jewett's lovely, comfortable office. She knocked once, then, unable to wait, swept through the door.

Holding the note aloft like a torch, she announced, "Mr. Jewett, Algernon Okrent must be arrested at once!"

CHAPTER FOURTEEN

Algernon Okrent?"

The editor gazed at her, uncomprehending. This made Edith feel foolish, which she disliked. Awkwardly, she thrust the note at him. He recoiled at the suddenness of the gesture, then read the words.

"Is this . . . ?"

"Yes." She laid the note on the desk. "The language is dull, but the message succinct."

"'Do not write this.'" He was careful not to touch the paper. "This was sent to you personally?"

"At my hotel. Do you still have the note that was sent to Mr. Phillips?"

Nodding distractedly, Mr. Jewett unlocked one of the desk drawers and placed the note alongside hers. The characteristics of the handwriting—the rich black ink, the swooping copperplate, the placement of the words in the dead center of the page—all the same.

Jewett looked heartsick. "You must take this to the police, Mrs. Wharton. Please. Take mine with it."

"Of course, but you must come with me."

"I?"

"To tell them about Mr. Okrent." She sat down. "It will mean much more coming from you. You argued with him. You know his work." Waving toward the outer office, she added, "The young man at the front could come as well . . ."

"Forgive me, Mrs. Wharton. I don't understand. Why Algernon Okrent?"

"Because he shot Mr. Phillips."

He laughed. Briefly, but he did laugh. Then, clapping a hand to his chest as if to contain his amusement, he said, "My apologies, Mrs. Wharton. But I cannot imagine how you came to that conclusion."

She pointed to the notes. "The term *vampire* and the command not to write this—doesn't that indicate someone of a literary bent? Someone who wants to keep the story all for himself?"

The editor's face became indulgent. She felt an *Oh, now* coming.

Letting the edge of impatience into her voice, she said, "When I was here yesterday, wasn't Mr. Okrent screaming at you in a way that can only be described as deranged? Didn't he say that publishing *Susan Lenox* would ruin him?"

Mr. Jewett collected himself. "We have postponed his book. He is naturally upset."

"Aren't the two books similar?"

"Perhaps, broadly speaking, in their subject matter. Which is why we thought it unwise to publish them at the same time. One can only put out so many revelatory novels about fallen women at one time. And Graham's is the superior volume."

And he has just been killed in spectacular fashion. Strange, she thought, how many men wished to be seen as the sole teller of truths about women. Apparently, it was a title much coveted by male authors.

Then Jewett said, "But to suggest that a little competition between writers would lead to murder . . ."

"Oh, but David Graham Phillips was *such* an exasperating man. As his editor, Mr. Jewett, you might not have seen it, but he was exactly the sort of person to inspire jealousy. He practically insisted on it," she added, remembering the dead man's complacent *the* when speaking of great American writers.

"He was arrogant, entitled, belittling. And successful. That sort of person is enraging to most—but to writers?" She lifted her hands to underscore the point. "There is so little success to be had, someone who hogs the lion's share and is less than gracious? Particularly galling! And of course the publisher cannot support all books equally . . ."

"Surely then I would have been the target and not poor Graham."

"You are the giver, Mr. Phillips the competitor. And he was *very* competitive."

"The threats are written on Crane's stationery," he noted. "If I may be indiscreet, Mr. Okrent's advances would not stretch to such costly writing paper."

"You said yourself you use Crane's at Appleton. How difficult would it be for an author to take a few sheets?"

He smiled. "We make it a policy not to publish murderers, Mrs. Wharton. The odd thief, a forger here and there, perhaps a bigamist. But we draw the line at killing."

She smiled at the joke. And wondered how to get around the man's charm.

Then, in a more serious tone, he said, "Let me show you something, Mrs. Wharton. I think you'll see what I mean."

He went to a handsome oak filing cabinet. Peering into the top drawer, he picked through several folders before pulling out a fat sheaf of yellowing foolscap.

"Here we are." He laid it on the desk. "*No Shame but Ours: The Trials of Marigold Loveless.*"

Turning the manuscript around so she could read it, Edith felt an immediate stab of disappointment. The handwriting was small and crabbed, the letters poorly formed, all nervy vertical spikes and shriveled ovals as opposed to the graceful arcs and proud ballooning *a*'s and *o*'s of the notes. The words crowded one on top of the other as if Okrent were trying to prove he had so much to say, he must use every scrap of space. The ink, more brown than black, was uneven here, so thick it blotted, there anemic and barely visible. Looking from the notes to the manuscript, she tried to persuade herself this was a deliberate disguise. But the man who scratched his pronouncements on foolscap was incapable of the bold elegant line of the notes. They were the product of an altogether different personality. An altogether different . . .

Education. The elegant handwriting of the notes was not naturally acquired, she realized; it was taught. And practiced. She herself could recall hours of carefully copying out letters, the surge of frustration when her hand wobbled or the ink ran thin, ruining the line.

In fact, the handwriting of the notes was not unlike her own. Were there differences, she wondered, between men's and women's handwriting?

Mr. Jewett murmured, "As an editor, one is familiar with the handwriting of one's authors. Especially when it is as hard on the eyes as Mr. Okrent's."

"Yes," she sighed. "I see what you mean."

Mr. Jewett steepled his fingers. "For all his volatility, Mr. Okrent is a shouter, not a shooter. Moreover, he is worldly enough to know that the surest way to make *Susan Lenox* a success is to kill its author. No writer would willingly give another such a boost of publicity."

There was truth in that. Phillips's murder would greatly help the sales of *Susan Lenox*—no doubt one of the reasons Appleton was rushing it into print. The man's name hadn't left the newspapers' front page for days.

"Who do you think murdered David Graham Phillips?"

He sighed. "Graham was a combative personality. He made enemies and relished doing so. And he passionately believed that a writer should be candid when discussing sexual relations between men and women."

Remembering the raging introduction to *Susan Lenox*, Edith nodded.

"As such, he incurred the wrath of Anthony Comstock and his ilk. Any book more salacious than a nursery rhyme, they attack with a vengeance."

Edith was aware of Anthony Comstock, founder of the New York Society for the Suppression of Vice. "You're not saying Comstock killed him."

"Of course not. But his group attracts madmen, the sort who see Satan everywhere they look. My theory is some lunatic decided to stand in as the wrath of God."

"But has anyone read *Susan Lenox*, outside of Appleton?"

"I shouldn't think so. But Graham's earlier novels were also very frank."

"Why kill him now?"

"Fanatics don't always act on schedule, Mrs. Wharton. They can nurse their grievance for months, years. Then someone steps in front of them in a queue or their employer shouts at them, and they decide, 'I know, I shall go shoot that writer and feel better.'"

Edith was skeptical. "Do you really believe it can be as impulsive as that?"

Mr. Jewett's gaze shifted to his bookcases, in particular the shelf that held several of David Graham Phillips's books; Edith suspected they had been moved to the center as a sort of memorial.

"Yes, perhaps it was more deliberate. Not the work of a madman at all. You see, Graham wasn't just a novelist, he was also a journalist. A fearless one. I can think of one other book that might have inspired someone to kill him, *Treason of the Senate.*"

Edith saw that that title had been placed face out in the center of the collection. Brownell had mentioned the book at tea, with that affected little wave of his fist. *Here is the man who rakes the muck.*

"Is that his most recent book?"

"No, it was published as a series of magazine articles in 1906."

"Even for a fanatic, that seems a long time. And the title hardly sounds salacious."

"It caused quite an uproar when it came out. Graham accused the Senate of conniving against the interests of the American public on behalf of a few wealthy families. But you're right, it was five years ago; most people probably don't remember it these days." He grinned. "Except of course the Big Four."

The term was not familiar to her and she shook her head.

Slapping his hand on the desk to apologize for his thoughtlessness in presuming a lady followed political matters, Jewett explained, "The four senators Graham exposed for their corruption and self-dealing. Spooner, Aldrich, Gorman, and Depew."

"Senator Depew?"

"New York's very own," said Mr. Jewett. "Or, in Graham's inimitable words, 'the sleek, self-satisfied American opportunist in politics and Plunder.'"

Before she could make an acid remark about the late Mr. Phillips's obsession with alliteration, Jewett became, once again, the affable, enamored editor. "But I didn't mean to bore you with politics. Tell me—what can the world expect next from Edith Wharton?"

She felt the beat of a changed subject. Wondered at the shift. But she acquiesced, saying, "I am wayward in my affections at the moment. Like Mr. Phillips, I find myself drawn to the subject of marriage. But those are seldom happy stories and readers are so vicious toward women who are unhappy in marriage."

"Don't we feel pity for Anna Karenina? Madame Bovary?"

"Do we? They choose such poor men as lovers, you doubt their capacity to be happy." The moment the words were out of her mouth, she had the uneasy feeling she had strayed into confession.

She looked again at the notes on the desk—the elegant curve of the letters, the word *vampire*—and thought of HJ's novel *The Sacred Fount*. Lovers as predators, feeding off their loved ones. He wrote of sharp beaks and tearing claws. Those who thrived and those who withered.

You are a vampire. So personal. Almost . . . erotic.

On impulse, she asked, "Did Mr. Phillips have no one but his sister? No other lady who mourns him? He was not unattractive."

The editor shook his head. "The relationship between Graham and myself was purely professional. But I'm not sure he had any gift for intimacy. Or inclination. He was a busy, ambitious man. Everything was pared down to the essentials."

That wording—*pared down*—struck her. At one time, she had tried to live as David Graham Phillips had: self-contained, existing solely for work, friends, things she could control. Morton Fullerton had put an end to that. But Phillips had talked so expressively of love, its power to launch one into a new existence. How could a man say such things and live a pared-down life? She sensed something had been left out. Jewett was only telling her the things he felt safe, not everything he thought. Or perhaps knew.

Wanting to disarm him, she said, "You must forgive my fancies about Mr. Okrent. When dreadful things happen, I search for the cause so I may place the dreadful thing into a neat little box and say, 'There, that shall not happen again.'"

He smiled. "Were I in charge of such things, Mrs. Wharton, your command would be enough for me."

Then he became serious. "But I will certainly understand if you don't continue with *Susan Lenox*."

The implication of cowardice offended her. "I promised Mrs. Frevert I would read it, and read it I shall." Rising, she added, "Besides, I'm returning to Europe soon. I doubt very much our letter writer will follow me there."

"I don't want him following you *anywhere*, Mrs. Wharton. I feel responsible enough for poor Graham."

As she reached for her note, Mr. Jewett put his fingers on the edge. "I would be happy to take this to the police along with mine . . ."

It was a sensible offer. And yet she resisted, as if surrendering the note meant surrendering her interest in the murder. Putting it in her bag, she said, "I'll keep it. If nothing else, it will be a macabre memento."

Then, wishing to end the meeting on a more cheerful note, she said, "Perhaps I shall write a tale of an unhappy marriage and everyone will feel terribly sorry for the spouse who wishes to escape because I will make him a man."

"And will the unhappy spouse find freedom and live happily ever after?"

She thought of Teddy. "That remains to be seen, Mr. Jewett."

CHAPTER FIFTEEN

It was late afternoon and already dark as Edith emerged onto the street. Pulling her furs around her, she considered finding a taxi, but that felt extravagant given the short distance to the hotel. And she did not deserve a taxi. Her theory about Algernon Okrent had collapsed like a badly made soufflé. She felt embarrassed and dissatisfied. A walk would do her good.

Her conversation with Mr. Jewett couldn't have gone more poorly. She had made a fool of herself accusing Okrent—waving the note in the air like that, what *had* possessed her? And her ignorance of American politics! Mr. Jewett might take it for granted that a lady paid no attention to such things, but to venture an opinion about a writer's murder and know so little of that writer's most famous work. Not to mention Jewett's light dismissal that there had been a woman in David Graham Phillips's life. *The ladies*, she imagined him thinking fondly, *always dreaming of romance.*

Oh, and worst of all, that Mr. Jewett had *worried* about her. Gently tried to dissuade her from reading further, even trying to take the note from her as if it were beyond her ken to go to the police (although she had no intention of doing so). The patronizing concern in his eyes when he said, "I don't want him following you *anywhere*, Mrs. Wharton."

In the middle of the street, she stopped. Perhaps it was the power of suggestion.

But she felt someone was following her.

She went still, tried to capture the source of the feeling. As she did, the weight of someone behind her evaporated.

No, she corrected herself, not evaporated, because it was never there. Clearly all this Mary Roberts Rinehart–ing was making her fanciful. She resumed her walk.

And immediately felt it again—the presence. Like someone who wished to approach but hadn't quite got up the nerve. That happened, she told herself; she was occasionally recognized. Anna Walling at the funeral, for example.

She turned and saw no one who looked concerned with her in the slightest. *Edith*, she rebuked herself, *you have become conceited*.

Still, she began to walk just a bit faster.

When she had the sensation again, she told herself she was being absurd. Nervous, she made random connections. The word *absurd* led to the word *funny*, *funny* to the word *joke*, then the question *Are you making a joke?* That strange stone-faced young man.

No, she wasn't imagining it. Someone was there. Behind her. That too-close presence . . .

At a cigar shop, she paused to survey the offerings in the window. In the reflection, she watched those who passed behind her. A couple, fully captivated by each other. A nursemaid pushing a carriage. A portly man sunk deep in his own thoughts.

Embarrassed, she continued her walk.

And was immediately aware that the person behind her had done the same.

It was, she counted, three blocks to the Belmont. They were busy blocks, close to Grand Central, not a place you would randomly attack a woman. For a moment, she breathed easier. Then remembered David Graham Phillips had been shot in broad daylight on Twenty-First Street in the presence of many witnesses. A crowd was not protection.

Where was she now? Depew Place. Of all the streets to be on.

Turn around, she instructed herself. *Turn around and let this fellow know you are not afraid.*

Instead, she turned the corner where she didn't need to. After a few steps, she listened.

He had also turned. He was still with her.

Terror began to take hold. She felt it in the hard pounding of her heart, the shallowness of her breath, the tingling instability of her legs. She was aware of the back of her head, the unprotected expanse of her shoulders. If he did shoot, where would the bullet strike?

What would happen to Choumai if she didn't return? To all the dogs? White—White would care for them. Or Anna, her secretary, although she was elderly now. She would make a list when she returned to Paris. Things that should be attended to in case . . .

She knew she was walking quickly now, a mistake; it would alert her pursuer that she knew he was there. But she couldn't help it. Had David Graham Phillips known? She didn't think so. Often, you didn't see the danger until it was upon you. Anyway, the man was so self-absorbed, he wouldn't have noticed a rhinoceros behind him.

Another corner turned. The hideous, marvelous, never-to-be-detested-again Belmont Hotel came into view. Almost hysterical, she waved in greeting to the doorman in his resplendent purple overcoat. As she hurried toward the doors, she babbled to him as if he were an old friend. Such weather! And the noise from the construction on the new station, just terrible. Poor man, his ears must suffer . . .

Pushing through the revolving doors, and into the warm bright light of the lobby, the ping of the front desk bell, the purr of the concierge, the rumble of other guests filled her with bone-deep relief. It was comparable to sinking into a hot, scented tub in February; one relaxed so quickly, one almost passed out.

Harried, she made her way to the desk clerk and asked for her messages. Her housekeeper had telephoned from Lenox to say the elevator was stuck between floors. Her butler had sent word from Paris about a leaking pipe. Walter had called. Twice. Was she coming to this opera or no?

"Also a Mr. Brownell," said the clerk. "He inquired after Miss Spragg and said he hoped she was doing better."

"So kind of him."

Her heart had eased; it felt safe to ask, "Was that all?"

Grimacing slightly, he held up an envelope. "This. It was dropped on the desk a few minutes ago. I'm afraid I don't know who left it. I was attending to a guest and didn't get a good look at the individual. But it is addressed to you."

So it was. On the front of the envelope, her name. Written in a fine round hand: *Mrs. Edith Wharton.* Opening the envelope, she took out the note. Quality paper, undoubtedly Crane's.

A WOMAN WHO LEAVES HER HOME WALKS THE STREET. SHE IS NEITHER PURE NOR PROTECTED.

This time, there was no feeling of playfulness. No glee. She felt violated, as if someone had put a hand up her skirt. *Who knew?* she thought, heart pounding. *Who could possibly know?*

A woman who leaves her home . . .

Only three men knew her desires, and none of them would send her such a message.

No, four men. But even he . . .

Hurrying to the elevator, she asked the operator to take her to the twelfth floor.

O h, that's dreadful. Pure and protected. Oh, it's . . . quite, quite bad."

Seated opposite Henry in the darkened hotel room, Edith waited for his further thoughts. The fire was burning nicely, but she was still chilled. She knew she looked dreadful. When she had arrived at his rooms, Henry had been in his dressing gown, fully indignant and prepared to tell her to leave. One look at her face and he pushed the door wide open.

Now he asked, "I gather you are the woman in question?"

She showed her hands: *I must be.*

"The emphasis on purity," he suggested.

"Well, 'a woman who leaves her home.'" Distressed, she gestured to the note. "How could they know, Henry? I have only confided in you, Walter, and Mr. Fullerton."

"Now, let us not leap to conclusions." He gave her a stern look to remind her: She had done a lot of leaping of late. "This terribly danger-ous book you are reading, is it about a woman who leaves her home?"

Trying to calm herself, she thought. "Yes. And walks the streets . . ."

"Well, then."

"But Phillips, to his credit, does not judge her. In fact, he seems to be on her side. Everything she does, she does out of great love. She loves recklessly. Desires to see the world . . ."

"But if the person writing to you is the same person who shot Mr. Phillips, we can assume he does not approve of such stories. Or such women. Or"—he added gently—"know you to be one."

She was desperate for reassurance—too desperate to fully believe it. She fingered her neck. The note, with all its apparent knowledge of her deepest secrets, had struck her like a blow to the throat.

"But who could have sent it, Henry?"

His cheeks billowed as he thought. "You went back to Appleton?" She nodded. "To accuse the ugly little writer?"

She nodded again. "But I was wrong. Mr. Jewett showed me one of his manuscripts. Entirely different handwriting."

"I warned you. Still. We can assume this note does not come from Mr. Okrent. You received the first one before you accused him."

"And only a handful of people would know I went to read *Susan Lenox*. Which is dreadful, by the way."

To cheer herself up, she recalled the awful dialogue—*"Go—go!"* she begged. *"Please go. I'm a bad girl—bad—bad!"*

Then she realized.

"Also obsessed with a woman's virtue. What makes a woman a good woman." She examined the note. "You could even say the style is similar."

"The murderer trying to imitate the dead man, perhaps?"

"And, in doing so, take his place?"

"In revenge for Mr. Phillips taking his."

This she did not understand and shook her head.

"The vampire," HJ reminded her. "The creature who takes life that does not belong to him."

"Ah, yes."

HJ's theory had the ring of truth to it. But there was something missing: women. Previously, she had thought it a contest between men: Okrent and Phillips. But Phillips wrote obsessively about women, and it seemed his killer also felt he had things to say on the subject. Especially women he felt were bad or impure. Women who left their homes. Or betrayed them . . .

"There is also the cuckold," she said. "The loathing one man might have for another who takes his place between the sheets."

"You said Phillips was unmarried."

"Unmarried *but* good-looking."

"Ah." HJ raised his eyebrows to acknowledge the danger of such a creature. "And the ladies in his life? Are they pure and protected?"

"I can think of only two, one of whom is his sister, who stays firmly put in the home they shared."

"And the other?"

The other, thought Edith, was also safely at home. But her husband, judging from that little melodrama on the street, might not be. She remembered Walling's face, wan and pale as he watched his wife charm another man, something she felt sure he had witnessed many times before.

"It would be interesting," she said, "to look at the other notes sent to David Graham Phillips. See if the theme is similar. I wonder if his sister has given them to the police yet."

"No doubt she has and no doubt you have better things to do."

Stung, she indicated the note.

"Throw it away," said Henry irritably. "Burn it. Put it out of your mind."

Matching his irritation, she answered, "We cannot all burn or destroy what we share, Henry."

They had stumbled onto matters more thorny. For a moment, each considered retreating. Then Henry said, "On the subject of better things to do—does Mr. Fullerton still have *your* letters?"

She sighed to indicate that he did.

"You must get them back. Before you do anything."

She knew *anything* referred to Teddy. If she asked for a divorce, the letters could be used against her with disastrous consequences. Seeking innocent reasons Fullerton had not returned them, she said, "Perhaps he is distracted over his sister's wedding."

"Such a tragic girl," mused Henry. "Beautiful. Gifted, but almost destined for unhappiness." He paused. "You do know she is his half cousin? Not his sister?"

Edith understood her old friend. In return for his solace and advice, Henry sometimes took a tiny morsel of pain. It was his right, she supposed. Thinking—wishing—the conversation over, she rose and went to the door.

Behind her, she heard, "He is *not* kind, our Mr. Fullerton."

"I am aware," she told him.

As she entered the elevator, her own words floated into memory: *I won't believe it's the end, no, I am going to fight for my life—I know it now!* So felt at the time, and felt still. But scalding when she thought of the man who held those words in his hand and how they would seem to others. The thought of her letters becoming public made her ill. It was not only the fear of scandal. Or blackmail. That a self she no longer recognized—passionate, slavish, delighted and deluded— was somewhere in the world, beyond her control, terrified her.

The elevator stopped. As she said good night to the operator and started down the hall, she wondered: How did one *not* think about something? She felt the need to take hold of her own brain and wrench it sharply in a fresh direction.

She heard a clock chime eight.

Good. It was not too late to call Carolyn Frevert.

CHAPTER SIXTEEN

Returning to the suite, she carefully opened the door. If Teddy was sleeping, she did not wish to wake him. If he was still sitting on the floor facing the wall . . .

Truthfully, she did not wish to know.

Entering her room, she called to Choumai. *Had he been lonely? She was so sorry, poor creature all alone, but still, he had been spared reading a dreadful book. Was he hungry? She was sure he was. Would he wait a few minutes while she made a telephone call? Just one small call to a lady named Mrs. Frevert.*

As she waited, Edith peered at the note, the accusation that she was neither pure nor protected, and wondered who Carolyn Frevert might have told that Edith Wharton had promised to read her brother's last book. Who might have taken exception . . .

Then she heard Mrs. Frevert's voice, high and excited, "Mrs. Wharton—have you finished?"

"I have begun."

"You see its quality. What an achievement it is."

"Oh, yes." *Achievement* was broad enough—writing so much without one's hand snapping at the wrist was an achievement.

"But also how it will anger certain people." Mrs. Frevert spoke in a low voice as if those very people were at her door.

"Yes, on that subject, may I ask—who knows that I am reading *Susan Lenox?*"

"No one. Aside from myself and Mrs. Walling."

"Then presumably Mr. Walling also knows."

The slightest delay in answering. *Was this a sensitivity with regard to difficulties in the Walling marriage or something else?*

"I don't know. But you needn't be concerned. William Walling is a man of fine character and a fervent believer in Graham's work."

A fervent believer who seemed to be living apart from his wife. A thought came to her. After the funeral, in that jumble of jostling bodies and heightened emotion, had she noted any frisson between Mr. Walling and Carolyn Frevert?

She had not. Of course that did not mean there had not been a frisson. Only that she had not noticed it—entirely possible in the crush.

She said, "His editor, Mr. Jewett, told me that your brother received several notes from the murderer prior to the shooting. Do you still have those notes?"

There was a pause.

"No. I burned them."

Edith was stunned. "Why would you do that?"

Mrs. Frevert's voice became shrill and unsteady. "Why would I keep such awful things?"

"But you should have given them to the police."

Over the line, a weary sigh. Smarting under the condescension—

These wealthy women who put their faith in police—Edith grew sharp. "Mrs. Frevert, don't you want to see your brother's murderer brought to justice?"

"The murderer will never be brought to justice, at least not by the police. Of that, I am certain."

Certain or hopeful? Edith bit her tongue on the question, reminding herself that whatever else, Mrs. Frevert was devoted to her brother.

But it was also true that she had been strangely apathetic about the arrest of his killer when she and Edith spoke in his study. At the time, Edith had thought her overwhelmed by grief. But she was not such a fragile creature, this Mrs. Frevert.

"I don't think you should give up hope. Your brother was a beloved public figure . . ."

Mrs. Frevert interrupted her. "My one, my *only* hope is to see my brother's last novel published as he wished it to be. *That* is how we will thwart the person responsible for his death. If you wish to help in that endeavor, Mrs. Wharton, I welcome your assistance. If not, I bid you good night."

She hung up. Smiling in bemusement, Edith held the receiver to her collarbone. Fine words. Dignity and depth of feeling nicely balanced. Who could possibly question the sincerity of Carolyn Frevert?

Mrs. Frevert mourned her brother—of that she felt sure. But if that were the case, why burn the only evidence that might implicate his murderer? Her tone when challenged suggested the mere presence of the death threats in her home was intolerable. But she might have disposed of them by giving them to law enforcement. Or, if she distrusted the police that much, she could have released the death threats to the newspapers, appealed to public outrage. New Yorkers delighted in outrage. With those notes, she might have had the whole city demanding to know who killed David Graham Phillips. Why had she destroyed them?

Unless she wished the person who sent them to remain unknown.

Pacing about the room, she asked Choumai who in a woman's life might retain her loyalty, even if he killed the person dearest to her?

Rapidly, she went through all the men who had been at the funeral. There was the other brother, Harrison. But Anna Walling said he had arrived after the killing. William Walling intrigued her. But would Carolyn Frevert call him "a man of fine character"—not to mention "a fervent believer in Graham's work"—if she believed him guilty of killing her brother?

Possibly, if she did not want people to suspect him. But when Edith speculated as to why Carolyn Frevert would protect William Walling, she could only come up with a romance, and here, her imagination failed. To be brutal, Carolyn Frevert was twenty years older than William Walling. She had a certain faded prettiness, but her manner was plain and earnest. Moreover, if Mr. Walling were, however improbably, in love with Mrs. Frevert, his wife would be the obstacle, not Mr. Phillips.

As she tried to recall the faces of the men who had been in that cramped, inadequate apartment, her thoughts leapt to another man whose face was unknown to her. Yet in his absence, he had been strikingly present. Carolyn Frevert's estranged husband. Anna Walling said he was still in New York—why had he not attended the funeral? Had he disliked his brother-in-law? Or had Carolyn Frevert forbidden him to come?

Carolyn Frevert was both married and unmarried, a state Edith would have thought the province of a more audacious personality. That suggested that Mr. Frevert was so odious—perhaps even dangerous—that his wife thought it worth any price to escape. The fact that she had retained the good opinion of her friends and family was another indication that Mr. Frevert's behavior was beyond the pale. And of course she had been able to leave him because she had her brother's support. Maybe even . . . encouragement?

How angry would a man be if he had been thrown out of his marriage by his arrogant brother-in-law? What might such a man do?

A woman who leaves her home walks the street . . .

But why would Carolyn Frevert protect such a man? Why *not* enlist the police, Edith wondered, for one's own safety? The answer was disturbing: Carolyn Frevert would not be the first woman to be terrified into silence by an abusive husband. She might well believe that the best she could manage was to ensure her brother's posterity, rather than avenge his murder. No wonder she had become almost hysterical when asked about the death threats.

She was about to call Carolyn Frevert back—she would apologize, explain that she too had received a threatening note, ask if perhaps they faced a common enemy?

When she saw it. Right there on the bed.

A white envelope laid against the pillow.

Beside it, a sprig of witch hazel.

CHAPTER SEVENTEEN

It was perfectly safe, she told herself. A piece of paper and some words. Where was the danger in that?

Also, she realized, her breath easing, it was not from the murderer. Unless the murderer knew things about her only one person in the world knew.

Taking up the envelope, she held it to the light and saw a shadow, a card or piece of paper that did not match. Briskly, as if the letter were nothing more than a bill from a bad seamstress she did not wish to pay, she opened the envelope and tugged into view a folded piece of blue paper, which she registered at once as a "petit bleu." They did not have them in America. Only in Paris.

His little words.

Once they had come several times a day, traveling from Fullerton's home or office to hers at Rue de Varenne. Sometimes they arrived scarcely after he left her, as if his need was so urgent, he must reach out minutes after parting. He would scribble them in cafés, at his office, or on the tram, dropping them in boxes all over the city, where they were picked up and winged to her breakfast tray or desk. Petits bleus were safer than telephones, where one might be overheard. Sometimes they contained plans; he would come to her at such and such a time. Other times, pleas. He had not heard from her. Did she still love him? She sent reassurances; she had just now written him a long letter; he would have it within the hour. Did he doubt her? Could he? It was that time when they could not bear separation. They *must* keep speaking. And so hundreds of petits bleus flying all over Paris. In the time before the broken talk. Before the silence.

Avoiding the card, she took up the witch hazel, twirling it between thumb and forefinger. It was called the "old woman's flower" because it bloomed in late fall. It was rather bold, with its blood-red core and garish yellow tendrils. She and Fullerton had discovered it buried in snow, on one of their early motor flights; later he had sent her one. It was then she started writing about him in an old leather diary, which she called "The Life Apart" and he teased her was really a love diary.

She didn't have to read the petit bleu, she told herself. She could rip it up, throw it away. But the idea of tearing it up lasted only long enough for her to admit she was not strong enough. She had to know. She opened the blue paper. And read:

> *Nothing else lives in me but you—I have no conscious existence outside the thought of you, the feeling of you.*

Beautiful sentiment. Lovely words. Hardly surprising—she had chosen them with great care.

He was quoting one of her own letters. The letters he still had. Distressed, she took up the witch hazel. Was this a reminder? An invitation?

. . . Blackmail?

Under her words were his.

I missed you. Call again?

Choumai whined. Suddenly reminded of where she was, she thought: How had the letter gotten here? Had he actually been in her suite? She could imagine it. He was appallingly persuasive, able to charm most people into doing what he wanted with that lovely tilt of his head as if he were the only person able to see you properly. A few words, murmured in a deep, honeyed voice. Any chambermaid at the Belmont, she thought savagely, would have succumbed.

She stared at the petit bleu. *Nothing else lives in me but you—I have no conscious existence outside the thought of you, the feeling of you.*

What had she been thinking, writing those words to him? Answer: She hadn't. She had lost herself entirely. It was insanity.

Weary, she undressed for bed. It was an uncomfortable chore; she missed her maid. Alone, she had to think about the body she was unwrapping, actively avoid the sight of it in the mirror. As she slipped off the last scrap, she had a memory of a long-ago bath, slim pale thighs and sturdy knees beneath her chin, slippery with soap.

Impulsively, she turned. Saw a woman who had waited too long.

Once she had been slim, once fresh and firm and new. Now she was heavy, sloping; at once corpulent and withered. When had her skin become so thin and papery? The circles under her eyes so dark? That webbiness at her neck, when had that come? Her waist had been a lovely slender bow; now she was one flabby line from armpit to hip.

Only now that her breasts were soft and slack did she suspect they had once been quite lovely. Lightly she had dismissed the possibility of Carolyn Frevert's allure. Now she was reminded: They were probably the same age.

As a girl, she had thought of her body as she would a paper doll. Something to dress and adorn. Sometimes, when making up, she would feel agitated. Feel a need to stalk about the room, book in hand, for hours, a practice that greatly disturbed her parents. Other times, it was important to sit absolutely still so that the mind could take over and she could forget she even had a body.

She had understood that her life would involve a husband and then children, and bodies played a part in all that. But the closest she came to understanding pregnancy was that she would serve as some sort of chifforobe; after a time, one opened the door and a baby was taken out. How the baby was put in or what served as the door was a mystery.

After she and Teddy had arrived at their mutual decision, she forgot about her body altogether. Except when it was sick. The times when her body was queasy and aching as if it were punishing her for setting it so ruthlessly aside.

The first time Morton Fullerton had said how he loved her and how he wanted to be loved by her, she had been terrified; surely he knew, he had to know, what a failure she was. It was cruel to ask her. They had argued. He had been angry.

The first rushed attempt in the countryside, she knew he was disappointed. As she undressed, she felt him smiling. *Look at the sagging old thing, she'll drop to the floor like a sack of laundry any moment. Dear God, has any woman ever been so unnatural?* Humiliated, she had seized up. Then begged his forgiveness for being so awkward. When he would not concede that she was wholly inadequate, forcing her to say it, she had thrown something at him and stormed out.

The one bright spot, she had thought, was that now it was all over. She had been her absolute worst, and she knew from experience, few people cared to approach after that. Fullerton, who vanished on the slightest pretext, had a perfectly rational excuse never to speak to her again.

The very next day, there was a petit bleu.

He was sure she could never forgive him. But it was . . . too real. Too strong, what he felt. He had failed her, he knew, but perhaps he might be forgiven? *I love you so much Dear that I want only what you want.*

The next time she had traveled to America, she had passed through London and allowed him to take her anywhere he wished. This turned out to be a hotel room near Charing Cross station, as transient as a space with a bed could be . . .

There, she stopped the memory. Drew on her nightgown. Hastily, she thrust the Crane's paper with its snide admonition and the petit bleu into the same drawer and slammed it shut. Then she huddled under the blanket, Choumai beside her. The silence terrified her. It was the ominous quiet of unspeakable things.

A woman who leaves her home . . .

. . . is neither pure nor protected.

She had no home. She had sold her home. She was in this absurd hotel with a sick husband. Whom she had hurt and who would be no help if she was attacked. Yes, she was unprotected. Against a gun, everyone was unprotected.

But strangely, the thought of the gun chilled her nerves. The ugliness, the *cowardice* of shooting someone—how dare he. Rage, blessed and consoling. How dare he. Threaten her. Remembering her stumbling terror on the street, she was furious with herself.

Shoving back the covers, she turned on the light. He lived in the city—that she knew. She would show him who she was. She would go directly to him, look him square in the face. Perhaps even hand him his ridiculous little missive. *"Do not write this,"* she sneered at the imaginary Frevert. *Who are you to tell me what I should and should not do?*

She was half aware, even as she stalked about the room, that she entered that old state of making up, a world where emotions flowed hot, courage was limitless, and anything, *anything*, was possible. Chin held high, body poised on tiptoe, she was like a conductor, able to pull miraculous feeling out of the air with an imperious wave of her hand.

However: She was not a child but a middle-aged woman. And this was not make-believe but a very dangerous proposition.

If a middle-aged woman was going to confront a dangerous man, she needed another dangerous man with her.

Once, she had asked Fullerton if they might be *camarades* rather than lovers. Comrades told each other things. They were honest; they did not degrade each other with secrets. They shared thoughts, experience, adventures.

Taking up the telephone, she asked the operator to connect her. As she waited, she prepared excuses, both to him and herself. He *had* asked that she call. And there were precious few people she knew who were adept at gathering the dull, basic facts. Walter had no use for the dull and basic. Henry refused to leave his room. Who else could she turn to but a journalist?

This time he answered himself. As she had known he would.

"I wish to do something I've been told I shouldn't, and I need you to help me."

She knew all his silences; this one, she judged open. Still, she waited until he said, "Tell me?"

"The murder of a writer. A journalist, in fact. But lately a novelist."

"So we both have cause for concern. This is the Phillips shooting, I take it."

His voice was still marvelous. "It is."

"And why do you need me?"

The silence of the suite deepened. "Would you be able to find someone if I gave you his name?"

"Of course. You know I love finding people."

His voice was light, intimate. Happy. He was pleased that she had called. It was insanity to take any pleasure whatsoever in his pleasure of her.

Well . . . let it be insanity then. A little more could hardly hurt.

CHAPTER EIGHTEEN

❧

Edith had spent too many hours waiting for word from Morton Fullerton before to put herself through another day of hoping and pacing. The next morning, she decided to go out. Not to Appleton; she still felt awkward that she had accused one of their authors of murder. Instead, she would investigate Mr. Jewett's theory that David Graham Phillips had been shot by an enraged supporter of Anthony Comstock.

After she had finished writing, Edith traveled to the New York Society for the Suppression of Vice and presented herself as Mrs. Edith Jones, a lady profoundly distressed by the damaging effects of today's fiction on young minds. At first, she worried one of the suppressors might recognize her from her author portrait; then she realized it was unlikely any of them had ever read a word she had written. She was taken to the office of a Mr. Sumner, a former stockbroker. (Mr. Comstock was not available due to ill health. The personal cost of battling for the morals of the nation!) Mr. Sumner began the meeting with the statement that novels were feeders for brothels.

Mystified that a man could be so stupid and walk upright, Edith said, "Well, not all . . ."

"*All*, Mrs. Jones. Novels are fiction. Fiction is fantasy. Once people are allowed to create their own worlds, they create their own mores. How can we stay faithful to the morals of this world if we permit engagement with the temptations of the illusory worlds of our own making? Once anything is possible . . ."

He paused for effect.

"Then *anything* is possible."

"My mother would have agreed wholeheartedly," said Edith. "But what are we to do, Mr. Sumner? How do we stop people from writing this filth?"

Not wanting to give him ideas, she waited.

"We apply pressure on the publishing houses, Mrs. Jones. And in the case of those women spreading obscenity through the mail, we prosecute!"

It took Edith a moment to realize that by *those women*, he probably meant people like Margaret Sanger, who sought to educate on matters biological.

"Do you win?" she asked.

"Not always. But we make things difficult enough that the next filth-monger thinks twice. And these people are unstable, Mrs. Jones. Once pressured, they often succumb."

". . . to?"

"Suicide."

Shocked, she said, "They kill themselves?"

"Oh, yes. To date fifteen women exposed by the Society have taken their own lives. A guilty conscience is a hard thing to live with."

"And you feel no guilt over driving them to such a desperate act?"

"Writers who do not take care that their work does not offend or corrupt . . ." He shrugged. "There are consequences."

His smugness was unbearable, as was his conviction that the despair of another human being meant a job well done. Edith knew that vulgarity existed, as did bad taste. But so did terror of people who told stories, and it seemed that those most eager to stamp out obscenity were the ones least equipped to do so.

However, Mr. Sumner seemed confident that the traditional levers of power—the courts, the police, public outrage against publishers—were sufficient to carry out the Society's mission. If the Comstockians were able to imprison or impoverish their enemies, even drive them to suicide, there was no need to shoot them. Moreover, Mr. Comstock and his horrible committee would have nothing to do without works like *Susan Lenox*. It was in their interest that books like that were published so that they could throw their stones.

Dispirited, she made her way back to the Belmont, wishing that when she got there, she would find her trunks packed and a taxi waiting to take her to the docks.

She arrived at the hotel at checkout time, and the lobby was crowded and bustling, making it difficult to see any one individual. Not that she had any hope that he had come. It would take Fullerton some time to find Henry Frevert, and even if he had found him, well . . . who knew when he would choose to turn up. Or if he would. Morton Fullerton had done that many times—promise, then vanish—and she would be a complete fool not to know it was possible this time. Sometimes, relations between them felt like that old childhood game of plucking petals off flowers: *Il m'aime. Il ne m'aime pas.* Ruthlessly, she forbid herself pleasurable anticipation.

But then she saw a dark-haired man seated on one of the tufted borne settees. He held his shin in clasped hands, his foot twisting elegantly in its pebble-gray John Lobb boot, as if to remind its owner not to tarry.

The son of a minister and a minister's daughter, Morton Fullerton had been blessed with a handsomely structured skull, silken black hair, and a resplendent mustache. He was not tall, but that added to his naughty allure; life could never quite catch the clever, diminutive Mr. Fullerton long enough to weary him. Neither could those who cared for him, and their numbers were legion. He knew everyone by the various meanings of that word, from Verlaine to Wilde to George Santayana. The ranee of Sarawak had been infatuated, Blanche Roosevelt charmed. He had dabbled in marriage only once, with a French opera singer called Ixo, leaving her a year later for three possible women—no one was sure which.

Before she took the final step of attracting his attention, Edith asked herself: Why? Why had she called him? The operatic defiance of last night was gone. The quick and easy answers—he was a journalist; she could hardly confront a killer alone—all true. Also true, she had called him because she wished to see him. Alone.

Really, she just wanted him to have something none of the rest did.

She moved closer, a little to the left. Made herself known.

Seeing her, he rose immediately. In the crush of people, she smiled.

His lips curled under his mustache, as if he had spotted something delightful but forbidden.

"Have you found him?" she asked.

"Would you believe it? I have. I confess, it wasn't terribly difficult. You might have done it yourself."

"I might have." She wanted very badly to put her arm through his, line herself alongside him. She could feel he wanted her to. Even after everything, he made her feel any hour not spent in his company was a shadow existence.

"He's at 18 Dey Street," said Fullerton.

It was a shabby, mercantile area, ugly buildings and stores that sold cheap goods. A comedown, she thought, from the gentility of Gramercy Park. It would seem Mr. Frevert had not fared well in the separation.

"Well, then," she said brightly, "shall we pay a call on a murderer?"

"By all means."

He offered his arm. She took it. Thought, *Il m'aime.*

As she had expected, 18 Dey Street was a hovel, faced in that drab brownstone that was everywhere in New York. The glass of the front door was smudged, the oak scratched and battered. The windows of the upper floors showed the shabby lack of harmony of a home converted to a boarding house. Next door was Brunswick Books. In the store windows were large signs: "Liquidation Sale! Going Out of Business."

The landlady's eyes widened at the sight of Edith and Fullerton, dapper beside her. Her response when they asked for Henry Frevert: "He owes you money too?"

She showed them to the parlor. The rugs were threadbare, the furniture greasy to the touch. Edith kept her hands in her lap, her back away from the upholstery. The landlady shooed the other residents out, then said she would fetch Mr. Frevert.

"He's not at work then?" Fullerton inquired.

"Work?" she scoffed. "Him?"

As they waited, Fullerton whispered, "What am I to do if he starts waving a pistol about?"

"Knock him over?"

She spoke lightly, but their surroundings unnerved her. This seemed so ramshackle a place, one might scream, *Help! Murder!* only to have people shrug and say, *They've started early today.* Also, the planned attack, settled upon in the taxi, now seemed certain to provoke. *Tell me, Mr. Frevert, how much did you detest your brother-in-law?*

A large individual entered the sitting room. For a moment, he loomed, blocking the way out; Edith wished she had not been so flippant in her answer to Fullerton's question.

Rising, she said in her best hostess voice, "Ah, Mr. Frevert!"

She inclined her head in greeting, he responded in kind. He did not seem vicious, but neither did he put one at ease, moving from one foot to the other, looking over his shoulder as if anticipating the need for escape. His thinning gray hair was combed, but scarce. His hollowed cheeks shaved, but not recently, leaving a dirty scruff. He looked wrung out, as if life had taken him in its grip and twisted hard. With one hand, he held the edge of his trousers; with the other, he pulled at a grubby tie. That hand he offered to Fullerton, withdrawing it with embarrassment when Fullerton did not extend his.

This was not a husband one would want back, Edith thought as she sat down. But was he a husband one would protect, either out of fear or loyalty? The show of manners and the attempts at grooming indicated a man who had been raised to expect better things—a sharp spur for grievance. She wondered how she might get a look at his handwriting.

He asked, "You're not bill collectors, are you?"

"No, Mr. Frevert."

"Police?"

"Why would you expect the police, Mr. Frevert?" asked Fullerton.

A hitch of one bony shoulder. "Well—Graham."

Edith and Fullerton glanced at each other. As the gentleman had come to the point, she felt it time for introductions. "My name is Mrs. Edith Wharton. I was a colleague of your former brother-in-law." She saw her name meant nothing to him.

He squatted on the chair next to the settee. "Still is my brother-in-law. Or . . . was."

Not terribly bright, she thought. Easily overwhelmed. But probably murderers weren't bright. If they were, they'd find less risky solutions to their problems.

Fullerton gave the story they had planned. "I'm writing an article about the shooting."

A sharp shake of the head. "I can't tell you anything about that."

"We'd be happy to pay you for your time," said Fullerton. "We don't expect a busy man such as yourself to give his thoughts for nothing."

Frevert glanced at the hallway where the landlady lurked. "How much?" Fullerton named the amount they had agreed to in the taxi. Frevert accepted it with a nod.

"What was your reaction when you heard Mr. Phillips was dead?"

"Sad," said the other man swiftly, as if relieved the question could be answered in a single word.

"Surprised?"

"Not really. Graham wasn't the sort to make friends."

"Were you his friend?" Fullerton asked artlessly.

"How many in-laws you know who call themselves pals?" He slid his palms over his thighs. "No, but I was sorry to hear it. I'm sure it's grieved Carrie terribly."

Intrigued, Edith asked, "You call her Carrie?"

He colored. "I know she prefers Carolyn now. But we started with Carrie, and I got into the habit."

"Where did you 'start'?" asked Fullerton.

"Indiana."

His leg had begun to jiggle. Wanting to put him at ease, Edith said, "I understand you were a businessman."

"One of Madison's most promising."

"And what brought you east?"

"Oh, well . . ." The hands hanging limply between his knees came together. "That would have been Graham. He came to work for *The Sun*. Carrie was worried about him alone in a big city, felt he should have someone to look after him. It did make expenses easier, all of us sharing a place."

Feeling she had gained his confidence, she said, "Expenses might be easier, but surely living together made other things difficult."

Mr. Frevert squirmed. "How well did you know Graham, Mrs. Wharton?"

"Enough to know that I would not have enjoyed living under the same roof with him. He seemed a domineering personality."

"That about sums it up. Carrie—excuse me, Carolyn—used to say to me, 'Don't start fights.' I said, 'I'm not the one starting them.'"

"What did you fight about, Mr. Frevert?" Fullerton asked.

"Graham just took up so much space. Always going on about the corporations and the crooks in Albany and Washington. I don't say he was wrong, but you know how it is with people of strong opinions: If you don't go along with every last thing they say, they make you the villain."

And are *you the villain?* wondered Edith.

"You could have told him to leave," said Fullerton.

"Couldn't afford to. New York is expensive."

"So you were the one to go," said Edith softly. "What happened, Mr. Frevert?"

He glanced nervously from her to Fullerton. "Like I said, he took up a lot of space."

"But there must have been a breaking point," said Fullerton. "As you say, it's expensive in New York." Pointedly, he looked about the wretched sitting room. "For you to leave your home, the situation must have become intolerable."

Frevert exhaled. Looked again to the door. Under normal circumstances, Edith would see this as a natural reaction to being asked to share intimate details of a broken marriage. But these were not normal circumstances.

Finally he said, "I just got tired of the man's posturing. If I mispronounced something or said a topic of conversation wasn't suitable, he'd sneer. He had a lot to say about how a husband should act. One night, I lost my temper and told him if he was so interested in being a good husband, why didn't he find his own wife? Turned into a real battle. I told Carrie she had to choose. Took her about two seconds. That was ten years ago."

He raised his hands, letting them fall back to his knees. Perhaps unwittingly, he had made a point in his favor, she thought. If the Freverts had been separated for a decade, why would he shoot his cantankerous brother-in-law now?

Fullerton asked, "And you've been living here since?"

"No." Frevert pulled at his tie. "Hit a rough patch in the panic of last year. Had to change the living arrangements."

Well, there was the why. A sudden downturn in fortune might have inflamed Frevert's resentment against the man who was the reason he had left a prosperous business back home to come to a city he didn't care for—only to be turned out of his own home.

But why did he not return to Indiana, she wondered. Why stay? Unless he had hopes . . .

"Have you been in touch with Mrs. Frevert since her brother's death?" she asked.

"No, I'll go see her when the time's right."

"Right for what?"

Fullerton had posed the question in his smoothest, most neutral tone, giving Frevert no clue as to what the answer should be. Flummoxed, Frevert said, "When she's had some time. To grieve and get past . . ."

"The loss of her beloved brother."

Mr. Frevert gazed at him, not seeing the trap clearly but knowing it was there.

Fullerton said, "You must admit, his death presents an opportunity for you."

Frevert's fingers curled around the edge of the armrests. "I don't at all."

Edith said hastily, "I think what Mr. Fullerton means to say is that perhaps something good might come out of this tragedy. If you and Mrs. Frevert were able to reconcile. If nothing else, now that her brother is dead, how will she support herself?"

"I imagine Graham left her provided for. Didn't have anybody else to leave it to."

"But he wasn't a wealthy man," said Edith.

"By your standards, maybe not. But he did all right by Madison standards."

It was one of Fullerton's gifts to say the unsayable. "But that's even worse, Mr. Frevert. A brother-in-law you disliked, a man who got you evicted from your home, then took your wife as his companion, has been killed. You have recently fallen on difficult times. His death means you not only get your wife back, but she has become a rich woman. By Madison standards."

Edith glared; that last insult was unnecessary. Ready to apologize, she looked to Henry Frevert and was astonished to see him smiling.

"Sure, it makes sense," he said. "Couple of things wrong with your theory, though. First off, Carrie wouldn't have me back. It was never a love match. I think her folks wanted the marriage more than she did. Graham was always telling her that her mind and spirit were going to waste, married to me. And while she never said it, I knew she pretty much agreed."

"How awful," said Edith sincerely. Then recalled the times she had thought the exact same thing about being married to Teddy.

Frevert nodded to the outer corridor where the landlady was swatting the floor with a broom. "Finally you can ask Mrs. Krauss. I was here all that day hanging wallpaper for her. I'm a bit behind on the rent, so I pay her in odd jobs. I was covered in paste, so she made me take off everything and go back to my room wrapped in butcher paper. I was a sight. I remember it because when I heard, I wanted to go to Carrie, but every last stitch I had was drying on the line."

Fullerton bestowed his most beguiling smile. "You won't mind if I do ask the charming Frau Krauss."

"Be my guest," said Frevert.

As Fullerton went off in search of Mrs. Krauss, Edith felt the sudden intimacy of being left *à deux* and wondered how to use the situation to its full advantage. She didn't think Henry Frevert had the imagination to concoct the story of hanging wallpaper; most likely the bilious landlady would confirm it. True, he would not miss his brother-in-law, but he did not seem bitter toward the woman who was once his wife. Therefore, probably not a man to rail against impure women who left their home.

If Carolyn Frevert had not inspired such rage, who had?

Then she remembered: David Graham Phillips did not detest women society might condemn. His contempt was for women whose only passions were for luxury or status. Women such as Grace Vanderbilt, for example. Remembering the writer's wistful expression as he talked of love and burning bridges, she wondered again if some lady—or a woman who was not at all a lady—had captured his heart.

"Mr. Frevert, may I ask an indelicate question?"

"Another one?" The hands between the knees bobbed. "Go ahead."

"When you asked Mr. Phillips why he didn't find a wife of his own, what did he say?"

"Said he didn't have time for it. And that he had a duty to his sister."

"Certainly, as a loving sister, she wanted to see her brother happily settled."

Frevert nodded. "When I lived with them, she'd invite ladies over for supper, encourage Graham to show an interest. Every one, he dismissed as a noddle-head or doodlewit. But a short while back, I stopped by the apartment and Carrie was all excited. She told me Graham had finally found a woman who could match wits with him."

Edith waited for the name. When it didn't come, she asked, "Mrs. Frevert didn't say who it was?"

He shook his head. "It was all very hush-hush for some reason."

Edith surmised she knew the reason. "What happened?"

"I suspect it ended badly. Graham still had plenty of invective for fat cats and politicians. But after that, he built up a real rage against women of a . . . certain level of refinement," he finished tactfully. "Women who *liked* money. Put it before love, in his view."

Refinement—that fit, thought Edith. But avarice? That hardly described the woman she had in mind. Although she was certainly beautiful.

Then she remembered Anna Walling laughing as she said, "He once rebuked me for riding in a motorcar. He feared I was becoming an aristocrat." Perhaps avarice was in the eye of the beholder. A woman who refused to leave her wealthy husband might be described as such, if one was unkind. Or disappointed.

There had been some kind of rift in the Walling marriage. An affair could cause a rift. As could the suspicion that your husband had killed your lover.

She asked Henry Frevert, "And you don't know when it ended?"

He shook his head. "I spent a lot of time being aggravated by David Graham Phillips. I'm not inclined to give him another minute's thought."

Fullerton appeared at the door. A short nod indicated that the landlady supported Mr. Frevert's account of wallpapering.

Edith had one last question for Henry Frevert: "Did Mrs. Frevert keep a tidy house?"

He blinked in surprise that she had guessed. "Yes. Yes, she did. She liked things orderly. Everything in its place, and if it didn't have a place or use, out it went."

He smiled sadly and Edith understood he felt himself to be one of those things. Still, he had confirmed that it was not out of character for Carolyn Frevert to have destroyed the notes. Desiring dominance over her own small space in the wake of a catastrophe, she wanted them out of her domain as quickly as possible. That, Edith could understand.

Then she heard Henry Frevert say, "I don't suppose Carrie mentioned me at all." And before she could devise something suitably pleasant, "I didn't think so."

Mr. Frevert's humility spoke well of him, she decided. As did the butcher paper. As did the fact that he seemed a simple, plainspoken man, not given to words like *vampire*. And she doubted he knew the Belmont existed, much less that she was staying there or was a writer who must be warned off a story.

Rising, she said, "Thank you for your time, Mr. Frevert. If it is any consolation, I don't believe Mr. Phillips respected me very much either. He was stingy that way. And mistaken."

Hands in his pockets, Frevert bobbed his head in thanks.

Going out into the corridor, she found the landlady. In German, she asked, "How much does Mr. Frevert owe you, Mrs. Krauss?"

"Seventy dollars," she said indignantly. "Six *months*, he has not paid."

Taking out her purse, Edith handed her the back rent. Then she realized they had not paid Mr. Frevert and instructed Fullerton to do so. He waited a moment. Noting the hesitation, she raised an eyebrow. He said yes, of course.

As they left 18 Dey Street, Edith glanced back at the parlor window and wished Mr. Frevert better fortune.

CHAPTER NINETEEN

꧁✦꧂

I t's not unheard of," Fullerton said.

After Dey Street, Edith said she wanted to see where the murder had occurred. Now she and Fullerton stood side by side gazing up at the dull beige brick of the National Arts Club. She tried to imagine the currents of three lives in that ungainly space—was it always the same two against one, or did the alliances ever shift? As she envisioned Carolyn Frevert moving from room to room and man to man, she was so absorbed, she forgot Fullerton was with her until he spoke.

He had been ominously quiet in the taxi over. She suspected it was something to do with the money she had asked him to pay Frevert, but surely he understood that she had given over a much greater sum to the landlady. Anxious, she had tried to engage him by pointing out sights that had changed; he had not even bothered to look. His only contribution to the conversation had been to remark that

Henry Frevert was a complete nonentity and Carolyn Frevert a wise woman to have left him. His instinctive siding with the leaver left her on the side of the abandoned. Tartly, she responded that if *decent* were deemed a synonym for *dull*, it was a sad world.

She noted that Fullerton had not specified *what* was unheard of; she was meant to ask. Asking would give him permission to say things she might not wish to hear. She sensed that his mood had turned malicious. Recalling Henry's snipe about cousins and half-sisters, Edith decided not to respond.

Instead, she envisioned David Graham Phillips's last journey. He would have come sauntering out of the building, preoccupied by his own greatness and the world's wickedness. His head would have been down, she thought; hers was when she was thinking hard. And as it was a walk he had taken many times, he would not need to look where he was going. So he hadn't seen the man with the gun until it was too late.

The quiet homeliness of the block, the brevity of the walk, struck her as painful. David Graham Phillips's life had ended so quickly after he left this place. He had died so close to home.

That felt important. She reiterated the thought: *He died close to home.* And the letters had come to his home.

"What?" asked Fullerton.

"I am thinking of letters."

In her preoccupation with David Graham Phillips's home, she had forgotten that letters were a charged subject. The word hung, awkward and twisting, between them until she broke the mood, saying briskly, "Prior to his death, David Graham Phillips received several threats. Some were sent to the Princeton Club. Others came here."

"Which means the killer knew his address," said Fullerton, catching her line of thought.

"More than that, he knew his movements, the precise times he came and went. Not easy, even with a man of habit such as David Graham Phillips."

"So, the killer was watching the house."

"Precisely."

But where had the killer stood as he charted the writer's movements? It would be difficult to stand for hours in such a quiet neighborhood and not be noticed. Especially in the frigid air of January. If he had waited on the street, why hadn't David Graham Phillips noticed him? A man who was receiving death threats would surely be aware of anyone watching or following him. A man idling close to his house would be suspicious, especially if one saw him repeatedly.

Turning, she gazed up at the surrounding buildings, then across the street where a row of drab, anonymous houses slumped along the block, interrupted only by a large, squat building that seemed to be an institute, judging by the plaque bearing the name RAND SCHOOL. The upper floors seemed to be lodgings. From a distance, she peered into windows. Saw nothing more incriminating than curtains and pane glass.

But there was a second possibility: The killer knew David Graham Phillips's habits because he knew David Graham Phillips. A stranger would be noticeable on these streets, seen as possibly dangerous by a man who was being threatened. But a friend, a relative, a colleague . . .

But Fullerton was restless. "Is it a large apartment?" he asked.

It was the same artless tone he had used with Frevert, but she heard the subversion. "Not especially. Let's walk his path to the Princeton Club."

She started on ahead. He remained where he was.

"Two bedrooms," he clarified.

"Yes, two bedrooms," she said shortly.

She hoped her tone was a warning. But he smiled. She had answered; that was all that mattered.

As they approached Gramercy Park, she was careful not to look at him. She partly guessed what he wished to spring on her, and she hoped to avoid the trap.

Princeton, she realized, was also a charged subject between them. As were sisters. She had always known she was not the only woman to exchange letters with Morton Fullerton. Sometimes he read them in her presence, smiling as he did so. Always, she feigned lack of interest. But once, unable to resist, she peeked and saw the words "Ah, my own, my own!" She never looked again.

Several months after that, Fullerton's adopted sister, Katharine, arrived in Paris. The young woman was ardent and literary, quite without the defenses of wit or irony. She had studied at Radcliffe, lectured at Bryn Mawr. She sent Edith a poem on the subject of Dante and Beatrice. Edith was unsure: Was it a confession? An inquiry? Or was she simply looking for affirmation? In the end, she sent praise, and an invitation to see Isadora Duncan.

"Does she know?" she asked Fullerton afterwards.

"Of course not."

Do I *know?* she had wondered, and elected not to ask. She always felt lies were the worst humiliation he could inflict upon her. And yet he could use the truth—toy with it anyway—to unsettle her as well. Always, he . . . reversed things. If she did not beg for him, he called her cold. When she showered him with adoration, he accused her of suffocating him. She declared him free to do as he wished; he insisted she did not mean it. And now when she wished to discuss a murder, he wished to discuss love between brother and sister. And not because he truly believed it was the motive for the murder, but because he wished to see her off balance. *Il ne m'aime pas.*

Last year, Katharine Fullerton had married a Chaucer scholar at Princeton. Seeing the club rising above the gates of Gramercy Park, Edith thought to push it all out into the open. Lightly, she would say, *Don't you know someone at Princeton?* But it was not a fight she would win.

"The shooter," asked Fullerton. "Did he come up from behind or shoot him face-to-face?"

"As I understand it, they were face-to-face. The two witnesses were coming out of the building and they only saw the back of the shooter. One remembered a striped scarf." Had William Walling worn a striped scarf? She tried to recall.

"But Phillips didn't say anything?"

"Such as 'My God, so-and-so, why have you shot me, I thought we were friends'? Nothing so useful."

"But it was a man."

In his eyes, a focus that demanded he join her in his thoughts. She found it hard to resist. "Yes, of course a man. What are you implying?"

He put his hands in his pockets. "I find it interesting that Phillips's marital status was the subject of the final argument between the murdered man and Henry Frevert."

"Your point?"

"I wonder how Mr. Frevert felt, being kicked out of bed for his brother-in-law."

She had asked for honesty, she reminded herself. Well, here it was. *Camarades* should be able to negotiate such a conversation. But she felt his hunger for her distress. She would not give it to him.

"David Graham Phillips was complex," she said finally. "But rather pure-minded in that frank American way. I feel the arrangement you are suggesting would have struck him as decadent. Aristocratic."

"Hardly the first hypocrite to rail against what he desires."

"No, he disliked hypocrisy in matters of sex." She thought of that pompous introduction to *Susan Lenox*: *There are three ways of dealing with the sex relations of men and women—two wrong and one right.*

"He wrote about it a great deal in his novels. So much so that his editor believes one of the more deranged Comstockians might have killed him."

"So, he liked *writing* about it. Did he ever . . . engage?"

She thought of what Henry Frevert had told her. That there had been a woman possessed of wits "worthy" of David Graham Phillips. It was worth noting that Carolyn Frevert had not been possessive of her brother. To the contrary, if her husband was to be believed, she was pleased he had found someone.

Wanting the matter of Henry Frevert's innocence decided, she announced, "You think Frevert shot his brother-in-law out of jealousy and a wish to reconcile with his wife. But it is not as you suggest. For one thing, the landlady's account is persuasive. If she wanted a nonpaying tenant out of her house, what better way to evict him than to announce he was suspiciously absent the day his brother-in-law was murdered? Not to mention, the Freverts had been separated for some time. Why would Frevert suddenly take against his brother-in-law so violently as to shoot him?"

Fullerton shrugged, as if the loss of his Greek tragedy bothered him not at all. "Then perhaps a different jealous husband?"

"Perhaps," she said.

"Do you have a theory?"

She did, but not one she wished to share with him. To do so

would invite the possibility of introducing him to the person she had in mind. Which—one could call it jealousy; one could call it whim— she had no intention of doing.

Instead, looking through the bars at the slush-sodden grounds, she remarked on the hubris of building such an ungainly fence around such an unprepossessing bit of park. "It doesn't make it an Eden, keeping the sinners out."

"Was it sin?" Fullerton looked at her. "As I remember it was a choice. Ignorance and bliss. Or knowledge and exile."

"Poor Eve, if only there had been somewhere in Eden to quietly dispose of an apple core."

"Ah, but could she rely on the serpent's discretion?"

Again, he was teasing—no, insulting. *Ne m'aime pas.* It was time, she decided, to assert matters important to her.

Turning to face him, she said, "My letters."

"I cherish them," he said, his tone deliberately bland.

"You will have to cherish the memory. I want them back."

Theatrically, he patted his coat to indicate he did not have them at present.

Impatient, she said, "When you return to Paris, send them to me."

She waited for his *of course.* It did not come. What could she say that would not be pleading? *You returned Henry's letters.* Henry, so reserved in person, allowed his emotions full and free expression on the page, to a degree that would be shocking to those who did not know him and even some who did. His letters often came with the instruction "Commit this to the flame." Recently, he had made a bonfire of much of his correspondence, some of it from her. She had grieved, but also felt deep relief.

Now she had a disquieting thought. Last year, she and Henry had rescued Fullerton from his own epistolary folly, giving him the money to retrieve letters of a sensitive nature from a vicious little blackmailer named Madame Mirecourt.

Had Fullerton taken an ugly lesson from Madame Mirecourt?

"If it is money," she said with difficulty.

"Ah, here it is!" he cried, suddenly furious. "Always with you, it is money. It is what gives you power, so again and again, you brandish it over my head like a whip. How can you say this . . . to *me*?"

So—she *had* been wrong to tell him to pay Frevert. She cringed with remorse, even as a small, exasperated part of her thought, *Because you are often in need of money. It should not be heresy to say so.*

"Does this mean you've decided about Teddy?" he asked. "You're afraid the letters could be used against you in a divorce?"

His interest surprised her. Intrigued her. But she must not be drawn. "It means I would like my letters back."

"Why?"

"Because they are mine." And before he could object, she said, "You have no use for them. You've made that clear."

"Then yes, of course," he said, straightening. "When we return."

His careless acquiescence hurt, as it was meant to. And she knew: He was lying. When she was in Paris, the letters would be in London. Or Boston. He meant to keep them, she realized. For what purpose she didn't know. He would keep her letters, keep her raw, exposed self. And there was nothing she could do about it.

Except one thing.

I will write this, she thought. *I will write you and understand you and make you a thing that I create. And I will write that other woman too, that young ardent girl, because I am not afraid of her. I can look at her. I can even look at myself in the reflection of her youth and your obsession with her. I can do that. That power, I do have.*

Spotting a taxi on the other corner, she suggested that he go and fetch it.

As she watched him go, she thought of writers and lovers. Really, it was almost unfair that writers could take revenge in print on those who had wounded them in life, twisting the story and its characters any way they liked.

But that was not exactly true, not if the writer was good. Which was to say honest. Something authentic about the beloved usually appeared on the page. Something perhaps even . . . recognizable.

Susan Lenox. Had she been inspired by a real woman? A real love—and loss? Had Phillips written so much about her so he could, in some way, spend time with a woman he cared for but could not have?

Getting into the taxi, she instructed the driver to take her to Appleton. It was several blocks before she realized she had not said a proper goodbye to Morton Fullerton. In fact, she had all but forgotten him.

CHAPTER TWENTY

Susan Lenox did not improve with further reading. Sitting in the execrable armchair, Edith read purely for story, following Susan from the horror of her wedding night to her escape on a steamboat with an idealistic journalist named Roderick Spenser. The steamboat wrecked and the journalist got typhus. Arriving in New York, Spenser tried his hand at playwriting, and Susan worked in a house of bondage, "abandoning her body to abominations beyond belief." Spenser drank. Susan took opium. Then she met a powerful, successful man named Robert Brent. He was also a playwright. Apparently, there was no other profession to which one might aspire in New York.

Searching for clues to Susan's identity, Edith found many descriptions of her. Her eyes were "starlike," her lips "crimson," her features set in "the clear old-ivory pallor of her small face in its frame of glorious dark hair." She was slender, she was sensuous, she was perfect. Edith tried to match this paragon to the women in David

Graham Phillips's life. In beauty, perhaps Mrs. Walling. In devotion, perhaps Mrs. Frevert. But in truth, like no woman who had ever actually walked the earth.

Restless, she went to the stack of earlier novels and began leafing through them. Here, she found more women. Bold women, craven women, generous women, selfish women. Saints, harlots, harridans, shrews, helpmeets. But they did, she noticed, have a few things in common. Certain sorts of names came up repeatedly. Certain character traits. *Yes*, she thought, *she is here after all.*

Turning the pages of *The Fashionable Adventures of Joshua Craig*, she read, "She has some brains—the woman kind of brains. If I had the time and it were worthwhile, I could develop her into a real woman." Insufferable. Perhaps Fullerton was right and a woman had murdered David Graham Phillips . . . Then she heard a knock and called, "Yes?"

The door opened and Mr. Jewett appeared. "My apologies, Mrs. Wharton, they just told me you were here. I am anxious to know: What do you make of our *Susan Lenox*?"

Weighing tact and candor, she said, "I am uncertain as to whether Susan Lenox genuinely exists on the page. But she certainly existed for Mr. Phillips. Do you have any idea as to who might have inspired her?"

"Graham once told me that when he was fourteen years old, still living in the Midwest, he saw a beautiful young woman in a wagon. He felt she had breeding. Culture. Next to her was an older man, perhaps a farmer. His suit indicated some level of wealth, but no refinement. He put a hand on the girl and she shrank. Graham said he couldn't forget the look of noble resignation on her face. To be such a person as she was, yoked to a man who would only appreciate . . ."

Delicately, he concluded, ". . . one aspect of her being."

"So he wrote a novel about her."

Jewett spread his hands: *Apparently so.*

Edith considered. Fourteen and living in the Midwest strongly suggested Carolyn Frevert. But Susan Lenox was beautiful. Even in youth, Carolyn Frevert would not have been a beauty. Moreover, Susan was physically alluring. Erotic. That too pointed elsewhere.

And the dull, unworthy man who had claimed her? She could not imagine William Walling in a wagon. But perhaps the man had not been William Walling.

What, precisely, had Anna Walling been back in Russia? The image of a girl bundled off in a wagon could be American. But it also had a certain Slavic feel to it.

Jewett broke her thoughts, asking, "May I know the reason for your interest?"

Thinking of Morton Fullerton, she said, "In every novel, there is a touch of vengeance. I'm curious to know who is avenged in *Susan Lenox.*"

And who, she thought, might wish to take vengeance in return.

The Belmont lobby was particularly frantic when she returned. She turned toward the front desk when several things happened. A bellboy passed carrying four cases, and two small dogs took noisy exception to each other, which caused a martyred-looking nurse to wheel her ancient charge's chair around a gold velvet sofa to avoid them, thereby startling a young chatterbox who was announcing her devotion to Maynard's fudge. Assailed by the barking of the dogs, the squeaking of the wheels, and the calls of "Excuse me, sir, pardon me, madame," Edith was momentarily flummoxed.

Then she felt a sudden blow to her shoulder as someone shoved past, jostling her sideways. Furious, she searched through the crowd for the precise person to blame, and saw a dark-haired man, his long slim legs scissoring as he made his way to the elevators. He carried his hat in his hand, so she saw his glossy hair, ever so slightly receding from his high pale forehead. The elevator doors opened just as he approached; he got on with the ease of a man accustomed to doing so.

William Walling, it seemed, was a guest at the Belmont Hotel.

The day before, that might have surprised her. Now she only wondered when he had arrived.

Going to the desk, she asked for her messages. The desk clerk handed her an envelope. Opening it immediately, she read:

A man in this world who does just about what he wishes is liable to be a social outcast, a very prominent member of the Four Hundred, or both.

Perhaps it was vanity, but it almost sounded like an imitation of her style. There were two signifiers: "social outcast" and "member of the Four Hundred." *Which are you?* she wondered.

Based on what she now knew, she suspected the answer was both. William Walling would have had an excellent education, which would have taught him proper handwriting. And despite his proletarian pretensions, she suspected he used quality writing paper, such as Crane's.

She had suspected William Walling when she received the warning to women who strayed from their homes, only to reconsider when Carolyn Frevert insisted that Walling supported Phillips's work. Why, if that were the case, would he warn her off reading *Susan Lenox*?

Unless that novel revealed truths about his wife he wished to keep secret. The cultured young girl in the wagon who later became a prostitute—had Anna Walling shared stories of her sordid past with Phillips that he then turned into *Susan Lenox*? A novel her vain, fragile husband felt humiliating to her—and, more importantly, to him? A disgrace compounded by his wife's affair with the author? She remembered Mrs. Walling entrancing Walter with her bold black eyes while Mr. Walling looked on, her own certainty that Walling had endured that torment before. Had he watched the same scene in that very room of the Phillips apartment, between his wife and the man who lived there?

All was quiet in the suite on the top floor. As she opened the door, Choumai hopped off his pillow and trundled over to greet her. Taking up the telephone, she asked to be connected. When a woman's voice came on the line, she said, "Mrs. Walling. This is Mrs. Edith Wharton. I would like to invite you to tea here at the Belmont. Shall we say two o'clock tomorrow? Excellent."

CHAPTER TWENTY-ONE

Edith Wharton sat alone in the Palm Garden of the Belmont Hotel and considered the question of beauty. Not with regard to the room, which she found deeply unattractive, but in people. What made a face and form beautiful? One knew it when one saw it, but it was not always easy to say why. (Whereas deficiencies were easy to categorize—she had done so often enough with her own slab of a face.) When creating Lily Bart, she had imagined freshness. A purity that was just beginning to show the traces and smudges of being on display for years. Lily Bart suffered from exposure; unclaimed too long, she had grown just that bit stale.

Seeing Anna Strunsky Walling, nervous and defiant at the room's entrance, Edith decided she *was* beautiful. And yet she was a woman who had most certainly been in the world, and Edith guessed she had not always been protected. As she came into the tearoom, her movement suggested power and vigor, but she was not coarse. Her face was uncrowded, her features boldly drawn—strong dark brows; eyes rich and brown as the center of a sunflower; ears that stuck out slightly from her lovely round head; a nose that was a genuine nose, although Edith's mother would have had something to say about its length, and Edith noticed it herself. Her black hair was parted down the middle; her long white neck was ravishing. Her figure was extraordinary. Yet she was not merely beautiful, thought Edith. She was romantic. A woman to dream on.

Which men had dreamed of her? In Russia, who knew? But in this country, Walter had mentioned a long friendship with Jack London. London was also a journalist, politically minded, a good-looking rough-and-ready sort from America's West Coast. There were similarities, she thought, between him and the deceased Mr. Phillips.

But unlike Lily, Anna had been claimed, although she would probably resent that statement, insisting marriage had been her choice. But her husband's presence at the Belmont suggested she had cause to regret that choice. What Edith wished to know was: Where had that regret led her? Where had it led William Walling?

As she made her way into the tearoom, Mrs. Walling's clear and creamy brow was furrowed with confusion at being summoned to such a place and by such a person. But she gave a cry of delight when presented to Choumai, immediately babbling to the dog in Russian, then French in a way that made Edith feel that even if Mrs. Walling was a socialist, she was at least a dog lover.

"I am reading *Susan Lenox*," Edith told her.

Mrs. Walling smiled. "And?"

"I am not sure I share your"—this word Edith had planned beforehand—"ardent admiration of his style. But certainly he has things to say." She sat back in her chair. "You are quite the champion for David Graham Phillips. Have you known him long?"

"I met them in Paris a few years ago."

Edith noted the switch in pronouns. Purposely evasive as to the significance of Mr. Phillips in her life? Or more evidence that brother and sister were a single entity?

"He and his sister?" Anna Walling nodded. Edith said, "They seem extraordinarily close."

"Oh, yes." Mrs. Walling's eyes shone with genuine fervor. "I remarked the very same thing when we were in Paris. It was unlike anything I had ever seen, this love. It was like the sun."

In Edith's experience, the sun warmed, but also burned and wore one out. Still, Mrs. Walling had her theme and she let her continue.

"The way she supported him—and he her! They lived in perfect harmony, every step in life they took together . . ."

Wishing to introduce the topic of alienated husbands, Edith said, "Not her marriage, certainly."

Halted in her passionate endorsement of the Phillips siblings, Anna Walling said, "I couldn't say."

"So you liked Mr. Phillips immediately. He was not so . . . directive then?"

The other woman laughed. "Oh, no, he was. Many opinions. He despised fashionable women who were motivated by a desire for material comfort and status rather than genuine love and sensuality."

Both women became aware of Edith's coat, its collar and cuffs trimmed in sable. Hastily Mrs. Walling added, "But he felt that men and women were both responsible for the degrading barter of women. And he candidly confessed to liking luxury himself. He worked as he did partly to avoid the lure of frivolity and indulgence.

The way he talked, the things he thought about—he had a luminous intellect. His mind could go here, there, anywhere his reason took him. 'Make your mistakes a ladder, not a grave,' he said. He seemed to me a boy, a wondrous boy."

"You sound smitten."

"He fired my heart," said Mrs. Walling simply.

Edith found herself touched by the other woman's vulnerability. Her passion for the dead man was such she could not help showing it.

"And Mr. Walling? What of his heart? Did he share your fondness for David Graham Phillips?"

A clumsy little shrug. ". . . Of course."

Edith raised an eyebrow. "I pay you the compliment of saying you are a sincere woman and a poor actress. I find it rare that spouses agree on friends of a certain kind."

"I don't have 'kinds' of friends, Mrs. Wharton. Only friends."

Oh, yes? Such as Jack London? But Anna Walling was already bristling. A direct challenge could provoke a departure. Edith decided to retreat to safer ground.

"Tell me, how did you and Mr. Walling meet?"

"We met in San Francisco," said the other woman. "We were both members of a group opposed to tsarist tyranny in Russia."

"Ah, yes, your homeland."

"I would not call it that. My family came to America when I was nine years old."

Nine years old. Far too young to have been the despairing beauty in the wagon. Her vision of a lurid past on the Russian steppe spoiled, Edith recalled Henry Frevert's words: *Graham had finally found a woman who could match wits with him.* She still felt strongly that Phillips had revealed his illicit attraction in his work.

She said, "Mrs. Walling, it's your view that David Graham Phillips was murdered to stop the publication of *Susan Lenox*."

"I said I felt he was murdered to silence him," she corrected.

"And yet I don't find *Susan Lenox* a specifically political work."

"The lives of women in this country—the insulting conjunction of personal and economic—the way we are all forced into prostitution of some kind? You don't find that political, Mrs. Wharton?"

Edith noted the reference to prostitution. But she would not be distracted. "I do find that Mr. Phillips was obsessed with a certain kind of woman. One thing I observe: Often the woman who inspires great passion in our hero has a name that begins or ends with *A*. She is Anita or Alice or Viola. In one novel, she is Russian, the captivating Baroness Nadeshda."

"I assure you, I am not a baroness."

"In another, she is Selma, who also happens to be Jewish."

"And hardly the only Jewish woman in the city of New York."

"The women he deems worthy of love defy convention. They are driven. Unwilling to live off a man's largesse and reputation. Didn't you say you prefer to write under your maiden name, that you deplored having to live under your husband's shadow?"

"Mrs. Wharton, are you implying I am the inspiration for Graham's heroines?"

"I am wondering how a man who never married became so intimately acquainted with passion. The dialogue is laughable, but the mechanics seem to be in order."

"And you think I am Graham's dark-haired lady?"

"You are certainly dark-haired and certainly attractive. As well as married."

Anna Walling's aspect became brittle. "I see. In your little story, it is William who shoots Graham for love of me."

"At Mrs. Frevert's house after the funeral, you said you hoped the murderer was not anyone who knew Graham. Then you added, 'knew his work.' Meaning, I think, that you actually are worried that he was killed by someone who knew him. An acquaintance. Even a friend."

". . . Not in the slightest, I assure you." Edith noticed that Mrs. Walling's hands were tight in her lap. "Also, I think this is none of your business."

"Very little of what we concern ourselves with is our business, Mrs. Walling, that's a poor dodge. And let me remind you, you asked me to involve myself in the matter of David Graham Phillips."

"His work, yes. Not his private life."

"He was a writer, Mrs. Walling, his work and private life are hopelessly intertwined. Who *was* Susan Lenox? If not you, then who? Do you know?"

"I do," whispered Anna Walling.

Edith leaned forward.

"She is a figment of Graham's imagination."

"Beloveds, real or fiction, usually are. I know your husband is staying at this hotel, Mrs. Walling. May I ask why?"

Here Mrs. Walling grew less confident. "We have four children," she stammered. "It can be difficult to work at home . . ."

"That's what offices are for."

Anna Walling took a deep breath. "Mrs. Wharton, as writers, we see things others don't and have the courage to put them on the page so that others can see as well. But in this, your vision is clouded. My husband is not a violent man. And he was very fond of Graham. He would never have killed him." She stroked her throat as if it ached. "No matter what had passed between us."

It was not, perhaps, to the point, but Edith couldn't resist asking,

"What did pass between you, Mrs. Walling? Were you very much in love?"

Did you lose your head? Your dignity? Did you do things of which you never imagined yourself capable? And yet, rather than die of shame afterwards, you were exultant?

"He was more so," Anna Walling said carefully. "But I had more to lose."

"When did things end between you?"

The other woman hesitated; Edith wondered if she did not wish to give a time frame that might implicate her husband.

"I'm not sure it ever really began, Mrs. Wharton. This was not an affair, you understand. Really, I would call it a pantomime."

"That is the first time I have heard that euphemism."

"It's true. Graham had never been in love, at least in the traditional way, and I think he decided that he should be. It was something he needed to understand for his work."

Morton Fullerton had told her the exact same thing—that she needed to know not just the glory of love but the pain as well. That she would write better as a result.

"I think you underestimate your appeal, Mrs. Walling."

"I do not, believe me, Mrs. Wharton. Things were written. Things were said. Finally, I proposed a meeting. Alone in a place where we would not be seen. Graham went into a fever of anticipation."

Edith knew well the logistics of infidelity could be a challenge. "And?"

"And then he did not come. We never spoke of it again. From that time on, he was . . . cool to me. Angry. As if it were somehow my fault."

That tallied with Henry Frevert's observation that Phillips had become rageful against women of sophistication.

"Forgive me, Mrs. Walling, but I did and do dislike that man."

The other woman smiled sadly. "He was afraid. It is frightening, isn't it? To give love? Even to *want* love?"

Much as she detested yielding to Mr. Phillips's views in anything, Edith knew: Love gave no quarter to dignity, especially when you embarked on it late in life.

Still, she exclaimed, "Oh, dear! Poor Mr. Phillips! How terrifying for him! To emerge from behind his sister's skirts and the edifice of his own pride. Why, he might have discovered that we are more than the meager roles he assigns us."

Leaning in so she might whisper, she asked, "Whatever drew you to him?"

"He was vital. He was talented. He was . . . not unattractive."

Perhaps not, thought Edith, recalling the dark hair, cleft chin, and intense arrogant eyes. Still, she retained the memory of an angry boy.

Then she heard Anna Walling say, "And at the time, I was unhappy."

"I am sorry," said Edith, meaning it.

Tugging at the tips of her gloves, Anna Walling said, "You have seen that William and I are living apart. Perhaps, not living in America, you are unaware that my husband has been accused by a young woman of promising her marriage. Two years ago, she sued him for breach of promise. The trial will begin soon. Of course, the woman's claim is entirely untrue."

She delivered this official statement with a lofty toss of her head Edith did not believe for a moment.

"But as a family, we have been distracted. *I* was distracted. And injured, I suppose. William says it is his fault, my distraction. That I became enamored of another man to strike back at him. I feel patronized when he says this. My passions are my passions. I don't feel them out of spite."

"But perhaps as an escape?"

"Perhaps." Mrs. Walling looked down at her knotted hands. "In truth, I'm no longer sure why I am angry at William, only that I can't stop. And so we have found it beneficial to live alone for a time. But *that* is why we live apart, Mrs. Wharton. Not because my husband"— here she lowered her voice—"murdered Graham."

Edith found herself intensely sympathetic to Mrs. Walling— but suspicious. Gently, she said, "Mrs. Walling, don't you agree that a man whose pride has been wounded can be a very dangerous animal?"

"I do. But William never knew it was Graham."

"What do you mean?"

"No one thought Graham interested in that sort of thing. My husband is not a man of great imagination." Edith heard the unspoken *or insight*.

Taking last night's note out of her reticule, she laid it on the table. Mrs. Walling peered at the paper, then frowned.

"You don't recognize it?" Edith asked.

The other lady shook her head.

"It is on the same paper and in the same handwriting as the notes David Graham Phillips received before he was killed. I received it yesterday."

Anna Walling looked genuinely appalled. "Mrs. Wharton, you must believe me, I never actually thought they would dare. Not with you . . ."

"*Who* would not dare, Mrs. Walling? And why not with me? Why should a jealous author or jealous husband, for that matter, show any regard for my well-being?"

Anna Walling shook her head, deeply distressed. She waved her hand over the note as if willing it to go away.

Edith pressed. "You put me into this situation the moment you invited me to the Phillips home, knowing Carolyn Frevert would ask me to read *Susan Lenox*. Now I have read it and I am receiving threats. The first note was a blunt instruction not to write this story. This one is more nuanced. It shows some knowledge of society, yet it was clearly written by someone who feels cast out of society. The paper is excellent, as is the handwriting, suggesting a level of expensive education. Does that remind you of anyone?"

"Mrs. Wharton . . ."

Anticipating evasion, Edith insisted, "The very *least* you owe me is a candid answer as to who you believe is responsible. Even if that person is dear to you."

Her tone had become imperious. Mrs. Walling turned cold. She took her time in answering.

"Not dear to me, Mrs. Wharton," she said finally. "But perhaps to you."

She tapped the note. "You think the person 'cast out of society' is my husband. But I think it is you. The people you write about—you think it inconceivable that they see you as one of their own, and yet a person 'who does just about what she wishes'?"

It was absurd, thought Edith. *Entirely* absurd. Anna Walling was trying to lure attention away from her husband. And yet she could not speak because she was stuck on another thought: Her poor placement at dinner. Alice's pointed greeting to Teddy. Nannie's endless carping. HJ's snipes about talons . . .

Many did see her as a woman who did just what she wanted.

She heard Anna Walling say, "In *The House of Mirth*, you wrote about the cruelty of these people. I would have thought you have some idea of what they're capable of."

Edith recovered herself. "Yes. But this is not how they deliver their warnings."

"Then why are you receiving threats, Mrs. Wharton?"

It was so obvious that for a moment, Edith was lost for words. "Because I involved myself in *Susan Lenox*. Because I wish to know who killed Mr. Phillips . . ."

Another toss of the head. "Do you?" As Edith scoffed, she spoke over her saying, "You are questioning the wrong people and asking the wrong questions, because in your heart, you don't want the answer."

Too astonished to be offended, Edith asked, "And where should I be looking, Mrs. Walling?"

"Closer to home."

"I have no precise home at the moment. It shall have to be a name, I'm afraid."

Anna Walling looked slowly around the opulent tearoom. Turning back to Edith, she said simply, "And what if the name I gave you was Vanderbilt?"

CHAPTER TWENTY-TWO

I *would say you were a liar or a fantasist* was Edith's preferred response.
But she settled for "What on earth would the Vanderbilts have to
fear from *Susan Lenox?*"

"Not from *Susan Lenox*, Mrs. Wharton. From *Treason of the
Senate.*"

Now she did laugh. "The Senate? To my knowledge, no member
of the Vanderbilt family has ever joined that august body."

"Of course they haven't. Gentlemen do not engage in politics. It
would never do for them to sully themselves by courting the good
will of the people. Instead, they court a few specific men who will
persuade the public that the people's interests and those of families
like the Vanderbilts are one and the same. Men like Senator Depew.
In return, to quote Graham, these men are 'rewarded with scant and
contemptuous crumbs.' If you can call Senator Depew's three magnificent houses crumbs."

"Are you accusing Alice Vanderbilt of murder?" It was so ridiculous, Edith allowed herself to smile.

"Of course not, Mrs. Wharton. Women like Alice Vanderbilt, like yourself, do not have to act in order to protect your interests. You have men to do that. Lawyers, accountants, doctors, butlers, valets—as well as politicians."

"And yet Senator Depew told me himself he is about to retire."

Even as she said it, she realized that was not exactly true. He had *talked* of retirement. And Alice had said, "We shan't let you." Then he had made some twinkly remark about strange doings in Albany . . .

Anna Walling said, "But only a year ago, he was confident of reelection. Even as late as this summer, he said he would like another term."

"Well, these grand old men. It can be hard to persuade them to leave the stage."

"The Vanderbilts do not wish him to leave the stage. If he does, they lose their influence in government. They will have to break in an entirely new lapdog. But the old guard is falling, Mrs. Wharton. The Big Four who controlled the Senate on behalf of the wealthy are losing their grip. First John Spooner left the Senate. Then Nelson Aldrich, so-called boss of the Senate and Rockefeller retainer, announced his retirement. Now Depew's power is in jeopardy. Do you know what these men have in common, Mrs. Wharton? Graham wrote about each of them in *Treason of the Senate*."

"That book was published years ago. Why kill Mr. Phillips now?"

"Because its effects are being felt now, Mrs. Wharton. Five years ago, Senator Depew's seat was secure. Now, his allies are falling. People are asking questions. 'Why does my senator oppose direct primary elections?' 'How does a public servant live like a prince?' Who would have thought a nobody from Indiana would threaten the fortunes of the Big Four? And in doing so, the families they serve, the Rockefellers and Vanderbilts?"

"So it is your opinion that David Graham Phillips was killed not to stop *Susan Lenox* from being published, but to avenge the ruin of Senator Depew's career."

"And to make it clear to others what happens to those who dare to expose the corrupt influence of wealth over the American government."

"Senator Depew must be in his seventies. A man of his years—not to mention fame—could never hope to shoot a man in broad daylight and get away unrecognized."

"Even lapdogs have lapdogs."

Her grim certainty was such that Edith found herself flummoxed. "But why try to stop me from reading *Susan Lenox*? These are not people who read widely, Mrs. Walling. I can't imagine how they would know the book even exists . . ."

But then she remembered Alice's dinner. Herself, bored and flustered, desperate to make conversation with the monosyllabic tombstone opposite. *David Graham Phillips. Apparently, he's about to publish some huge novel. Been working on it for ages. Explosive, explosive! Will expose the hypocrisy and evils of . . . well, everything, I suppose . . .*

She heard Anna Walling say, "The Vanderbilts and Depew don't need to know what it's about, Mrs. Wharton. They will have heard that David Graham Phillips, the man who wrote *Treason of the Senate*, has completed the book it took him a decade to write, in which he exposes corruption and hypocrisy in America."

Yes, thought Edith, *they do know that. Because I told them*. She who had such terror of saying the wrong thing might have made the greatest conversational blunder of her life.

"And if Edith Wharton, one of their own, decides to defend that novel, how much harder will it be for them to deny that everything it says is true? No, much better if she is scared enough that she stops reading, flees back to Paris, and the Comstocks and their verminous allies can stop it from ever seeing the light of day."

For a brief moment, Edith was persuaded. Then shook herself. No. It was both too tidy and too outrageous. A neat little bundle of conspiracy that pulled in the wealthiest families, famous politicians, and bigoted censors: all the people Anna Walling despised. And yet when Edith tried to find the loose thread so she might tug the other woman's argument apart, all she could think of was the younger Depew, with that strange flat voice: *Are you making a joke?*

Edith was tired. Her head ached. She felt Mrs. Walling must be in error, but she could not find the right words, except to say, *These people who horrify you, they are so mediocre, you cannot imagine.*

And—stubbornly, she came back to it—the word *vampire* was not a political word.

Although the theft of someone's reputation could also be seen as taking a life that did not belong to you.

The younger Depew did take offense easily. If he had any prospects beyond his father's employment, she could not imagine them.

And he had frightened her. Briefly. But frightened her nonetheless.

She heard Anna Walling say, "You don't believe me."

"I am thinking. Of course I wonder if you're making these accusations in order to protect your husband. You have four children. And, if I'm not mistaken, you still love him."

Anna Walling dropped her gaze. Smoothing the napkin on her lap, she said, "Shall I tell you the thing I love most in William?"

"Please."

"William's family created its wealth through the enslavement of other people. I am not speaking poetically of factories. I am speaking of human beings that they owned. Much of what William has—his education at Harvard, his security and freedom—comes at the cost of other people's lives. There is a reason he fights for complete political and economic equality. There is a reason he works for the American Federation of Labor. And that is because he knows the burden of sin."

Anna Walling looked at her. "William Walling is a man conscious of his crimes. He has dedicated his life to atonement. Does that sound like a man who would shoot a man he admires, then walk away?"

"It depends on how badly he felt that man had betrayed him. No matter how selfless, there is always something—or someone—we wish to call our own, to whom we demand absolute rights."

"I am not property, Mrs. Wharton. No human being is."

"One's emotions do not always match one's ideals."

She expected an argument, full of abstractions and platitudes. To her surprise, Anna Walling nodded, wearily conceding the point.

"What *is* a happy marriage, Mrs. Wharton?" asked the Russian woman. "How is it achieved? Do you know? If so, please tell me."

"Travel," she said. "Either together or apart. If together, you may be the same people, but at least you are in a different space."

"Travel involves so many of the choices of marriage: Where do you wish to go? Change—is it exciting or tiring? How long do you wish to stay? May others join your journey . . . ?"

Edith knew that Mrs. Walling was asking if she had ever been distracted. For a moment, she longed to say yes, to make the Russian woman a new HJ, a better one, who would understand that at times it felt impossible to be a woman and love—passionately, heedlessly— and not be degraded. Men seemed to manage it, loving but keeping themselves intact. Why couldn't women?

Taking up her teacup, she said, "I find three a very difficult number to manage. A natural pair occurs and one is left to sulk." She met Mrs. Walling's eye. "Or worse."

"I have told you who is responsible for Graham's murder, Mrs. Wharton. If you read *Treason of the Senate*, you will see I am right." She stood. "But perhaps, unlike my husband, you are incapable of confronting the cruelties of your people with courage or integrity. It's difficult, I know. We see . . . and we make excuses. The careless young fellow who runs someone down with his motorcar—well, he drinks too much. The gentleman who fondles the little housemaid—a bit of a bore. The lady who fires that housemaid without pay—somewhat rigid. They do bad things, people we love, but we insist they are not bad people. Or some of them are bad people—we'll say so just between us late at night—but they're not dangerous. It would be ill-mannered to take offense at their behavior. To call it what it is: criminal.

"I had hoped that the woman who wrote *The House of Mirth* might be braver. But now I see the author portrait was correct. You are a grand society matron who takes the viciousness and brutality of her friends and makes of them a charming comedy. They are appalling, these people, and you admit as much. But in the end, you present them as the only people of any real interest or importance. Good day, Mrs. Wharton."

It was a dare, Edith told herself as she ignored Mrs. Walling's departure. A silly one. *Do not look at me, but at yourself.* What a convenient thing the wealthy were; one might blame them for anything.

But Mr. Jewett had also mentioned *Treason of the Senate*. Him, she could not dismiss as a grief-stricken radical. As much as she resented Mrs. Walling's accusations, she could not lay them aside until she had shown she was not afraid to face . . . well, the muck.

In the distance, she noticed the hotel manager directing one of the bellboys in the removal of the last of the holiday garlands from the lobby. The Christmas festivities were finally over. It made her think of a Christmas long ago—celebrated at the largest, most splendid house in America, an estate to rival Versailles or Blenheim.

A house only a Vanderbilt could build.

At Appleton, the youth was surprised to see her. "Soldiering on with *Susan Lenox*?"

"No, actually."

Briefly, they smiled in shared loathing of that work.

"I wonder if you could bring me a copy of another of Mr. Phillips's books. Not the novels, but *Treason of the Senate*—do you have that?"

He said he would bring it to her straightaway.

CHAPTER TWENTY-THREE

No, Edith—no!"

HJ peered at her through the three-inch crack between the door and its frame. His face was flushed with the effort of keeping her at bay, his eyes bright with determination.

"It is late," he announced. "I am tired."

"It's nine o'clock." She held up *Treason of the Senate*. "And I bring a book."

He looked at the title; his eyes were poor and he had to squint. "That's not a book, it's a pamphlet. Is this more about the Phillips business?" The door shuddered, threatened to close.

"Partly. It's also about George Vanderbilt and Biltmore. Christmas 1905."

She had surprised him. More than that, she had given him the opportunity to be eloquent in complaint, a thing he loved. His grip on the door relaxed.

"I *detest* Biltmore," he said. "It's a space utterly unaddressed to any possible arrangement of life. But what do the Vanderbilts have to do with your dead writer?"

"I don't know yet."

Allowed in, she took her customary chair. While HJ poked at the fire and settled his foot properly, she thought back to their visit to North Carolina. A French château in the Appalachian territory might have struck some as whimsical, and others as crazed. But when one had the Vanderbilt millions and the assistance of Frederick Law Olmsted and Richard Morris Hunt, one could turn such outlandish fantasies into even more outlandish reality.

Christmas of 1905, she had been festive and full of herself. It was the year of *Mirth*, when her book was published in the astonishing number of forty thousand copies—a count that later rose to one hundred thousand. At last, she stood secure on the one pedestal bearing the title that mattered most: author. When George and his wife asked her to the most extravagant house in America on the most extravagant of holidays, she had known it was precisely the place she should be and dragged HJ along for good measure. She had gamboled around the estate, reveling in its spectacular collection of books and jovial St. Bernards, who left whorls of slobber on all the rugs. She delighted in the thirty-foot-high tree, the vast brimming punch bowls, the brightly wrapped presents, and the gardens of jasmine and juniper, honeysuckle and cascading fruited ivy over the stone terrace walls. It seemed that everyone agreeable was there and they all wished to congratulate her.

Now, reclining in his chair, HJ recalled, "My room was half a mile from the mile-long library. And there were people one didn't know. And one didn't like."

"On that subject, do you remember Chauncey Depew?"

"Notable gasbag and senator?" HJ consulted his memory. "A friend of your friend Mr. Roosevelt."

"A friend to many, apparently. He was at Biltmore that Christmas. I thought it odd at the time that George, normally so discerning with his guest list, would mix artists and politicians. When I asked him, he said Willie insisted."

"George's older brother who married the harridan Alva," Henry remembered. "She left him, and he went horse mad. And house mad. And yacht mad."

"Naturally, I made every effort to avoid the senator and his party. But one night, I went looking for George in his study. A Renoir was badly placed, and I felt he should know. I was in the corridor when I heard a man shouting about some writer and people named Spooner and Aldrich."

"And you didn't care so you walked away."

"Almost. But then I heard someone say, 'He's just throwing muck to see if it'll stick. But anything he throws at me spatters you as well.' A few minutes later, Depew and Willie came out of the study."

". . . and?"

"Soon after that, Mr. Phillips published *Treason of the Senate*. In which he accused Senator Depew of acting with impropriety on behalf of the Vanderbilts."

HJ looked dubious. "You're not suggesting an elderly politician hobbled down Twenty-First Street, shot Phillips, and managed to limp away without being caught? More than five years after being attacked in print by him?"

"No. But he has a son. Who is nearly twenty years younger than I am, so presumably capable of running up and down streets and shooting people."

"I return to my earlier question: Why?"

"Because he knew Mr. Phillips was about to publish an explosive new book. He knew it because I told him so the day before David Graham Phillips was murdered."

In vain, she waited for Henry to absolve her with *Oh, don't be ridiculous*. But he was silent.

She added, "And, although I met him only briefly, his manner was strange."

"One hears of these people called police. If Senator Depew's son shot Mr. Phillips, surely they will discover as much."

"But the police would be inclined to look the other way, wouldn't they? If the son of a famous, influential politician was involved?"

HJ's eyes narrowed. "You make an unlikely Jacobin."

"It's hardly revolutionary to suggest that public figures enjoy a certain amount of leeway."

"Also an unlikely detective. You were only asked to read a book and say something nice about it. You were not asked to solve the man's murder."

"The man was a writer, Henry. Maybe not a writer to my taste. But even in New York, the killing of writers seems a new outrage."

HJ's face lightened. "Ah, now Socrates might disagree."

Dimly, she recalled the Jacques-Louis David painting of the philosopher sentenced to die by drinking poison. "What was the charge?"

"The moral corruption of Athenian youth." When she nodded knowingly, he said, "No, unlike Plato, Socrates did not indulge; he was very ugly. The jury found him guilty of encouraging the young to disrespect the established gods. Socrates felt that their society had grown lazy, apathetic. A plodding horse, it needed a good sting. Not surprisingly, the state did not appreciate it. Like a mule, it kicked."

It took her a moment to decipher the analogy. "So, Depew and the Vanderbilts are the mule and Mr. Phillips is Socrates?"

"Surely the Vanderbilts are our established gods," said HJ slyly. "Senator Depew the workhorse. Still, I don't see what you can do about it. I don't even see why you'd want to." He pulled a face of mock horror. "The Vanderbilts would never ask you to dine again!"

"Well, if they've taken to assassinating writers, I'm not sure I want to."

But it was a poor joke and her problem remained unsolved. Settling her chin in her hand, she thought. It was obviously not a thing she could discuss with Alice. Or even George. Who had, she now remembered, called Depew "our senator." Such a task was not something one would put in writing, the way she gave instructions to staff. *Morning: drive senator to speech. Midday: shoot writer.* It seemed most likely that the son would have committed the murder on his own initiative. Perhaps he had been spurred on by a "Who will rid me of this turbulent priest?" outburst from the senator. Young Depew didn't seem particularly gifted or competent. But that, he could do.

But how to prove he had done it?

HJ spoke, deep and round as if from the bottom of a well: "You have become enamored of the extreme."

And you have become terrified, she thought. It showed in his work. All that brilliant language winding around the characters like a fog. Discreet coughs and ellipses where there should be candor. Or . . . truth. Irritatingly, Mr. Phillips's favorite word came to her. She had not liked HJ's last novels. The delicacy of language, which, like the most elaborate lace, had once revealed the intricate patterns of human existence, was now cotton wool, muffling and suffocating. The ability to set life at a remove so that the reader might see it in all its complexities had become a refusal to examine life up close. HJ held life aloft on a long branch, as if it were a hornet's nest, fascinated by its gray bulbous shape—something so ugly *must* be organic—yet terrified of the agony that might come flying out of it at any moment.

Perhaps, she thought, that was one reason the *New York Edition* had failed. The world had moved on.

"So," he said, "will you invite Alice to tea and suggest that the man who has served her family faithfully for his entire career is a murderer? Or his son is?"

"I might see Alice tomorrow night, as a matter of fact. Walter has asked me to the opera."

"Is Walter still in the city? Such the world traveler, one expects him to wing off elsewhere."

He widened his eyes. "I wonder what keeps him."

Ignoring this, she continued, "It is quite the event. The New York debut of *Natoma*. No doubt the senator will be there. With his son."

Smiling, she stood and gave him her hands. Henry gazed up at her. "Please don't get shot," he said. "I should miss my Devastating Angel."

"I am sure she has nothing to fear," she lied.

W alter was not at all grateful when she accepted his invitation to *Natoma*, clearly feeling she should have said yes ages ago and spared him the nagging.

"Who will be at the gala dinner?" she asked.

"Literally everyone," said Walter, using the words accurately given his definition of *everyone*. "The mayor. Thomas Edison. Mrs. Fish. Minnie. Various branches of the Vanderbilts. I believe Senator Depew is giving the toast. The man's running for office, even if he pretends otherwise."

"Delightful."

"Well, delightful or dismal, I think *Natoma* will be an excellent distraction for you. It is an 'American' opera set in California." She heard the amusement in Walter's voice. "I suspect there will be much to criticize."

Edith made an agreeable sound. But she knew women like the one he imagined her to be: cantankerous old vultures hovering, wishing for catastrophe so they might have a good feed. She did not wish to be one. At least not for many more years.

Thinking of Alice and her hallowed spot in box three of the Diamond Horseshoe, she asked where they were seated.

"We shall be sitting in Mrs. Robert Goelet's box."

She paused, then asked, "With Mr. Goelet?"

"I believe Robert is away."

So this was why HJ had made a point of wondering why Walter was still in the city. Cross, Edith thought to say she didn't much like being used as cover for Walter's liaison. *For God's sake*, she thought, *couldn't you have chosen someone less vapid?* Elsie Goelet was nearly half his age.

No, that was not why she was disappointed. She felt inside herself, pressing here and there for the bruise. The places of loss felt tender—too tender—and she left off exploring. *Of course it is Elsie Goelet*, she thought. *Young, voluptuous, eager for life—why shouldn't she be, there is so much of it left to her. Who would not want to embrace that?*

Walter had revealed his secret. Should she tell him hers? If so, which one? She thought of telling her oldest friend about the notes delivered to the hotel. Her sense the other evening that she was being followed. She thought to ask him if they were now so old they shouldn't mind dying. If he still felt as fiercely about living as he had when he was twenty-one. Or if, at the half-century mark, they were supposed to recede like spirits, fade through the walls and be heard only occasionally as moans and whispers, easily mistaken for wind through the trees.

"Tomorrow then," said Walter.

"Yes, tomorrow."

Predictably, Teddy did not want to go to the opera. He also did not want her to go to the opera. He especially did not want her to go with Walter Berry.

"I shall not enjoy it," she promised him.

"But you'll enjoy it more than an evening with me."

I am sorry, she thought wearily, *that my life is full and yours is not. I am sorry that you take joy in so few things. It is a large world, with so much to do. Why do you not go in search of what will make you happy?*

She remembered Teddy's actress. Had she made him happy? She rather hoped so. If she had not been exorbitantly expensive, it might have been worth it to keep her on.

Later, she met with White in her room. While she was at the opera, perhaps it would be best for Mr. Wharton to dine at the hotel and have an early night.

"Mr. Wharton does not care for the food at the Belmont," said White. "In any event, he has informed me he has plans for the evening."

"Plans?" White nodded. "But what—?"

"He did not inform me as to what they were," he clarified. "Only that he would be out."

"I see."

She thought of the night she had returned to her room to find the sprig of witch hazel and the petit bleu on her pillow. Had Teddy made similar plans that evening? Did they involve young actresses?

Investments? He no longer had access to her funds, so she supposed it made no difference. Even if it did, she could hardly ask White if her husband was consorting with other women because he thought she was consorting with other men.

"Thank you, White."

CHAPTER TWENTY-FOUR

E dith, dear, how lovely to see you!"
   "Mrs. Wharton, such a surprise . . ."
   "Darling Edith, how we've missed you."
   "Do give our love to Teddy . . ."
   "What are these dreadful rumors that you're leaving us?"

To everyone in Edith's New York, the opera was the buzzing center of the winter season. The city's elite families gathered at the Metropolitan Opera House, ostensibly to hear music, but in truth to make matches and do battle. The boxholders in the Diamond Horseshoe enjoyed lengthy intermissions that allowed them to pay calls on one another, going from box to box just as they would from home to home to pay their respects. Careers were promoted, reputations enhanced or destroyed. The Metropolitan Opera had been founded in a fit of pique when Alva Vanderbilt was denied one of the eighteen boxes at the old Academy of Music, and Edith often wondered where American cultural life would be without New Yorkers' thin skin. Someone was always starting something because they had been snubbed and wished to keep someone else out.

As Edith and Walter made their way into the house from the private carriage entrances reserved for the patrons and their guests, she found it difficult to breathe and she was not sure whether it was the sheer number of people or the people themselves. They were all here. The Vanderbilts, the Belmonts, the Harrimans, the Fishes, the Clewses, the Wilsons. She reminded herself that the person who unnerved her the most was probably not in the crowd. The Depews would come with Alice, and she never arrived until the first aria was underway, and she departed halfway through the finale. But the Depews would stay for the gala. The thought of confronting the hulking, dull-eyed junior Depew set her heart pounding and she wondered: Would she be relieved if he did not come?

No. She would not. Guilt over having blabbed about *Susan Lenox* weighed on her. If she was in any way responsible for provoking Depew into an act of violence against David Graham Phillips, it felt imperative to expose him. At least it felt imperative that she try.

Her plan, inspired by *Hamlet*, was to raise the subject of the murder and watch the son's reaction. He did not possess his father's gift for evasion. If he had a violent disposition, it would be easy enough to bait him into an outburst. Even now she was not entirely sure what she meant to say to him. When she imagined it, she had a vision of throwing David Graham Phillips in his face as you would a glass of water and watching him sputter into some sort of confession.

"Why did you change your mind?" Walter asked as they climbed the stairs.

"Did I?"

"I distinctly recall a reference to wild horses and their inability to drag you within a hundred feet of an American opera."

"Clearly the horses had more oomph than I realized."

As they entered the parterre, Edith steadied her nerves by noting the superficial things. Walter, magnificent in white tie. The new color scheme of the house—gold and maroon to replace the old ivory decor, which had been deemed unflattering to the ladies. Partridges were a popular motif for fans. Opera coats were gold and black, with touches of peacock. She put her ear to the buzz of conversation around her. Most of the opera's patrons were intensely preoccupied by the genuine stars of the evening, which were not the singers but the patrons themselves. They had managed to be in the most important place on this most important evening, when the most important event in the city was taking place: the debut of *Natoma*! People were keen to show off their knowledge of the evening's entertainment. One matron resplendent in emeralds looked forward to the "Dagger Dance." Her companion had heard that the production featured a papoose. Also vaqueros, although he was unclear as to what those were.

Escorted to the salon area of the Goelet box, Edith surrendered her wrap, then took a deep breath as she prepared to pass through the red velvet curtains into the heart of the house. As she did, she was assaulted by the thrumming excitement of more than three thousand people. Also the vast stage curtain of dazzling gold and the sight of Mrs. Robert Goelet. Barely thirty, Elsie Goelet was ravishing, with crystalline eyes, dramatic brows, and luxurious masses of dark hair. She made Edith feel approximately a hundred and nine years old.

Edith had heard that the enchanting Elsie was dallying with Henry Clews, who was here this evening with his wife. Watching

Elsie simper in Walter's direction, Edith told herself perhaps she had
heard wrong. But she inquired after Mr. Clews nonetheless. Just to
be polite.

They arranged themselves in the usual manner on the seats of
dark mahogany and black rattan: Edith and Elsie in the front, Walter
seated behind Elsie. While he made gallant and Elsie charmed with
her fan, Edith resented her assigned role as duenna. She had been
asked not for her company, but to give the appearance of propriety.
*My dear, I saw Walter Berry with Mrs. Goelet at the opera!—And you
saw Mrs. Wharton right there next to him, don't dramatize!* That she
had used HJ in exactly the same way when traveling with Fullerton
mollified her not at all.

She looked toward Alice Vanderbilt's box. The chairs stood
empty, the curtains still.

Then there was a storm of applause as the conductor took the
podium. The lights dimmed and the magnificent gold curtain rose.
Natoma was about to begin. As the overture played, she recalled a performance of *La Figlia di Iorio*. Fullerton had quietly joined her in the
darkness mid-act. They said nothing, and yet she felt suffused by him,
their minds and sensibilities so attuned they did not need words. This,
she had thought, must be what happy women felt. What a gift to be
found and rescued—late in life, to be sure, but rescued nonetheless.

Thoughts of rescue stayed with her as the first act got underway.
Edith considered herself receptive to the "new." At the very least, she
had disdain for people who weren't and a determination not to be
counted among them. She had attended Stravinsky's *L'Oiseau de Feu*,
admired Diaghilev, and thought Cocteau delightful. Her tastes were
in no way hidebound.

So she felt quite confident in her opinion that *Natoma* was terrible. The first time one heard the tunes, they had some freshness

and charm. By the second act, they began to bore. By the twentieth repetition, Edith strongly considered snatching the baton from the conductor's hand and thrusting it through his eyeball.

Restless, she looked about the darkened theater and saw that Alice had finally arrived. Dressed in her customary black, strands of pearls around her neck, she sat, a grand immobile totem, impervious to the lesser beings around her. Senator Depew, his old eyes large and brilliant, sat with his liver-spotted hands resting hard on the silver handle of a cane. Beside him, his son, gargantuan and gangly in his ill-fitting white tie, did not watch the action on the stage. From his expression, she judged that the young man was acutely unhappy to be at the opera.

Of course there, he was not alone. The rapturous applause that erupted when the last notes faded was the sound of a people liberated from torment. Huzzahs and bravos resounded throughout the house, although Edith heard a distinct menace in the bravos. The prima donna was pelted with orchids and violets. Then she brought on the composer, who, had the audience had offal on hand, might have been pelted as well. Afterwards, the crowds trailed out, wide-eyed in shock, aware that the gala reception—and reviews—lay ahead. The rush to the bar was so speedy it might have been the bell at Belmont racetrack.

Edith could see Senator Depew, waving and cheerful as he made his way through the crowd. To him, the opera itself was merely the overture. Now the real star would take the stage. Retiring or not, he still wished to show he was beloved in the hearts of New Yorkers, at least the ones who truly mattered.

Behind her, Walter whispered, "Do you want to stay? I think we've suffered enough."

"All that despair and recrimination? The descent into gloom when the reviews are read? I wouldn't miss it for the world. But if it is past Mrs. Goelet's bedtime, you may pop her into her cradle whenever you see fit."

The reception was held in the grand foyer of the opera house. Buffet tables laden with hams, lobsters, oysters, roasts, as well as acres of vegetables and every sort of bread and roll imaginable, surrounded fifteen tables, each of which sat ten prominent guests. At the center of each table was a basket of spring flowers. A vast American flag hung overhead, flanked by the flags of New York and California. The hall's columns were decorated with tiger lilies and crowned with forsythia. Enormous bay trees stood on either side of the entrance. The walls and ceilings were adorned with Southern smilax woven with pink and white azaleas and pink electric lights. American Beauty roses emphasized the national triumph of the occasion.

As did the guests themselves. Thomas Edison was in attendance, as were Mr. and Mrs. Charles Dana Gibson. The mayor and his wife were present. ("Is that the one who was shot in New Jersey?" Edith whispered to Walter.) Yet another wing of the Vanderbilt clan was represented by William K. and his new wife. As was her habit, Alice had departed during the last aria. But her daughter-in-law was reeling in every personage in the room, all of whom seemed to have dined at her home at one time or another. "I feel deeply for poor dear Marie Antoinette," Grace said to Prince Paul Trubetskoy. "If revolution came to America, I should be the first to go!"

Walter, who had found it prudent to separate from Mrs. Goelet for a time, chatted with Mrs. Schuyler Van Rensselaer. Edith greeted an obscure member of the Astor clan and a minor Stuyvesant. As she worked her way into the senator's orbit, her surroundings grew notably more masculine, with black wool replacing an array of silks and lace. Doleful, she took in wizened necks, pouched eyes, and flapping arm flesh. There was no denying it: They were an aging group.

"A pessimist," boomed Senator Depew to his admirers, "is a man who thinks all women are bad. An optimist is a man who hopes they are." The younger Depew lurked at a distance behind his father, as if he were one of the waiters attempting to seat people so the dinner service might start. As Edith inserted herself into the circle of syco- phants, she drew on her full display of regal entitlement. She was a Jones, a Schermerhorn, cousin to the Astors. She was not going to be intimidated by a Depew.

The senator greeted her with equanimity; he had spent enough time with people like her to know when to stand down. But he was canny, asking, "And where is your fine husband this evening, Mrs. Wharton?"

"Toothache, I'm afraid. But preferable, I daresay, to the evening's entertainment."

A round of masculine chuckles. The senator returned, "Ah, but we must embrace the new!"

"The new, by all means," she said. "The dreadful and earsplitting, perhaps not."

"Progress is often seen as disruption, Mrs. Wharton. Change is inevitable."

So it is, she thought. *In a matter of months, you may be out on your ear.*

Borrowing Alice Vanderbilt's stern tone and furrowed brow, she said, "Ah, but is change always *desirable*? If, for example, we were to rid New York of all that awful brownstone, I would rejoice. The city is now so crowded. And the level of crime *shocking*." Turning her gaze on the son, she added, "Just the other day, a colleague of mine was murdered in broad daylight."

The senator smiled benevolently; if women were not shocked by the world, his role as a gentleman able to navigate it on their behalf would disappear.

"It is regrettable," he said, "but so many women now insist on walking unescorted in the streets, there are bound to be difficulties."

A woman who leaves her home is neither pure not protected, thought Edith. One of the senator's witty aphorisms? That his son would have heard repeatedly?

"But it wasn't a woman," she said. "He was a writer. Shot dead in the street. David Graham Phillips. You must have seen it in the newspapers."

Turning, she addressed the son directly. "You remember, we spoke of Mr. Phillips at dinner the other evening. I've been reading his new book. It is indeed revelatory . . ."

"I assure you," said the senator solemnly, cutting her off, "that I shall make the safety of New York's citizens a priority should I return to the Senate. Now, if you will excuse me, gentlemen"—he glittered at Edith—"and Mrs. Wharton, I believe I am expected on the dais."

He was too good, she thought, watching him slip away. Too experienced in evasion. So intent was she on watching the senator, she only belatedly noticed that the son did not follow him to the dais but headed in the opposite direction. She tried to follow him, but Walter arrived to escort her to their table.

By happy surprise, Edith found Minnie seated near her. Once her sister-in-law, now one of her dearest friends, Minnie had taken the astonishing step of parting with Edith's brother after catching him in flagrante with another woman. To her mother's horror, Edith had sided with Minnie—as had many others. Such was Minnie's quality, her reputation had not suffered. When asked if she enjoyed the opera, Edith made a face of a silent scream. Minnie put her hands to her cheeks in feigned horror.

"But when the reviews are read," said Minnie, "you must say, 'Well, they didn't understand it.'" Then, unfurling her napkin onto her lap, she said, "Henry has come to stay with me. He said he found it difficult to rest at the Belmont."

"I was not such a menace, I assure you, that he needed to flee to Washington Square."

"Well, it is where he grew up," said Minnie. "He feels at ease there."

But Edith was not in the mood to discuss Henry's fragility. Glancing toward the dais where Senator Depew was seated at a long table at the head of the room with the soprano Miss Garden, the composer Mr. Herbert, and various other luminaries, Edith asked, "Is it your opinion that Senator Depew will return to Washington?"

"Heavens, how should I know?" Then, having made a proper display of ignorance about politics, Minnie added, "I understand he means to retire." She leaned in to be heard below the conversation. "Apparently, the levels of greed became ostentatious. Or perhaps he was pushed from the trough by younger, more robust swine."

Or by one writer, thought Edith, *who is now dead.* She saw that the younger Depew had landed at a table close to the doors. His fellow diners were mostly single men, with one couple she did not recognize. None of them greeted him as he sat down. It was what Edith called an odds-and-ends table, a place to seat people who had no friends nor people who wished to be their friend.

"And his son?" she inquired. "Does he seek a place at the trough?"

"Does he have a son?" asked Minnie. Edith cast a discreet glance in that gentleman's direction. "I know nothing of him. You often see it, dazzling father, dud son drawn along on his papa's coattails. Oh, speak of the devil—the senator has risen. The first review must have come in."

The tinkling sound of sterling on crystal brought the room to silence. Glass in hand, the senator said, "Ladies and gentlemen, we are gathered here to celebrate the premiere of *Natoma*, the first truly American opera!"

This was greeted by bellows of "Hear, hear" and the thumping of hands upon the tables.

"I think it appropriate at this time"—here Depew held up a sheaf of paper—"to read some reviews."

An apprehensive hush fell over the room.

The senator cleared his throat, then read: "'What happened last night in the opera house was neither opera nor drama. It was certainly not related to music in any way.'"

Glances ranging from shocked to gleeful darted around Edith's table. Every word was true, obviously, but to say so out loud?

The senator moved on to the next clipping. "'The performance last night at the opera was disgraceful and should not have been allowed.'"

The murmurs rose, became hostile. Everyone knew they had endured a travesty; why rub their noses in it?

Serene, the senator continued. "Ah, and here we have, 'The composer of the new opera may have talent for some things, but writing opera is obviously not one of them.'"

Then he grinned at the aghast assemblage.

"Ladies and gentlemen, I have just read to you the actual reviews of Bizet's *Carmen*."

A roar of relief was followed by a storm of clapping. Miss Garden and Mr. Herbert swooned. Crowds swarmed the senator, demanding to shake his hand. Cries of "Well done, sir, well done!" were everywhere. A call of Depew for president went up—Edith felt sure it had started at his table, but it lasted a surprisingly long time. Edith looked at William K. Vanderbilt, applauding vigorously, and thought, *Hail, thou good and faithful servant.*

She looked to the younger Depew's table. The commotion that greeted the senator's speech had given young Chauncey's dining companions an excuse to desert him. While everyone else was on their feet, he remained seated, scraping and scrabbling at his meal as if it were his last. Edith thought he looked morose. Which was a suitable aspect for someone at this ridiculous occasion. Also, what one might expect to see in a man who had shot another man only five days ago.

Excusing herself, she made her way to his table, inventing, as she went, a tale of a nephew who desired a position with a political personage. What would the work entail? How much travel? Depew Jr.—what did his day look like? Did he, by any chance, travel to Gramercy Park often? Taking a deep breath, she reminded herself that the mayor was present, which meant a number of policemen were also present.

"Mr. Depew."

He looked up, startled.

"A fine speech," she began.

His grip remained tight on his fork. It took him a moment to frame the correct response; when he did, it was almost a question. "Thank you."

On impulse, she discarded her story of a nephew who sought a position in politics. Hoping candor might unsettle the young man, she said, "I hope I did not offend you earlier with my remarks about Mr. Phillips."

"You didn't. But I would be grateful if you did not raise the subject again. It is not a happy one for my family. He wrote inflammatory and unjust things about my father. We are sorry, of course, that the man is dead."

"*Are* you sorry, Mr. Depew?"

He looked pained, as if she were twisting his ear. ". . . Of course."

"Where were you on that day?"

"I was in Albany."

"Why Albany? Your father is a senator, surely his business is in Washington."

The smallest smile at her ignorance. "Albany is where the real decisions are made, Mrs. Wharton."

Remembering the senator's joke about strange doings in that place, she said, "But it seems they have decided that they no longer require your father in the Senate."

"My father is retiring after many decades of service to the people of New York. As you can see, he is beloved." He nodded around the room. "That is all the payment he has ever asked."

That and three houses and who knows what else, thought Edith.

"And what will you do when your father retires?"

"I?" He seemed surprised. Clearly an inquiry as to his plans or feelings was a novel experience.

"Yes."

For a long moment, he considered. "I shall feel the greatest relief imaginable, Mrs. Wharton."

It was not the answer she had expected, and she took it for a lie. "You have no concern for your own future?"

"Oh, I expect something will be found for me."

His tone was complacent, almost bored. She looked about the room, the happy chattering crowd that swirled past their odds-and-ends table. There the mayor, there Thomas Edison, Walter and Minnie, and everywhere, everywhere, Vanderbilts. In short, everyone who mattered in New York.

Skeptical, she said, "But it will not be this."

"No, and it will not be a musicale at One West Fifty-Seventh

Street. Or Christmas at Biltmore. Or tennis at Newport. But I shall miss none of it."

Intrigued despite herself, she said, "Really? You feel you can simply . . . walk away? Live a different life entirely? You won't miss telling people 'I dined at Alice Vanderbilt's the other evening. I had the most fascinating conversation with her son Reginald'?"

Depew Jr. looked toward that young man who had stumbled into a waiter and was now laughing his head off. "Has anyone ever had a fascinating conversation with Reggie Vanderbilt?"

Why, that was an attempt at humor, she thought. And not wholly terrible either.

Then she heard him say, "Did you know that he's killed three people?"

Amazed, she could only repeat the number. "Three?"

"Driving. He killed two men in New York City, one in Cannes. He's hit many more, of course. In Cannes, he was particularly put out because the ambulance blocked the road, making him late to the casino."

Had she known this? She knew Reggie had accidents; she knew he drove badly. And yes, now that she thought of it, she had heard of people being hurt. But somehow the words *killed* or *dead* had never been used. She almost said, *But poor driving isn't murder*, when she remembered Anna Walling's remark about careless young fellows.

"He knocked over a messenger boy in Harlem. Injured him badly."

That she did know and she corrected him, saying, "No, but that was the chauffeur's fault." She remembered feeling rather smug about her own driver and thinking the Vanderbilts sloppy in their hiring practices.

"Yes, because the chauffeur was paid handsomely to say he was driving the car at the time."

She had known Reginald Vanderbilt his entire life. Inordinately fond of brandy milk punch, he was often drunk when she saw him and always quite stupid. She had thought he bumbled through life, as many youngest sons do. She had read about his wedding, his triumphs in carriage racing, a dinner with his sister, the Countess Széchenyi. Privately, she had heard about his gambling debts and his mistresses.

But she had never seen him as a killer.

"None of this has been in the papers," she said stupidly.

"No, none of it has been," he said. "Neither has the fact that Mr. and Mrs. Cornelius Vanderbilt"—he nodded to Grace and Neily— "own almost nothing. The Newport house, the jewels, the Chinese vases, the linens, even the grand piano—all rented to create the illusion of wealth. Nor has it been in the papers that your friend George Vanderbilt has spent a significant portion of his capital on that palace in North Carolina. He is also in debt. You will notice that Alice never opens the Breakers and her New York home in the same year. She cannot afford to. Perhaps you can understand why I shall be relieved when my father leaves office. Soon, all that will be left is the auction block and the wrecking ball."

Edith thought to assure him that he exaggerated. Then she remembered the Princeton Club. Which had once been Stanford White's house. Which might one day be known as the place David Graham Phillips, America's leading novelist, had been shot. Before that too was forgotten.

She thought back to the first time she had seen father and son. The senator using his awkward child like a prop to change the subject. The son cringing under his father's hand. Yet he had not shrugged him off.

"But you admire your father."

He considered. "Did you enjoy *Natoma*, Mrs. Wharton?"

"Not in the slightest."

"And yet my father found a way to make it seem just fine. Almost as good as *Carmen*! So rather than feel embarrassed or awkward"—he gestured at the room—"everyone is happy. They know it was terrible, but they've saved face. My father is a gifted flatterer. He makes Americans feel good about themselves. Do you know he gave the oration at the unveiling of the Statue of Liberty? I was eight years old. I remember being confused, as if my father and the enormous copper lady were somehow getting married."

He looked up at the dais. "When my father worked with old Cornelius Vanderbilt, they united New York through ferries and railroads." He looked to William K. and Reggie. "Now they buy things. Gamble. Build palaces no one needs. I do admire my father. But I know what he has become."

His disdain reminded her of the murdered man's loathing for those who lived to consume. "Then you don't blame David Graham Phillips for your father's . . ." She thought *fall*, said instead, ". . . retirement."

"Why would I blame David Graham Phillips?"

"Because he wrote *Treason of the Senate*."

"Oh, that." To her surprise, he looked apologetic. "Writers aren't all *that* important, Mrs. Wharton. People don't really care about books. If you'll forgive me for saying so."

Mildly piqued, she said, "*The House of Mirth* sold one hundred and forty *thousand* copies, Mr. Depew."

"Yes, and the population of the United States is ninety-two *million* people."

The calm assertion that books did not matter was such heresy to her that she had no idea how to refute it. As she tried to muster an argument, Depew gazed around the room as if taking a last look, then said, "Do you know? I should like to go to Paris."

Stunned, she said, "Oh. Well, you must. Everyone should." And stopped herself just in time from saying he must call on her.

W alter wished to go. Mrs. Goelet insisted they join her in her motor. Looking at Walter—lighter and livelier than she had seen him since his return from Egypt—the magnificent Mrs. Goelet beside him, Edith realized she was *de trop* and said she would go with Minnie.

"What on earth did you have to say to young Depew?" asked Minnie when she had given instructions to the driver.

She thought to say, *We discussed books.* But said instead, "Did you know Reggie Vanderbilt has killed three people?"

Minnie tugged at the edge of her glove. "I'm surprised it's so few."

And yet none of us have ever said anything about it. She remembered her fear when she considered the prospect of being in the same room as the man who had killed David Graham Phillips. Yet she had been in rooms—and cars—with Reggie Vanderbilt and thought nothing of it. It was not the same, she told herself. But why wasn't it?

Minnie said, "Henry says there has been much tension and excitement. That you are flying here, there, and everywhere about this man who was murdered."

"He died on my birthday," she said. "Of course I take an interest."

"He also says you asked him if you should part with Teddy."

"Yes."

Minnie put a strong hand over hers. She would not give advice; they had known each other too long for that. But the press of her fingers said, *I am here. I will always be here.* Edith squeezed her hand back to say, *I know. And thank you.*

Thinking again of Depew, she tried to cheer herself with self-congratulation. Anna Walling and Carolyn Frevert had been wrong. The person who shot David Graham Phillips had not been an agent of Depew or the Vanderbilts.

It did not cheer her. The man was still out there, twisted and stunted and ill. And he was not, she thought, as remarkable as she might wish. Unhappy young men, it seemed, were everywhere. Young Depew was disappointed and apathetic. Alice's worthless Reginald. She wanted to say to her sister-in-law, *These men who have had everything our world has to offer, these men who should be our future—what is wrong with them? Something has gone sour.*

"When do you return to Europe?" Minnie asked.

"As soon as Dr. Kinnicutt delivers me. I pray it is soon. New York seems so appalling to me now. It has lost all sense of its history and tradition."

They were approaching the Belmont. Minnie said, "I have come to the conclusion that New York is always appalling. That *is* its history and tradition. We all have our 'New York.' None of us gets to keep it. If we're lucky, we hold fast to our little bit as long as we need it."

She kissed her cheek. "Goodbye, Edith dear."

CHAPTER TWENTY-FIVE

I t was mere steps to the hotel. She was close enough that the doorman touched his cap and reached for the door. And yet she raised
her hand: *Thank you, but no.* The strain of the evening weighed on
her too heavily for her to lie down and sleep. If she did, there was a
very good chance she would never get up. It was the old debilitating
misery. Were she in Lenox, she would walk in her garden. In Paris,
retreat to her study. This was New York, where she had no garden nor
study. So she had to walk. Even if only around the block. Leaving the
doorman, she kept him firmly in mind. Should the killer suddenly
leap from behind a lamppost, the doorman would hear her screams.
Although whether he would reach her in time to stop a bullet was
doubtful. Those handsome purple overcoats were heavy.

When she heard the footsteps behind her, she told herself that it
was only because she was thinking so hard on murder that the hairs
on the back of her neck rose and fear uncoiled in her belly. New York

was a city of millions. Anyone might be behind her. The idea that Mr. Do Not Write had found her again was ridiculous.

Still, she began to walk faster. As she did, she calculated how far she had come from that comforting doorman. One corner turned. That meant two more before she was back within the doorman's sight. Two more corners and what now seemed to her two endless streets.

If she stopped, would he stop?

She couldn't risk it. It felt essential to appear unconcerned. Somehow, to acknowledge the threat would give him the excuse to strike. And so, no rushing. No shouting. Nothing unseemly. Without turning her head, she tried to find other people. The evening had been unforgivably long—truly, if she was not murdered, she was going to make sure not a penny of her money went to the Metropolitan ever again. The streets were largely empty. A pair across the street, but they had eyes only for each other.

Wanting reassurance, she slowed. Felt the person behind her slow as well.

One corner. The longest expanse of concrete ever laid in a city stretched before her. To her right, a darkened Grand Central Station, trapped like Gulliver under ropes and scaffolding. No travelers this late. Builders gone home. Surrounding the half-ruined, half-rising structure, a deep wound of excavated earth. A trench where a body might be hastily buried.

The fear was becoming intolerable. It clutched at her throat, attacked the sinews of her legs, leaving them rubbery. Every nerve screamed that she should run (something she was no longer sure she could do, her knees were so cranky) or, perversely, turn around and face it. It was the not knowing that was unbearable, the pretense that what was actually happening was not . . .

The final corner in view, she set her feet on the pavement. Turned. And saw her husband.

He started, hands raised, as if he were the one followed. Then he peered at her through the winter murk of fog and streetlamp. She looked for White behind him, but the poor man had obviously gone to sleep never dreaming his middle-aged charge would escape.

"Oh, Teddy."

Slowly she walked toward him, saw the old confused shame in his eyes.

"Have you been following me all this time?"

"Yes."

". . . Why?"

She saw him struggle with how to express it—words her power, not his. Watched as feelings of want, despair, and fear played over his face.

Finally he said, "You're leaving me."

"No." Even as she realized, *Yes*.

She looked down at his feet, saw that he was wearing slippers. His coat was open, showing his nightshirt. His poor, scrawny legs were bare, the withered flesh trembling in the cold. His face, already harrowed by age, sagged toothless on one side. What had she seen when she first met him? A large man, laughing. Oddly comfortable in himself, unaware that others found him faintly ridiculous. He was a friend of her brother Harry, and her mother liked him. But he was older than she, and although they moved in the same circles, they did not know each other well. Still, the sight of him in a crowded room always brought relief—*There's a safe spot*. Also boredom. He was not intimidatingly bright. Without paying much attention to him, she had absorbed that he sometimes laughed too late or too loudly. Other times, he seemed to drift from the conversation, a small frown on his face as if he'd forgotten something and then forgotten what it was he'd forgotten.

But then came the summer of the broken engagement. Everywhere, she was met with curiosity masked as sympathy. After the agony of that winter's Patriarch's Ball, where it was whispered that Edith Jones had broken with Henry Stevens for the sake of *literary ambition*, her mother had thought it best to avoid Newport, settling instead for Bar Harbor, Maine. One afternoon, Mamie Updike's tennis tournament had been spoiled by rain, everyone fleeing into the house, where towels were brought and tea was served. As there was now nothing to do but talk, Edith had found herself nibbled at by a variety of people, hoping for details of her mortification. She felt like a horse that had fallen at the first hurdle, and now everyone was awaiting her dispatch with a mix of dread and anticipation. Finally, she had taken refuge by a window. When she felt him settle next to her, she wondered, *Teddy Wharton, why on earth . . . ? I'm hardly a fishing rod, rifle, or racehorse.* She had pretended not to notice him.

Then she heard him say, "Poor old duck."

The words, not meant for her, surprised her; concern was not something she was used to hearing from young men. Edith looked up, and he nodded to point by the fireplace, where a spaniel was cowering under a stout leather wingback chair. It was difficult to see the dog at first; she was surrounded by a forest of legs, swaying summer skirts, and light striped trousers. The dog lay on her belly, head between her paws, eyes darting miserably with every sudden, careless movement. They were not aware of her, those young, laughing people. But she was deeply aware of them.

"I've been trying to rescue her for ages," he said.

Mamie Updike let out a peal of laughter. Terrified, the dog rose, tried to escape, only to discover she was barricaded by silk tea slippers and canvas tennis shoes. Mamie shrieked, "I'd simply adore to have him do me!" This in reference to a very fashionable painter. Edith and Teddy exchanged glances: One edition of Mamie Updike's face was quite enough—the world did not require more. And the dog was still trembling.

She had said, "No creature should have to endure that." Standing, she had nudged the chatterers away from the wingback—after the broken engagement, one more odd move made no difference. She moved the chair, caught the spaniel as it tried to flee, and brought it back in her arms to the window and Teddy Wharton's applause.

"Bravo," he said. "Joan of Arc."

She accepted the praise even as she thought Joan of Arc probably represented the sum total of Teddy Wharton's knowledge of women in history. But right now, she appreciated that he wasn't clever enough to be spiteful. If he ever heard gossip, he probably forgot it the moment he left the person who had shared it.

Together, they soothed the spaniel, Teddy stroking its ears with surprising delicacy. "I think she'd be happier outside," he said. "I agree," she answered. So, out they went. It was lightly drizzling, but she was happy to exchange the noise and close confinement for fresh damp air and the feel of earth giving under her feet. As the spaniel trotted ahead, they congratulated themselves for liberating it. The talk turned to summer: Was he enjoying it? Very much. Was she?

Here, there was a pause. Then he said, "Oh! I suppose not. I'm dreadfully sorry."

It was an apology, not a condolence; he was genuinely appalled by his clumsiness.

Kicking at the wet grass, she said, "I've decided to see it as an accomplishment. Any girl can suffer a mere broken engagement. But to be blamed for the break in *Town Topics* by one's almost mother-in-law? For an excess of intellectuality? That's a rare feat."

"Well, I'd say it is!" She smiled at his enthusiasm, laughing when he added, "Good for you."

"Yes, good for me."

"I gather you write."

"Just poems so far. Stories too. But some of the poems have been printed."

"Extraordinary," he marveled. "Extraordinary. Good for you."

He was so simple, she had laughed again. No one had ever called her extraordinary. No one else had ever congratulated her in this way, seen what a triumph it was for a girl of twenty-two to take the words that spun endlessly in her head and place them before people as worthy of attention. He was, she realized, a bit awed by her. Even better, he did not seem to mind it, her having that power. Perhaps because he was himself a bit strange, still unmarried at the age of thirty, despite having a good family and decent income. He was also strange in that he was *kind*. And when he said, "I suppose we're both off to a late start in things," she understood he meant marriage, and when he asked her to the Patriarch's Ball, she said yes, knowing what it signified, and when he stammered would she consider, might she . . . she had said yes straightaway, not making him go through the whole rigmarole. The right words, they agreed, were her métier. He called her writing a kind of witchcraft.

As she began to lead him back to the Belmont, she remembered them, herself so young, walking from her mother's home on Twenty-Third Street. They walked a lot in those first days—she was so desperate to be away from Lucretia. He had followed her, vast sums of money in his pocket, so that she could buy anything that struck her fancy. Back then, it was the only way she knew to escape: purchase the new, as if the arrival of something novel in the house might transform her world. Quietly, humbly, he had become her ally, trailing behind her as she restlessly wandered the city looking for a life she couldn't quite yet imagine. But she had started moving too fast. Gone to places where he got lost.

I have made you so unhappy, she thought. Something like a plea of forgiveness darted through her mind.

Removing a hand from her muff, she held it out. He took it, and she despaired at how cold and unsteady his hand was; the tremors radiated up his arm. ". . . freezing," she said, rubbing the back of his hand with her thumb. "Come, let's go in."

Gently, she tugged him along so that together, they turned the last corner. He said, "My mind is going and the doctors don't see." She said, "Then we must find better ones." As they approached the entrance, she wrapped her arm in his, aligning herself with him, and his shaking eased a little. To the doorman, she gave her loftiest nod, her grandest good evening, holding his gaze with her own imperious one so that he did not take in Teddy's naked legs and bedraggled slippers under the hem of his Savile Row overcoat. Although, of course, even if he did see, he would never have been so crass as to show it. This was, after all, the Belmont. Appearances were maintained.

CHAPTER TWENTY-SIX

I am attempting to reach Mary Roberts Rinehart. I have been attempting to reach her for some time . . . No. As I told the last young woman of dubious intellect, I do not have her telephone number. But she is a very famous writer. How many of those can you have in Pittsburgh? Someone must know how to reach her."

Edith was well aware there was no need to shout into the telephone. The distance between New York and Pennsylvania did not require amplification on her part. But she was frustrated; she had been trying to reach the celebrated mystery author for over half an hour, so she felt like shouting. To Choumai, she said, "Perhaps I should send word by carrier pigeon."

Last night, she had told herself it was time to set aside the matter of David Graham Phillips. She had suspected a number of people and she had been wrong. She could think of no one else to accuse. Yes, the notes were worrying, but she did not think they would follow her back to Europe. The thing now was to get Dr. Kinnicutt in New York and get herself out of it.

But when she woke up, her very first thought was that while she had been wrong, other people had been *more* wrong. Carolyn Frevert and Anna Walling's imagined plot of murderous aristocrats and their lapdogs was entirely wrong. As was, it seemed, her theory of a jealous husband. However, her theory of a frustrated writer had yet to be fully tested. Maybe she had been wrong to suspect Algernon Okrent. But a man as suffocatingly arrogant as David Graham Phillips must have offended *someone* else. Someone who saw him as a parasite, living off the life blood of others. Someone overwrought enough to use the term *vampire*.

But her theory was not proof. She needed evidence. More than that, she needed to learn how to *obtain* evidence. And for that, she needed to speak with someone whose métier was crime—but who was not an actual criminal. Or a policeman, for the simple reason she didn't know any. Given the nature of the crime, it made sense to put the matter before a fellow author. In America, there was no crime writer more celebrated than Mary Roberts Rinehart.

As she waited, Edith tried to recall everything she had heard about *The Circular Staircase*; when encountering new authors, she liked to begin on a simple and sincere note of admiration. It had been published three years ago, spawning what some called imitations and others a category called the "had I but known" novel, meaning that if the characters knew what horrors awaited them in the old house or dark woods, they would never have ventured forth. Irritably tapping her pen on the edge of the side table, Edith thought that everything might be called a "had I but known" story. Had she but known that her interest in David Graham Phillips's murder was going to lead to this interminable phone call, she would never have attended the funeral. Had she but known that the malingering Dr. Kinnicutt was going to take this long to get over a little cold, she would have packed Teddy off to California that first day, Nannie be damned.

"Hello?"

Startled, Edith barked back, "Yes, hello?"

"Is this . . . Forgive me, they said Mrs. Edith Wharton was on the line, I said surely not, it must be a joke . . ."

"No, no!" The woman was self-deprecating and deferential, two qualities that endeared her to Edith straightaway. "I apologize for the confusion. This is Edith Wharton." She realized she was still shouting; the woman wasn't deaf. "I hope I'm not disturbing you."

"No, not at all. I . . ."

"My congratulations on the success of *The Circular Staircase*. I long to read it."

"I so enjoyed *The House of Mirth*," said the other woman faintly. Edith frowned. *The House of Mirth* was not a biscuit or blend of tea, something to be blandly enjoyed. Still. She must allow for nerves. Mrs. Rinehart had not expected her call.

Then she heard an impressive crash and a cry of despair from Mrs. Rinehart, who said, "Excuse me, Mrs. Wharton . . ." before shouting, "Stanley, Alan, and Fred, take yourselves outside the house while there still is a house!"

Returning, she said, "Forgive me."

"Your sons?" guessed Edith, thinking you would never name a dog Stanley.

"Yes," said Mrs. Rinehart. "Marvelous, of course, and I adore them. But a challenge when it comes to finding time to write."

Edith thought the other woman had been about to say something along the lines of *as you know* before remembering that Edith did not know. The issue of time having been raised, Edith felt she should come to the point. But her well-rehearsed request that Mrs. Rinehart use her knowledge of crime to help her find a murderer now sounded overly bold.

Floundering, she said, "I suppose you have heard of the murder of the writer David Graham Phillips."

"I read about it in the paper. Terrible. Did you know him?"

"I only met him once, the day before he was killed." A sympathetic gasp from Mrs. Rinehart encouraged frankness. "And yet since it happened, I haven't been able to think about anything else. It's become something of an obsession. I do that, I'm told, become obsessed with things. Trips, motors . . ."

"I became obsessed with a house once."

Thinking of The Mount, Edith felt a rush of kinship. "Did you?"

"Yes, I sometimes felt I was writing just to pay for it. But you didn't call to talk about houses."

Edith would have happily talked about houses for hours. But she said, "No, I suppose I didn't. I thought since you write so well about crime, you might have some idea of how one might go about catching the person who did it."

A gentle pause. "Well, I would go to the police."

This was disappointing. Edith rallied. "Heavens, Mrs. Rinehart, where would you be if people believed the police solved every crime? Leave it to the professionals, where's the fun in that?"

The other woman laughed.

Remembering the reviews, Edith said, "In *The Circular Staircase*, a spinster in a strange house discovers a body at the bottom of the stairs. Then she finds a pistol in a flower bed. Now—she doesn't tell the police she found the pistol. She investigates on her own."

"True. But Rachel's nephew is a suspect, and she feels she has to clear his name."

"Well, isn't that dangerous? Doesn't she experience all sorts of peril once the killer discovers that she's looking for him?"

"Of course, otherwise nothing would happen in the story." Edith sensed Mrs. Rinehart smiling on the other end of the phone. "It *is* true that readers become impatient with a character who needlessly puts herself at risk."

"But what if she is already at risk? And the only way to feel safe is to catch the person who did it?"

"What do you mean, Mrs. Wharton?"

"I have been asked to read Mr. Phillips's final book. From the day I began reading, I began to receive anonymous messages at my hotel. Very similar to the ones sent to David Graham Phillips before he was killed."

A long pause. "Have you seen those notes?" Edith affirmed that she had. "And the handwriting is the same?"

"Yes."

"Really, Mrs. Wharton, I . . ."

Edith refused to listen to more advice to go to the police. "Mrs. Rinehart, isn't the appeal of your book that you write about a woman who wants to find out something? A woman who wants to know? She goes digging and asks questions and takes risks because whatever people might tell her, she knows that women live in the world and must grapple with its realities. Perhaps we don't serve on juries or fight wars, but we shouldn't be endlessly sheltered . . ."

"Many women aren't," said Mrs. Rinehart.

Edith heard the rebuke but ignored it. "And so we have a right to seek answers. Like the adults we are."

Mrs. Rinehart asked, "Mr. Phillips had loved ones, did he not?"

"Yes, strangely. He was a very abrasive man."

"Do they have any thoughts on who killed him?"

"They think he was murdered by the rich and powerful to stop the publication of his next book. I know the people they suspect, and their complacency is only equal to their incompetence. These are not assassins, Mrs. Rinehart."

"And what is your opinion, Mrs. Wharton?"

"At one point, I thought it a jealous husband and a love affair gone wrong. Mr. Phillips wrote a great deal about women, but more to scold than in sympathy. He felt very much like a man spurned. Honestly, if a woman did shoot him, I should not be in the least surprised."

"But you're sure the shooter was not a woman," Mrs. Rinehart clarified.

"Not according to the witnesses. They were very dull and unobservant, but that much they seemed to have noticed."

"And the jealous husband?"

Edith thought of Henry Frevert covered in paste and butcher paper. William Walling, desperate to atone. "One has what I think you call an alibi. The other seems temperamentally unsuited to murder. So I return to my original theory."

"Which was?"

"A jealous writer."

She felt mildly foolish in saying it. But Mrs. Rinehart offered a delighted "A-*ha*."

Encouraged, she said, "Someone who lives in the same area as Mr. Phillips did. The notes were delivered to his address—the killer seems to have been familiar with his movements. He was shot not very far from his apartment, outside his club. I've also wondered if that doesn't indicate that Mr. Phillips knew his killer. I mean, if you were receiving death threats, Mrs. Rinehart, wouldn't any stranger who got too close be cause for alarm?"

There was a long pause. Edith worried that she had strayed into fanciful thinking.

But then Mrs. Rinehart said, "I am more concerned with how the killer knows your movements, Mrs. Wharton. The notes to you were delivered where?"

"To my hotel."

"How did the sender know where you were staying?"

She thought to say, *Oh, he was following me.* Then remembered, no, that had been poor Teddy.

"How did they know you had taken an interest?" Mrs. Rinehart pressed.

"I went to Appleton. I was reading the book . . ."

"How did they know who you were? Oh, dear, I'm not saying this right."

"Well, I am Edith Wharton."

"Yes, but . . . how did the killer know you were you?"

Edith was about to snap that of course she was she, she was Edith Wharton, everyone knew who she was, even back to the time she had been Edith Jones, everyone who mattered anyway. Perhaps other people were unused to significance or relevance, but she was not . . .

Then she remembered her own words: *I don't know what Mary Roberts Rinehart looks like well enough to shoot her.*

And Anna Walling: *I recognized you from your author portrait.*

And if Teddy had been the person who was following her, how did the killer know she was staying at the Belmont?

Mrs. Rinehart's voice, anxious over the line. "Do you see what I mean, Mrs. Wharton?"

"Yes. Yes, I do."

"At the very least, you seem to be correct that the shooter is a book lover."

Or someone who hates writers. Although he may be unaware that he does.

To Mrs. Rinehart, she said, "Well, not a lover of the books of David Graham Phillips. At least not his last one."

"Then perhaps the answer lies inside the pages of his last book."

Edith heard a slammed door in the background followed by the stomping of careless feet, and Mrs. Rinehart directing the disposal of hats, coats, and galoshes.

Then her voice clearer as she returned to the phone. "Mrs. Wharton—I must say it again: If this person has killed once, please, be careful."

"Yes, thank you. And thank you for indulging me, Mrs. Rinehart. I hope we meet in person one day."

"I as well," said Mrs. Rinehart warmly. Then, after a brief pause, "May I ask if you support women's suffrage?"

"Good God, no," said Edith and bidding the otherwise lovely Mrs. Rinehart adieu, she hung up the phone.

CHAPTER TWENTY-SEVEN

Alone in her room, Edith pondered Mrs. Rinehart's warning. She thought of the killer's last note: *A man in this world who does just about what he wishes is liable to be a social outcast, a very prominent member of the Four Hundred, or both.*

It was rather funny, given her current situation. The entire point of the Four Hundred was that one should never encounter a person who was not known and approved by the right people. The definition of *stranger* was incalculably broad: Anyone who didn't possess one of a handful of names. Anyone who did not possess a comfortable income or live in one of the select areas of select cities—and of course, adhere to prescribed standards. She recalled her mother's sharp admonition to look away as August Belmont's mistress sailed by in her yellow brougham. One must only know August Belmont to a certain degree because he was Jewish. One must know nothing at all of his mistress.

She was astonished by how few strangers she encountered in life.

Every room she entered, familiar faces, with a few select new ones made known to her by association with the old. A woman of her class was never to be "known" by people outside of it, mentioned publicly only at the time of her birth, marriage, and death, and attendance at the opera. She had fought it, this refusal to associate only with certain people, to stay in approved spaces. When she traveled, she never wanted to go to the five places all Americans went, but to the small convent in the countryside, the caves known only to the locals, uncelebrated houses with beautiful, ancient roofs that spoke of ages past. She wanted to see what real life felt like to the people who lived there. Now she wondered: If her mother knew that Edith's face and whereabouts were known by a murderer, would she say, *Well, that is what comes of traveling to the Grotte di Frasassi?*

A person who had taken a life knew who she was. Where she was. And she knew nothing about him.

Or did she?

Now that she was certain neither the Vanderbilts nor the Depews had murdered David Graham Phillips, she allowed Anna Walling's accusation back into her mind: *Closer to home.* Who close to home might think her a woman who did just as she wanted? Who might think her too free and send her notes to let her know she was not protected?

It was difficult not to think of the one man whose notes had recently been her entire existence.

But Morton Fullerton had no need of a mystery identity to torment her. And it would hardly satisfy his vanity to unnerve her anonymously. He would want credit. Besides, he was a better writer than the note sender.

HJ? Normally, she would never think him capable of cruelty. But he had not been himself of late. His brother's death had been an enormous blow. And there had always been resentment on his part over the fact that her books sold better than his. He knew the details of the murder because she had kept him informed. In the darkness of depression, brooding in his room that he could not afford, would it have amused him to frighten her through words on the page, a thing so dear to both their hearts?

No. HJ was a gentle man, in every sense. A kind man. Also, *the* (she flung the word at David Graham Phillips's ghost) greatest American writer. He would be incapable of such clumsy prose. And . . . he was a good friend.

Walter, she dismissed. Sending anonymous threats was too tawdry a pastime for her fastidious friend. And it would distract him from the vapid charms of Mrs. Goelet.

Fearfully, she approached the possibility of Teddy. He had followed her; she must consider that he had written the notes as well. It was not unlike him to grovel one moment, lash out the next. And he was not a felicitous writer. But, she realized with great relief, the desk clerk would have recognized him.

The Vanderbilts, she thought, would not bother sending notes; their preferred punishment was to withdraw communication, not increase it. Young Depew thought writing a waste of time. Deplorable, but in this case exonerating. The first note had come before Henry Frevert knew of her involvement; also he would have no way of knowing she was staying at the Belmont. Anna Walling, altogether too forthright and ferocious for such sneaky dealings. Her husband, on the other hand . . .

But why threaten her if he hadn't shot David Graham Phillips?

She reminded herself that she had only his wife's assurance on that point. But however absurd Anna Walling's worldview might be, she had a stubborn integrity. Also William Walling was not a frustrated writer. In their poor attempts at epigrams, the notes begged for attention and applause. Walling might desire that from his wife—but not from Edith Wharton.

Thoughts of writers turned to thoughts of publishers. Editors.

Rutger Bleecker Jewett.

He knew she had taken an interest in David Graham Phillips's murder. He knew she was staying at the Belmont because she had told him so, saying it would be no trouble to read the book in-house. She had received the first note on the same day as their first meeting. She recalled her impulse to joke that he would never have murdered so successful an author.

And she still believed that.

But perhaps he had been careless about sharing her interest. Maybe, inadvertently, he had told the sender of the notes that Edith Wharton was eager to discover who had killed David Graham Phillips. Another writer, perhaps.

She should, she decided, ask him directly.

Almost unthinking, she left the suite and let the elevator lower her to the lobby. On her way, she stopped at the front desk to inform them that she was going to the Appleton offices. Should anyone inquire. If she did not return . . .

Well—should anyone inquire.

It was a very simple question, she told herself, one that Mr. Jewett should be more than happy to answer, given his stated concern as to her welfare. He had told her, hadn't he, that she must stop reading *Susan Lenox*, that it was too dangerous . . .

Those words sounded very different to her now.

But why should he not want her to read *Susan Lenox*? It was his author's book. It would create a sensation. That was precisely why they were rushing to publish now, after having delayed for so long. He had every reason to hope for its success. And what better way to improve its chances than to have the support of a celebrated author such as herself?

She remembered his remark about Algernon Okrent: *He is worldly enough to know that the surest way to make* Susan Lenox *a success is to kill its author. No writer would willingly give another such a boost of publicity.*

Also his remark about Crane's notepaper. *It is excellent paper. I use it myself.*

No, she thought as she went through the lobby doors, no. It was altogether ridiculous. She was a keen judge of people. Rutger Bleecker Jewett was a good man who cared about his authors. He had become emotional when speaking about David Graham Phillips. He had assured her that *Susan Lenox* would be published whole and unmucked with.

But had he meant it?

When had the decision been made that *Susan Lenox* was ready to be released to the world? She had always assumed the publicity surrounding the author's death had made them eager to publish. But she remembered now, the pages had been typeset before David Graham Phillips had died. And according to his sister, the text was as he wished it to be.

Mr. Jewett had promised her that he would resist any attempt to censor *Susan Lenox*. That he was ready to battle Anthony Comstock and his ilk. But he had also said Comstock's cause attracted people who were unstable. Violent. Comstock's own lieutenant had boasted that they had driven people to suicide with their threats and harassment.

Had they threatened Rutger Bleecker Jewett? How would they do such a thing?

The answer came almost immediately: money.

Appleton had been in financial difficulties in the past. Another round of bankruptcy might well be catastrophic. It was not beyond imagining that the Puritanical Postman could organize a boycott of all of Appleton's authors. A reasonable man might conclude that the fortunes of one writer were not worth the sacrifice of every other writer in the house. Not to mention its editors.

Taken me ten years to write, and almost as long to get the cowards at Appleton to publish. The public will not soon forgive me for this one.

Was that why Appleton had waited so long to publish? Because they were afraid of financial ruin? Still, it seemed braver spirits had prevailed.

But perhaps Mr. Jewett was not as brave as he seemed.

This she knew: David Graham Phillips would never have censored his own work, no matter what the consequences to himself or anyone else.

In the elevator at the Appleton building, she strove to recall her first, congenial impression of Mr. Jewett. His warm smile and penguin form, his affability and grave concern for writers. No, she was wrong; she must be. The difficulties of the past week were muddling her. Rutger Bleecker Jewett was a man of letters. The brute violent act of pointing a pistol at another human being and firing a bullet into them was simply not in him. And judging from the overheard argument with Algernon Okrent, he was as eager as anyone at Appleton that *Susan Lenox* get into bookstores.

But that was not to say he was incapable of passing on the information that she was reading *Susan Lenox* with an intent to support its author. She imagined him calling down the hall, *Mrs. Wharton is staying at the Belmont.* Some wag responding, *Of course she is . . .*

Yes, she thought, leaving the elevator. That was entirely possible. Such a decent, trusting man would not see the threat even when it was right in front of him.

"Mrs. Wharton."

The youth looked at her, puzzled. She had been so lost in thought, she had not presented herself properly as she came through the doors. Even now, she was not certain what she meant to say.

Guessing as much, he said, "Can I assist you?"

"No," she said, thinking she did not want to be any bother. Then changed it to, "Yes, I'm so sorry, yes. Mr. Jewett, is he in?"

"Regrettably, he's away at the moment."

"Oh, dear. When will he be back?"

"He didn't say. So I couldn't say. But if you wish to read *Susan Lenox . . .*"

He reached for the drawer that held the key to the spare room.

"No, no. I don't think I do want that."

He sat back down, a smile on his face. "No."

She answered his smile, taking small relief in their shared loathing. Then noticed that his overcoat lay on the desk.

"Were you about to go out?" He inclined his head to indicate as much. "Oh, then you must go. I'll just . . . sit . . ."

Sideways, she made her way to one of the chairs.

". . . and wait for Mr. Jewett. Hopefully, my mind will return before he does!"

The youth stood, gathered up his coat. "I'm sure your mind is as fine as ever, Mrs. Wharton."

She smiled her gratitude, watching as he slid into his coat. It was a very nice coat, actually. Good strong wool, charcoal gray. One wouldn't have thought an assistant could afford such a coat.

"It's cold out," she warned him. "It may snow."

"I am prepared," he assured her.

To prove it, he wound a long striped scarf around his neck.

"What a lovely pattern," she said after a moment. "Chevron?"

"Yes, I think so."

"Are you off to lunch?"

"I don't take lunch," he said. "At this time of day I like to have a walk around my favorite park."

"Lovely," she enthused. She did not have to ask which park was his favorite.

Turning in her seat to wave goodbye as he left, she saw that yes, he had left the scarf long and flowing down his back. Just as a young man of artistic sensibility would.

Just as the man who had murdered David Graham Phillips had.

She sat until she was certain he had reached the ground floor and left the building. She had no doubt that he was going to Gramercy Park, a little more than a mile away. She had no doubt that it was his lunchtime habit. David Graham Phillips had been shot on a Monday, between one and two o'clock.

Quietly, she went to the desk and opened the drawer where he kept the key. She was not surprised to see a stack of Crane's paper and a tidy batch of envelopes.

On instinct, she opened the lowest drawer. As a writer, she knew the impulse to tuck one's work away before it was ready to be shown. And there it was, a battered notebook, a single word on the cardboard cover: "Life." The handwriting was similar to the notes.

Under "Life," he had written his name: "Fitzhugh Coyle Goldsborough."

But this was crossed out. Underneath he had written "David Graham Phillips."

This was also crossed out and replaced by "Fitzhugh Coyle

Goldsborough." Then something illegible as if he had written one name over the other, again and again.

Edith shuddered. She was familiar with the nervous condition, but this was a different sort of madness.

Gingerly with one finger, she lifted the cover of the diary. Mr. Goldsborough's obsession with David Graham Phillips dated back at least several months.

July 11, 1910. Certain happenings recently lead me to think it advisable to jot down data. I believe David Graham Phillips is trying to fake a case against me, or to do me serious bodily harm, or both.

This surprised her. Had the men known each other beyond this office? Had they quarreled?

But the "harm" done to Mr. Goldsborough was made clear in the next entry.

September 3, 1910. There is no doubt in my mind but that he has slandered me with his novel of a Washington family. The sensitive, "eccentric" hero is clearly me. The degrading caricature of its heroine, Margaret, a fashionable "noddle-head," an insult to my own dear sister. He is an enemy to society. He is my enemy.

Another entry showed that Mr. Phillips was not the only person to attract Goldsborough's attention. Chilled, Edith read:

October 5, 1910. Yesterday I was sitting at the window when I noticed a pretty looking woman seated on the second-story window of the arts society building. She smiled at me in a pointed manner, lifted her hand and waved it. I could not decide if this was an involuntary motion or encouragement for me to start flirting with her. I got rather the latter impression.

Edith remembered the Frevert apartment had been on the second floor. The parlor had two windows. A later entry confirmed Goldsborough made the connection between the woman in the window and his "enemy."

January 5, 1911. Again, the woman appeared at the window and continued to take evident notice of me. I concluded it was Mrs. Frevert, D.G.P.'s sister . . .

January 19, 1911. I saw them leave the house. They were laughing. In his hand was my latest letter. I concluded they were amusing themselves at my expense.

After this, there were no more dated entries. The rest was notes for stories or aphorisms such as the ones he had sent her. An entire page was devoted to one observation, written in capital letters— DATA FOR VAMPIRE—as Mr. Goldsborough raved about writers who stole the flesh and blood of real people for their own use. Remembering that first note Mr. Jewett had shown her, *"You are a vampire,"* her stomach churned. Goldsborough had been sitting just outside as she talked with Mr. Jewett. He would have heard she was staying at the Belmont. Would have heard them discussing his . . . work.

That very day, he had written to her for the first time. Most likely, he had dropped off the note on his way home from work.

She smelled something. It was sweet, pleasantly herbaceous. Turning the page she saw a faded yellow flower, pressed flat, and a dark green leaf. Bay laurel, a keepsake or memento of some kind. Without thinking, she breathed it in, thought of sun, the sharp fresh air of spring.

She closed the diary.

She could, she told herself, return to the Belmont Hotel. She would write. Tend to Teddy. Walk Choumai. Play out the old comedy of care when Dr. Kinnicutt finally made his appearance. It was only a matter of a day or two. Then she would return to Europe. If she was feeling civic-minded, she might call the police. Or simply tell Mr. Jewett to look in the lower left drawer of the secretary's desk.

But she could not dismiss the feeling that she had been invited to something. The way Goldsborough looked at her when he announced his intention to walk around his favorite park. The way he had not named that park because he knew she understood which one he meant.

He could have locked this drawer, she thought. But he didn't. Like the notes, the diary was his work and he wished her to read it.

Did he intend to harm her? That was chief in her mind. Was he asking her to the place where he had murdered David Graham Phillips to reveal something? Or did he want to murder another writer? She saw no evidence in his diary that he was obsessed with her in the way he had been with Phillips. That didn't mean he wouldn't appease his wounded vanity by killing her.

But—the thought came stubbornly to her—they had agreed that *Susan Lenox* was bad. All he knew of her was that she shared his dislike of the murdered man.

Was that enough to keep her safe?

Quickly, she picked up the telephone. It could not be Walter, she told herself; he was simply too old. And it could not be poor Henry; he was simply too ill. Teddy she did not even consider, although it did occur to her that White might be summoned.

But then she heard a hello. She asked if she might speak to Mr. Fullerton. Told he was not available, she asked the lady if she might tell Mr. Fullerton that she needed to see him immediately. Now. He should meet her at Gramercy Park.

CHAPTER TWENTY-EIGHT

As she approached Gramercy Park, Edith asked herself: Why did they call it a park? Why not a garden? Really, it was too ugly to be a garden. But also too small for a park. She sometimes thought the gardens she designed were superior works of art to her novels, nature giving her so much more to work with than the ether of her thoughts. Here was seed and soil, infinite variety of color, shape, and height. She loved the rhythm of it, the glorious return year after year of dahlia and delphinium, cleome and hydrangea. Wandering slowly through the separate parts of her garden—she thought of them as rooms in a house—she was happily humbled by the knowledge that she could never write a line as pure as a lily. A garden required care and imagination. Respect for the fragile blooms that gave it life. One cultivated a garden. One stomped through a park. Gardens were private. Parks for the public.

And yet because so few people walked its paths, it was easy to think of Gramercy Park as a garden, albeit an inadequate one. She

remembered a summer afternoon she had been standing in her garden at The Mount when she heard an agitated thrum. At first she
took it for a hummingbird until one of the gardeners had pointed to
a heavy tan snake with black diamonds down its length of five feet,
sunning itself on the stone wall. Edith, who had thought rattlesnakes
lived only in deserts, had been mesmerized with terror. Yet rather
giddy that such a creature existed in her garden.

He stood at the northeast corner. As people hurried by him, cold,
tired, wanting to be home, he was still, gazing down Irving Place,
certain she would come.

She took a last moment, then stepped into his line of sight. "Mr.
Goldsborough."

"You finally learned my name."

"Yes."

"You should have known it before."

Foolishly she wondered if it might have made a difference if she
had bothered to learn his name, rather than thinking of him as "the
youth," "the smirky youth," "the infant." But no, he had killed David
Graham Phillips before they ever met.

"It is a fine name," he said. "Fitzhugh Coyle Goldsborough. Far
more elegant and distinguished, don't you think? Phillips—that's a
name for a fishmonger."

She could not find the breath to speak. Her heart was pounding
fast and hard; to ease it, she analyzed the accent: genteel, soft. A
touch of the South, a light, graceful overlay, the vowels only slightly
prolonged. Not the Carolinas. Virginia perhaps. Oh, yes—an old
Washington family. He had said in the diary. She could imagine it. A
place so genteel, one did not dream of illness. Of rage. And certainly
not violence. Even when it bloomed right in front of you.

For the first time, she looked at him properly. He was not as young as she had thought. He was willowy, with flowing, light brown hair, and almost frail—that made him seem younger. She could see the quality of his care in his strong teeth and the sheen of his hair. And yet, away from the office, his brokenness was clear. She saw it in his wandering gaze, the way he stood, stoop-shouldered, head swaying as he gazed at the ground, the twitchy hand, fingers spasming open and closed. This was a cracked brain.

She felt for the jagged pulse of violence in the space between them. For the moment, it was calm.

"Have you read my work?" he asked.

Did he mean the notes or the diaries? Was it safe to admit she had read the diaries?

Always, she thought, *begin on a sincere note of admiration*. "Riveting. An entirely fresh perspective."

"You see how much better it is. It has some wit, some style, I think."

She nodded.

"My writing doesn't just . . . harangue you like a backwoods preacher."

Harangue. She had used just that word when speaking of David Graham Phillips. Horrible to think she had tastes in common with this ill young man. But she also knew it might save her, his belief that they were allies. She must keep him thinking that. At least until help arrived. Surreptitiously, she took note of the people around them. There a man hurrying, there a lady walking her dog.

Of Morton Fullerton, she saw no sign.

To Goldsborough, she said, "I don't think I realized how much you disliked him."

"I didn't *dislike* him." He frowned, rebuking her poor choice of words. "He persecuted me."

Persecuted. In the diaries, he had written of being followed by Phillips, his impertinent stare. She was sure it had been the other way round. She thought of what HJ had said: *As if the murderer were the victim's victim.*

"Tell me how?"

He stared at her, astonished that she did not understand. "He was a *terrible* writer."

It was almost funny, but she sensed the threat. His trust was a wobbly thing, liable to tip over at any moment. The gun. Did he have it with him? Her eyes darted over his coat. As she searched, she distracted him by saying, "But my dear Mr. Goldsborough, there are so many terrible writers. Some of them, regrettably"—deliberately, she used a word he liked—"sell well. The best thing to do is ignore them."

"Ignore him? Do you think he would ever accept that? With that suit and the gaudy bloom in his lapel. His posturing and pronouncements . . ."

"Yes, I hated that suit as well. And I grant you, he was a man who insisted on being noticed. But the one recourse left to us as writers is to focus on our own work."

Hoping to persuade him to confess to the police, she said, as gently as possible, "If we tell the stories that reflect our deepest selves . . ."

Voice rising, he said, "He made that impossible, Mrs. Wharton. He stole my story."

Confused, she said, "You accuse him of plagiarism?"

"I accuse him of literary vampirism. He stole my life. That arrogant vulgarian stole my *self* and made a cheap ugly comedy out of it. And not just me, but my family."

"He wrote about you in *Susan Lenox*?"

"No! *The Fashionable Adventures of Joshua Craig.* That is why I brought you his books, so you would see. I left it right there on the top of the pile."

Agitated, she tried to remember. Which one had that been? Oh, yes, the novel set in Washington with the ambitious girl Margaret and the sensitive eccentric hero. Goldsborough had complained about it in his diary.

Wanting to calm him—and reassure him she was on his side—she said, "But Mr. Goldsborough, how could Phillips, a vulgarian as you say, from . . . Indiana, was it? I can barely remember. How could a tawdry little muckraker who wore white in winter and a chrysanthemum in his lapel know anything of your family? Your people are in Washington, aren't they?"

"Yes." He drew himself up. "Perhaps we are not members of the Four Hundred. But my father is a prominent physician, my mother widely admired. A Goldsborough was a delegate to the Continental Congress, another a senator who distinguished himself in the War of 1812."

She thought, *Ah, yes, the pedigree. How we cling to it.*

"And yet Phillips turned us into a farce for people to jeer at. A real writer, a genuine artist, would never use people like that. That is why I call him a vampire."

She nodded deeply as if she now understood. "I admire your choice of words, Mr. Goldsborough. *Vampire*—very evocative. A creature that feeds on others, taking life that is not theirs."

"Yes."

"I myself have known such a creature. Interestingly he didn't look like a monster. In fact, he was quite charming. Perhaps that is why they fascinate us. Unlike other monsters, vampires draw one in by promising a new sort of life. The destruction of the old one."

As she spoke, she heard an echo of something Phillips had said.

Before it could come clear, Goldsborough said coldly, "The person attacked by Mr. Phillips had no wish to be outraged and degraded."

The diaries had mentioned two "shes." Not wanting to provoke him with another error, she said in a low voice, "Who is that, Mr. Goldsborough?"

"My sister," he said. "A gracious, lovely woman, and he held her up to the world as you would a joint of meat in a shop window. He took his sister and made her a thing of his own imagination when she is so much more . . ."

He had gone from *my* to *his*. She thought to correct him but sensed that his faculties were breaking down. He was having difficulty keeping the sisters straight: his own and Carolyn Frevert. Nor could he quite disentangle his own identity from David Graham Phillips, so desperately did he covet that man's success and reputation.

She glanced about the park. Still no sign of Morton Fullerton.

"Who are you looking for?"

". . . No one. I thought I saw a friend. But I was mistaken."

"You know what it is like to be written about by people who sneer," he said suddenly. "To have people whisper falsehoods about you. That is why I warned you about making yourself conspicuous. If you put yourself out in the world, people might make anything of you."

A woman who leaves her home walks the streets. She is neither pure nor protected.

"How did you know I was . . . leaving my home, Mr. Goldsborough?"

"I read it in *Town Topics*."

She nodded: *Of course.*

It had begun to snow. As the white flakes flew between them, gathering on his coat and hat, making him look young and, yes, rather pure, she wondered if there had ever been a point where he might have been saved.

He said, "There must be consequences, Mrs. Wharton. Punishment for people who put evil into the world with their stories."

His echo of the Comstockians put steel into her spine. "We cannot be afraid of books, Mr. Goldsborough."

"We cannot accept lies, Mrs. Wharton. That man's books are not just books; they are weapons. Propaganda. He wrote about us with loathing and contempt, and people heralded it as the truth. It is a *violation*."

He peered at her, suddenly plaintive. "Do you see now, why I had to do what I did?"

Depew Jr.'s words came to her: *People don't really care about books.*

Oh, but they do, Mr. Depew. Once in print, words and ideas exist. They are discussed, repeated, debated—even by people who have never read the original work. That is why some people are so terrified of them.

She heard him say in a small voice, "They laugh at me, Mrs. Wharton."

"I do not laugh, Mr. Goldsborough."

"No, but she did. She laughed at me."

He nodded toward Irving Place, the path to the Phillips home. She remembered the diary entry, how he had seen Phillips and Carolyn Frevert laugh over his note.

"My sister . . ."

His sister, she thought.

"He showed her my letter and . . . they *laughed*. As if my words were nothing and I was a trifle."

He gathered himself, standing straighter, and she braced.

"That's when I realized how little they understood. He refused to see how great was his offense. No matter how many times I warned him. That's how I knew there was only one way to make him understand."

"And do you think he understood?" Edith asked. "Is that what you believe happened?"

"He understood that he didn't have the power he thought he did." Now there was a smirk. "He understood that well enough, I saw it in his eyes."

And that was enough for you, she thought. *That grisly few seconds of power that was not even yours, but the gun's. You rage that David Graham Phillips created a false version of you in the world. But you made him a fantasy nemesis, holding him responsible for your own failure. Then you stole his life with six bullets.*

Something inside the park had caught his attention. She looked through the gates and saw a young woman happily wrapped in her coat, sketching. The artist seemed oblivious to the cold, rapt as she gazed up at a tree, then back down at her handiwork. The one thing on which she and Mr. Phillips had ever agreed, thought Edith. The consolations of creation.

Goldsborough was also looking at the young woman with the sketch pad, his eyes narrowed, as if she were a puzzle he could not solve. Edith thought sadly how small he was, for all his pretension to greatness. Murder was such a final act, one fantasized that the person who committed it had some purpose or vision. Goldsborough imagined he did. But really he was just a bundle of grievance, insisting that he be heard when he had nothing to say beyond *Look at me!* He was nothing so majestic as a serpent. Rather, he put her in mind of a bad apricot she had once bitten into. The sudden slimy give of overripe flesh under the teeth, the bitter burst of rot, the awareness of tiny worms squirming on the tongue.

He said, "I want you to speak to Jewett about my work. He didn't like it before, but if you speak for it . . ."

Of course, she thought. *He submitted his own novel, only to be rejected, while his enemy was celebrated. Who fears and detests a writer more than another writer, Henry?*

"What would you like me to say?"

"That it is good, that they should publish it." As if it were obvious. "We must answer that posturing jackass. We must put the truth before the public!"

Heart wild in her chest, she was at a loss for an answer. *Ah, yes,* she thought hysterically, *the truth!*

She had tested his trust by not answering right away. Leaning to whisper, he said, "You're not going to speak for his book, are you? That would be a terrible betrayal."

His hand went to his chest. She understood that was where the gun rested.

"No. No, I'm not. But enough about Mr. Phillips—I'm tired of talking about the tiresome man. No, what we must think about is your novel, Mr. Goldsborough. I should like to think about how we get them to see your value."

Your value reassured him. The hand lowered.

She said, "I very much enjoy being helpful to writers. But as you know all too well, publishing has become a crass, commercial concern."

An idea came to her.

"However, your notoriety might be an asset. A book written by a man with your keen insight and capacity for decisive action. Someone who dared to do something . . ."

"You mean I should tell them what I did."

"Yes. The full story of how Mr. Phillips robbed you and how you made him pay for it. It is an important story, one people should hear. And it will increase interest in your work."

"The work is interesting for its own sake. My words are beautiful . . ."

"Quality of writing is no longer the sole criteria, I'm afraid. Look at Mr. Phillips's final work. It is tremendously long and twice as dull. And yet they are rushing to publish it. Why? Because you, Mr. Goldsborough, put him on the front page of every newspaper. But you could share in that fame . . ."

He gazed at her, uncertain. He wanted to believe her. For a moment, she fancied she had persuaded him to turn himself in to the police.

"Yes," he said. "Death does help move a book along, doesn't it?"

Clumsily, he thrust his hand under the lapel of his coat. When he drew out the gun, she had only a moment, but long enough to understand the weapon had appeared. Before she could scream or raise her arms or even remember the possibility of movement, he raised the gun to his own temple. A colossal shocking crack she thought would stop her heart. Then he was no longer standing before her. And the blood was everywhere, staining the snow.

CHAPTER TWENTY-NINE

What she *mustn't* do, thought Edith, was laugh. The policemen—there were two: one very young and very pale who had been sick at the sight of Mr. Goldsborough's ruined head, and an older man with a very impressive gray mustache. She kept thinking to compliment it, and then deciding, no, he would think that strange under the circumstances, but it really was tremendous.

The *policemen*—she refocused herself—were concerned. Even though she had assured them several times that she was fine. She had thought Mr. Goldsborough was going to shoot her, but he hadn't. Well, they could see that, couldn't they? But she was fine. Entirely unharmed.

She raised her arms to show them. Felt dizzy. The younger officer rushed in to prop her up; the older one steadied her by taking hold of her shoulder. Which she found rude and overfamiliar, but she supposed they meant well. In fact, the officer had probably stopped her from falling off the bench into the snow.

Someone had opened the gate. She didn't know who and she wasn't sure when it had happened. All she could remember was someone shouting that the lady needed to sit down, and a few minutes later, she found herself sitting on a wretched little bench in Gramercy Park. The younger officer had cleared the snow with his sleeve. Which was still wet, poor man. She was about to tell him he ought to change out of that coat—but perhaps they only had one, the New York City police wouldn't be in the habit of handing out multiple uniforms, but she did worry he would catch cold . . .

The older officer had asked her something. Embarrassed, she asked him to repeat it.

"You said his name was Goldsborough."

"Yes. Fitzhugh . . . I'm sorry, there was a middle name, but I don't remember it. He lived nearby, I think. Just over there."

She thought of pointing. But the prospect of raising her arm did not appeal.

"He lived opposite, you see. That's how he knew when he came and went. And how he knew where to send the notes." Suddenly, she worried. "I mentioned the notes, didn't I?"

Yes, they assured her. She had.

"He lives across the street, I'm fairly sure. Oh!"

She had almost forgotten.

"In his desk drawer, there is a diary. His desk at the office, not in his home. But if you read that, you'll see."

The two men exchanged looks. She felt annoyed. Were they not listening?

"See what, ma'am?" asked the older officer.

No—clearly, they were not listening. What on earth was wrong with the New York police? Teddy Roosevelt had mandated intelligence and competency standards *decades* ago; obviously, those had lapsed. She might have been talking to two cabbages.

"The diary," she repeated. "If you read it, you'll understand."

The younger man winced, as if struggling to hear. "Why he shot himself?"

"No!" Now she was really irritated. "Why he killed David Graham Phillips."

The younger man's eyes went wide. The older one got out some sort of little notebook.

"You say this is the man who killed David Graham Phillips?"

"Yes! Just over there."

She pointed to the Princeton Club. Which had once been Stanford White's old house. Which would probably be something else one day soon, knocked over, rebuilt, something bigger and uglier taking its place. Because this was New York, and everything would fall eventually.

Allowing the word *fall* into her mind had been a mistake. Too late, she gazed up the trees to center herself. Green, nature, freshness always did that. But all she saw were bare dark winter branches. They looked like bones, starved, old fingers clawing at the sky, wanting the sun, its warmth and brightness. But the sun wasn't there. Just gray, just slush, old snow, trod on by so many feet and no longer new. Even in Gramercy Park, the gate left open, she and the policemen, they'd left all these tracks where once it had been rather pretty. That girl who had been sketching, someone should tend to her.

She thought of the blood. And then did not wish to think anymore.

They all came; they all fussed. Minnie begged her to come and stay. Edith refused. "You have one invalid, you don't need another."

Henry was unable to come, although he sent his ardent wishes for her recovery. Walter came, more than once, mostly to demand what she had been thinking. How could she put herself at risk like that? Did she realize how foolish she had been? What might have happened? Did she understand, how he would have felt if . . . ?

Taking his hand, she pressed it and said yes, she understood.

The accepted story was that a deranged young man had taken his life in front of her, entirely by chance, and she was suffering from shock. Teddy was told only that she had become dizzy near Gramercy Park and needed rest. It had happened enough in the past that he didn't question it. In fact, she thought he rather enjoyed bossing the hotel staff on her behalf, instructing visitors that they weren't to stay too long, and sending White on errands to "fetch that mushroom soup you like, the one they do at the Waldorf" or buy new socks at Lord & Taylor's, "get something proper on your feet." Choumai was also pleased, allowed to be on the bed as much as he liked, curled protectively at her hip, gimlet eyes fixed on guests who might drop crumbs.

So much care and attention was wearying; one could only say "I'm fine" so many times. Surely that was why her head felt foggy. One afternoon she was dozing when she became aware of a gentle knock. Her eyes opened, and she saw Morton Fullerton at the door. He leaned halfway in—or out—of the room.

He smiled at her confusion. "Henry told me."

Yes, that made sense. What she didn't know was whether or not to be angry. Not, she supposed. She was too tired to be angry.

When she didn't order him out, he stepped into the room, closing the door. He took the liberty of sitting on the edge of her bed. Wary, Choumai resettled himself.

"Well," he said, taking her hand and examining it as if what had happened might show itself in her palm. "You've been wandering. What did you find?"

He looked up, gaze warm and intent. She remembered his mouth.

"A vampire," she said to surprise him. "No, I found an unhappy young man with a gun. An unexceptional thing in this part of the world."

"Was he what you thought?" he asked. He turned his attention back to her hand, his finger making its way along the ball of her thumb.

"I don't know what I thought he would be. So I can't answer that."

He waited for her to explain. When she didn't, he knew he had been denied something. Setting her hand down, he drew himself up by crossing one leg over the other.

"My letters," she reminded him.

"As I've said, they're in Paris. Quite safe, I assure you."

His reference to their safety was meant to remind her how dangerous they were. But she found his possession of her words and feelings no longer terrified her. If he made their existence known, he would be shunned by every person he valued, barred from every house he hoped to enter, because in doing so, he would reveal what he really was. She thought of the books she had encouraged him to write. The time she had arranged for him to meet Mr. Roosevelt—and he refused to come. Changes in his career he should have made. Every time, he avoided, evaded. Why should he make the effort?

He had not come when she needed him. And not for the first time. He was not really a man who did things, she realized. *And you will continue to do nothing*, she thought looking at the man known as the Beautiful Fullerton. *Create nothing. In years to come, you will be known for the people you seduced—and abandoned. The promises you made, never intending to keep them. You will be known for what you did not do.*

At long last, detachment came, like rain in a dry acrid summer. One cavorted in relief, aware that yes, some things like shoes might be ruined, but they were well sacrificed for an end to the brain-destroying heat.

Of course he wanted to keep her letters. They were, after all, the work of Edith Wharton.

On the third day, she grew tired of being fussed over and decided to be well. She took Choumai for a walk, allowing him to relieve himself directly below the Depew Place sign. Then she returned him to White and went to Appleton. It was only right to finish *Susan Lenox*. If she was going to speak for it, she didn't want any nasty surprises in the final chapters. And she supposed she did want to see how it turned out.

There was a new young man at the front desk, efficiently sliding paper into envelopes. Rejection slips, she imagined. So many of them. He asked if she wanted to see Mr. Jewett; he had said he wished to be notified if she came in.

She said, "Not yet."

Going to the spare room, she took up where she had left off: Susan's first encounter with playwright Robert Brent, a lion of a man with exhausting integrity who made all other men seem lesser, including Susan's current paramour. *Ah*, thought Edith, *at last we see the author in the story*. And, she assumed, Susan's happy ending.

But in the final chapter, Robert Brent was murdered by Susan's lover in a fit of jealousy. Disquieted, Edith read the lover's defense of himself.

> "I did it," continued he, "because I had the right. He invited it. He knew me—knew what to expect. I suppose he decided that you were worth taking the risk. It's strange what fools men—all men—we men—are about women. . . . Yes, he knew it. He didn't blame me."

For a long moment, she sat, trying to set the timing straight in her mind. *Susan Lenox* had been finished well before Phillips's death. He had worked on it for a decade. And yet he had ended it with an uncanny prediction of his own murder. Susan's happy ending was not marriage but liberty and financial security—gained when the murdered Robert Brent left her his fortune.

There was a knock on the door. Mr. Jewett's pleasant face appeared. "Mrs. Wharton!"

She smiled. "I thought I would slip in and slip out. I didn't wish to disturb you. But I did want to finish."

He looked at the pages on her lap. "And?"

"And . . . I think it now makes sense to me."

He offered her tea in his office and she accepted. As he poured, he said, "I am very glad you came today." He gazed at his door, presumably thinking of the young man who had sat outside just a few days ago. "I remember my boast that we do not publish murderers. It seems, however, we did hire one."

"When did he come to work here, Mr. Jewett?"

"About a year ago. Shortly after *Adventures of Joshua Craig* was published."

"And you turned down his book," she said gently.

"I did. It was tremendously old-fashioned stuff. Fine stalwart men rescuing helpless maidens of good virtue. Of course now I wish we had published it. Maybe if we had . . ."

"You mustn't feel guilty, Mr. Jewett. How could you have known?"

"I had no idea he was stalking Graham, even taking rooms across the street from him. Graham never said a word."

"I suppose it was not in his nature to show fear." She paused, then said, "I hope it's not terribly burdensome, working out the legalities of his estate. All his royalties . . ."

"Oh, no, quite simple. He left everything to his sister."

As Henry Frevert had predicted he would.

She said, "If *Susan Lenox* is the . . . sensation you expect, she will do quite well."

"Let us hope. I also hope you will join me in defending it from Comstock and his ilk."

She nodded: *Of course.* Then said, "I am curious about one thing: When did Mr. Phillips change the ending? I'm right, aren't I? That he rewrote it?"

Surprised, Jewett said, "Yes. About three months ago."

Thinking back to Mr. Goldsborough's insane diaries, she wondered how many notes David Graham Phillips had received by that point. Enough, clearly, to take them seriously.

"Mrs. Wharton?"

Shaking herself free of her thoughts, she said, "What a tragedy this has been."

As Mr. Jewett walked her to the door, she smiled a goodbye to the new youth, who seemed preoccupied by finding a particular key on the typewriter. On impulse, she asked, "What is your name?"

He looked surprised. "Halliwell, ma'am. Gerald Halliwell."

"Goodbye, Mr. Halliwell."

At the elevator, Rutger Jewett opened his mouth, prepared to say something charming. Then closed it on a smile.

"No last words?" she asked.

"Only that . . . I hope they're not."

She smiled approvingly. "*À bientôt*, Mr. Jewett."

CHAPTER THIRTY

E dith had instructed the police not to tell Carolyn Frevert that she
had witnessed Fitzhugh Goldsborough's suicide. It was a story
she wished to tell very few people, and after today, she wouldn't tell it
ever again. All Mrs. Frevert knew was that an old woman had been
near the park when it happened and fainted shortly afterwards.

Admitted to the apartment at the National Arts building, she explained to Carolyn Frevert that she had been the "old woman" who had
seen the suicide and that she had done a good deal more than witness
the event. The two ladies were seated opposite each other over a frus-
tratingly low, small table; one had to hunch in order to get at the tea
and a vague muffinish item on offer. The tea was overbrewed, making
milk a necessity. But there was little space in which to maneuver, and
Edith worried about tipping the tray over onto the worn rug below.

"I spoke with him, Mrs. Frevert. Do you wish to know what he
said?"

Mrs. Frevert's hand went to her throat. ". . . I don't know. Do I? I suppose I should hear it."

Edith began with the story that had been given to the newspapers. That Fitzhugh Coyle Goldsborough had shot David Graham Phillips because he was under the delusion that he and his family, in particular his sister, had been maligned in *The Fashionable Adventures of Joshua Craig*.

"That's false," Mrs. Frevert interrupted. "We never knew the family. I've never even heard of them."

Edith said yes, she was certain of that. If she might continue?

In short, Mr. Goldsborough was mad. It was just a tragedy that in his final collapse, he had become obsessed with her brother and taken his life.

"He took rooms across the street at the Rand School," said Edith. "A young couple said he often came to look out their window, which faces your building. They thought he enjoyed the view. But in reality he was watching this apartment. Your brother, coming and going."

She waited to see if Mrs. Frevert understood that she too had been seen. If so, she gave no sign of it, saying only, "How horrible."

"You had no idea he was watching the house?" asked Edith.

"None whatsoever." Carolyn Frevert shook her head. "All this time, I've been so sure that Graham was killed because of his work, but I never imagined it would be *Adventures of Joshua Craig*. If it were *Susan Lenox* or *Treason of the Senate*, it would be more logical to me. I suppose I was wrong to look for reason in an act of murder." A small apologetic smile. "I do want to thank you for everything you have done on my brother's behalf."

Edith said it was her privilege.

Mrs. Frevert sipped her tea. "May I now ask what you think of *Susan Lenox*?"

"I think it overlong. I think it moralizes." She paused. "But I think it is one of the most remarkable novels I have read in many years."

Pleased, Mrs. Frevert nodded.

"I am curious about Susan Lenox herself. A passionate, loving woman who must ensure her financial security by giving herself to men who are unworthy of her. The character was so real to your brother, I thought she must have been based on someone he knew. But who, I wondered, could have inspired this mythical, perfectly imperfect woman? Fallen yet saintly. Pragmatic yet selfless. Adored by men, used by men, yet somehow always alone."

Carolyn Frevert nodded to indicate that Edith had her attention.

"You are Susan Lenox, aren't you, Mrs. Frevert?"

Carolyn Frevert leaned down to set her cup on the tray, but she could find no space and was obliged to hold on to it. The saucer rattled ever so slightly.

"My life has not been as . . . adventurous as Susan's," she said. "But yes, Graham always said he wrote the book for me."

Edith nodded. "In the book, Susan is married off to a man she doesn't love because she has disgraced herself with a young man who let her down."

"When we are young, we are imperfect judges of a man's integrity."

"Even when we are not young, Mrs. Frevert. And your brother, I take it he was his own inspiration for Robert Brent, the blunt playwright of unimpeachable integrity?"

"Yes, the man Susan marries."

"Oh, but she doesn't. Perhaps that was the original ending. But your brother changed it. At the end of the book, Robert Brent is murdered."

Mrs. Frevert lifted the cup to her lips, then set it back in its place.

"Extraordinary, isn't it, that your brother's last work predicted his own death?"

"Graham had received threats throughout his career. The possibility of a violent death was something he lived with and accepted."

Invited, even, if David Graham Phillips was to be believed. It was still incomprehensible to her. Why would a man so obnoxiously pleased with himself court death?

As if guessing her thoughts, Carolyn Frevert said, "I believe my brother took a certain pride in being menaced. If no one threatened him, then he was a threat to no one. *That* would have been intolerable."

Gathering herself, Edith said, "The second great surprise of the novel is that Robert Brent leaves Susan his fortune. With that money, she finally obtains her liberty."

She paused. "Mr. Jewett informs me that Mr. Phillips left everything to you. All the rights to his work, all his royalties."

"Because Graham knew I would protect his legacy with everything in me. The preservation of his work will be my mission in life."

"What of your husband?"

"What of him?"

"You will not be reconciling?"

"No," said Mrs. Frevert with a smile. "I will not."

It was an interesting word, *reconcile*. It could mean a restoration of harmonious relations. Or dull acceptance of what cannot be changed. Mrs. Frevert intended to do neither, apparently.

"Will you mind it, living alone?"

Carolyn Frevert looked around the empty apartment that was now hers, her expression by turns solemn, affectionate, and, Edith thought, haunted. But then her brow cleared and she said, "I shall be curious to see whether I do or no. In any event, I shall do what I wish to."

Just about what you wish to, in fact, thought Edith, recalling the note she had received.

Mrs. Frevert said, "I am curious as to why you ask me that question, Mrs. Wharton."

Edith met the other woman's gaze and thought how simple it would be to confess nothing. There were any number of pleasantries she could offer: *Idle curiosity! One's life is so busy, one yearns for occasional solitude.* But she hadn't come for pleasantries.

She said, "I have a dear friend who finds herself yearning for separation. She has been married for many years. Perhaps neither of them are ideal people. But they were always poorly suited, and lately, she finds the mismatch has become intolerable. He is terrified she will leave him. She is terrified she never will."

"Does she have means?" asked Mrs. Frevert.

"Sufficient. I should add that the husband is unwell."

"And he requires her care?"

"He thinks that he does. She thinks she only makes it worse."

"Him worse or herself?"

". . . Both?" said Edith. "But then she feels a break is too cruel. He is not a brute. And she is not brave; she fears being cast out, the shame of divorce. So she thinks perhaps she can manage after all. At such times she thinks her complaints small. Petty."

But looking back, it had been a small, petty thing that ended the marriage. Not the women, not the theft of her money, not even the fits of madness. It had been an offhand question. Now she recalled the precise moment she had, in her heart, broken with Teddy. She had arrived in America, having spent the crossing reading *Heredity and Variation*. She had brimmed with excitement, eager to discuss what she had learned. But when she began, Teddy cut her off, asking, "Does that sort of thing really amuse you?" The question, his use of the word *amuse*, took the breath from her. And she had thought, *I cannot bear it any longer.*

She said, "His father took his own life, you see. She worries if she leaves, it may drive him to despair."

"But what will she be driven to if she stays?" asked Carolyn Frevert softly. "One can care for someone—yet still wish to be free of them."

The women's eyes met. Questions came, essential and unspeakable. Edith recalled her words to Henry Frevert about the dead man. *He seemed a domineering personality.*

And Goldsborough's accusation. *He took his sister and made her a thing of his own imagination when she is so much more.* In the moment, she had assumed the murderer's use of *his* instead of *my* was another sign of his madness.

"May I, as a writer, ask you a question that was recently posed to me, Mrs. Frevert?" The other woman nodded. "We often assume people like to be captured in our books. Or, truthfully, we don't care if they do or no. This person felt it was very wrong to use people in this way. As the inspiration for Susan Lenox, what do you think?"

"I can only say that for me, it is a very great honor."

"Truly? You don't think it exhausting to live as someone's creation? Endlessly twisted to suit their needs?"

The smile stayed in place. "In fairness, I think we all do it."

Three questions lingered. *Those notes you burned, Mrs. Frevert. Were all of them sent to your brother?*

Not a single note to you, the woman at the window?

And if there were such a note, did you ever answer?

Then she thought, *No.* The time for questions and answers was done. Rising, she said, "I hope I haven't presumed too much on your family's devotion to the truth. But I thought you would wish to know something of the man who took your brother from you. I shall miss Mr. Phillips. I would have wished him a longer life. I will do what I can for *Susan Lenox*. It is a . . . deeper work than I once thought it. I anticipate it will have great success."

They pressed hands. As she turned to the door, Edith noticed a vase of greenery between the two windows of the sitting room. The dark leaves were a long oval, with a sharp point. The sight of them brought a memory, although at first, she could not place it.

Then she said, "Bay laurel."

Carolyn Frevert turned to look. "Yes. In the spring, it has a lovely yellow flower. But I like the scent, so I have it year round."

"'I change but with death,'" Edith quoted. Mrs. Frevert looked questioning. "Bay laurel's symbolism. In other words, victory achieved at great cost."

Mrs. Frevert laughed. "I just thought it was pretty."

Edith came out onto the street to find the sun had emerged; it was a bright, cold February day. From somewhere, she heard children shouting as they played one of those games where glee and cruelty are blended—tag or blindman's bluff. One must be eliminated so that the other might win. The swift, the clever, the strong separating themselves from the weak, hesitant, and no-good-at-games. Edith had always thought herself the latter. But now she recalled running in Maine. She and Walter had been hiding from their aged hostess and raced from the house. She had been faster than he, stronger, and ran ahead.

Looking up, she saw Carolyn Frevert at the window. For a long moment, Mrs. Frevert stood gazing at the broad blue sky above her. Then she looked at the Rand School across the street and drew the curtains.

CHAPTER THIRTY-ONE

At last, the doctor came. Gentle, kind Dr. Kinnicutt appeared at the Belmont as if they had summoned him only that morning. He and Teddy had known each other for many years. The start of the examination, held in Teddy's room, seemed more like two old friends catching up than a medical consultation. Then Dr. Kinnicutt asked Edith if she would leave so they might talk in private. He would come to her when they were done.

Edith repaired to her room. Speaking out loud to Choumai, she imagined drapes that would better suit the space. Replaced its rug, widened the windows, knocked all the faux frou from the fireplace moldings. Then she abandoned the game. She had no desire to redesign the Belmont; she only wished to leave.

Settling by the window, she gazed down at Grand Central Station, still overwhelmed by girders and planks and workmen. The ground all around it excavated, the structure itself was held up by supports that seemed they would splinter any moment, causing the great station to lurch forward like a wedding cake sliding from a tipped table. The promise was that the future station would be grander, greater, altogether more suited to a modern New York, and she supposed it would be. But difficult to see that future now among the wreckage of rebuilding.

In her mind, she traveled back, to another station, another hotel, a room that was filthy, a space she would have refused to enter under any other circumstance. So of course he chose it. She remembered him smiling as he pulled her through streets crowded with grim-faced tired Londoners, all of whom seemed to be going from a place they didn't much care for to another not much better. She had been leery at first, of the grime and spots on the mirror, the deep well of the mattress, the stickiness of dust on the bedside table, brass dull with fingerprints, the chintz spread shiny and greasy in spots—everything touched by something it shouldn't be. But then she had reveled in the creeping intimacy of things that degrade— dirt, soot, hands, wet mouths. Delirious and laughing afterwards, she had thought how useful trains are! How noisy in their clacking, the great hiss of steam and self-important whoop. One could howl the roof down and not be heard—the freedom it gave. Why did everyone not make love near train stations? The world population would double within a year. Giddy, she had imagined it, pair after pair coming, rutting, going, speedily, one after the other, the gully of the bed growing deeper and deeper, posts rattling, until the bed collapsed in on itself, exhausted.

And yet it was also quiet. She could hear him breathing deeply as he slept, offering for now only the pale expanse of his shoulders, the slope of his neck. She had traced them, his slopes and curves, finally brushing the edge of his hair. This simple little thing, the feel of another person's skin under one's fingertips.

Had he ever known such a miracle, David Graham Phillips? She thought the answer was no, sadly. That chrysanthemum—a heart left in desolation. She had been so certain he didn't know its meaning. Now she thought otherwise.

Oh, but he would have liked this coming-into-being station. It had the feel of him: noise, steel, crackling electricity, rushing, rushing, rushing. And yet, she thought, poor man, rushing headlong into six ugly pellets of metal that took his life. To satisfy the vanity of a sick, stupid boy who, because he could not *do* anything else of significance, decided he must kill someone.

A burst of laughter from beyond the door brought her back to Teddy. It was a sound she was entirely unused to, yet once he had laughed a great deal with her. Her mother had called him "sunshine in the house." Another thing Lucretia had been wrong about.

Or had she? Certainly not at the time. Maybe Teddy might have kept that old happy bumbling-bear spirit if he hadn't married a woman who, in the eyes of many, clapped a halter around his head and led him about on a leash, dragging him here and there, far from the Boston he loved, where he was comfortable. He had never learned to speak French, giving up after a few frustrating lessons. But maybe she should never have expected it of him: change, growth, effort. Perhaps, she thought wearily, it was her fault.

A knock at the door. She said "Yes" and looked up to see Dr. Kinnicutt.

In Edith's experience, the good doctor's success lay in his ability to tell his patients and their families what they wished to hear. He was as smooth and comforting as a bar of butter, and as malleable.

"Well," she said. "How do you find him?"

"He should have his teeth removed."

Startled, she said, "All of them?"

The doctor nodded sagely. "Not straightaway. But they do pain him a great deal."

False teeth, another indignity. She came to the point. "He can travel then."

"He can."

"And . . . you don't feel I should accompany him?"

A swift, decisive shake of the head. "Absolutely not, Mrs. Wharton. In fact, I would strenuously advise against."

This, she thought, was overdoing it. It was what she wished to hear—the words had been given to her to repeat to Nannie if necessary—but *strenuously*? She frowned, asking the question, but leaving room for him not to answer if he judged the response impolitic.

He did not answer, saying instead, "I would suggest returning to The Mount. It is the place that gives him the most pleasure."

She looked out the window again, Grand Central, workers crawling over it like so many ants. She had begun Lily Bart's journey in that terminus. She recalled the image, her heroine poised between one point and the next, observed by a man who loved her, but not enough. Lily had come from Tuxedo, was on her way to Rhinebeck, but had missed her train. And so she was stuck, because she did not know what to do with herself.

To the doctor, she nodded agreement to his suggestion of taking Teddy back to The Mount.

"But after his trip. I have a book to write."

The dinner, long planned, finally came to pass. Sitting in the vast dining room of the Belmont, styled to suggest the ducal palazzos of Mantua, Edith looked around the table and reflected that never before had the four of them dined together in America. She did not contribute much to the discussion at first, preferring to enjoy her friends and their enjoyment of one another. Fullerton was witty on the subject of the Millet paintings, insightful on the peace agreement between Haiti and Santo Domingo. When Walter made Henry laugh with a story of Cairo, Edith thought it was the first time in a while she had seen that miracle.

Pleased with the response, Walter escalated the absurdity and the loucheness of the tale, until Henry said, "No, no, you mustn't say these things."

"Oh, why not?" drawled Fullerton.

"They are magnificent, but they're not—well, discussable or per-missible or forgivable." Henry paused. "At least not all at once."

A roar went around the table.

"But—" said Walter, turning to her.

"Yes," said Henry, doing the same.

Fullerton swung in his chair, tilted his head in her direction.

She said, "I've decided, actually."

Walter looked surprised. "That you will leave him."

"That you won't," guessed Henry when she didn't answer.

"You've decided not to decide," said Fullerton.

"I have decided that while I greatly value your advice, I no longer require it. I know my mind. Shall we have cheese?"

Fullerton left first. As she touched her cheek to his, she sighed to herself, *Il m'aime, il ne m'aime pas.* But she had gotten a great deal from him, whether he meant to give it or not. She thought of the revenge novel she had planned, and thought instead she would write, or attempt to, the truth. As she decided, she heard an echo of David Graham Phillips: *The truth, Mrs. Wharton!*

A *truth, Mr. Phillips. Because there would be three in this story. Mine, his, and the young woman's. A young woman who acts in accordance with her desires—without shame. An older woman who faces her regrets, also without shame. And, perhaps, begins to act in accordance with her desires.*

Henry was complaining to Walter about rampant construction around Washington Square. "So much building. You wouldn't believe how the university has grown. They've destroyed three old buildings to make room. One of them just happened to be my childhood home. I always thought I might have a plaque there: 'Here lived Henry James, the author.'"

They recalled trips they had taken, proposed ones they should like to. Noting the way Henry's face sagged slightly on one side, the grunting, sighing strain of the smallest movement, Edith thought how gallant he was. And how ill. When she called him to New York, he had come. And always, he had listened. At their first meeting, she had worn a pink Doucet dress, hoping to impress him. That had been a long time ago.

The dining room was nearly empty. The waiters did not bother to hide their yawns. She said, "I think it's time."

Walter went to tell the concierge to fetch a taxi. Suddenly animated, Henry said to her, "Ah, but tell me, before you go—" She moved around the table to take his outstretched hands. "Your own great drama—*do* you have the ending?"

"I cannot quite see it yet. I think the next chapter shall be exciting."

She saw that the word *exciting* worried him. He said, "Once again, I advise you to wait."

"I cannot wait, Henry. I am nearly fifty years old. I shall see years David Graham Phillips never will. I mean to make use of them."

Bending down, she kissed him on both cheeks. "You don't need a plaque in Washington Square to immortalize you, Henry. It's you who have immortalized Washington Square."

You have his handkerchiefs?"

White nodded. "Cotton, Turnbull and Asser. Not the Irish linen."

"Possibly a new straw hat. A wider brim. The sort he wore in Italy. If you can find it."

"Yes, ma'am."

Edith looked at the luggage, piled high on the trolley at Grand Central Station.

Teddy stood some distance away, entranced by the scaffolding.

"And you'll telegram, should you need me. I'll send word once I've settled. Where I am."

"Very good, ma'am."

"Thank you, White. I don't know what I'd do without you."

"It's kind of you to say so." He looked at his charge. "He's looking forward to the sea lions."

Pressing White's arm, she went to say goodbye to Teddy. She stopped just short of his perimeter, watching as he watched a flock of pigeons leap into the air flapping. He turned to follow their flight, then stayed staring off . . . at what she could not imagine.

"Teddy?"

He turned.

"Have a safe journey."

The shadow of a smile around his ruined teeth. She took in his thin, craggy neck. The scant hair—poor thing, like an old coconut—

the dim, tired eyes, bruised and wrinkled from squinting at the world, the effort to see it clearly, at least as everyone else did, and the pain of failure.

The planned farewell—*Be good*—came to her. Approaching, she kissed him on the cheek. Whispered, "Be well."

And then she left him.

CHAPTER THIRTY-TWO

Summoned to a last tea with Mrs. Wharton at the Palm, Brownell was surprised to see that her chaotic stay in the city had done her much good. She looked far better now than at their last meeting. There was color in her cheeks; her eyes were clear. Her head no longer sank on its stem. She was brisk and confident in her speech and movement. He had the feeling her next book would be very good.

When the napkins were laid, cakes selected, Choumai provided for, and the tea poured, she said, "Mr. Brownell, do you anticipate my next royalty statement will be something above a dollar and thirty-seven cents?"

Immediately, he began to demur, and she interrupted. "'Bearing in mind the vagaries of the marketplace and the wickedness of the world and the fact that readers are faithless and fickle and their tastes growing coarser by the day,' so on and et cetera . . . will I have money coming to me or no?"

He sipped at his tea, frowning because it was hot. Then said, "Yes, I should think so. Quite a bit."

"Enough for a significant advance?"

He smiled. "I can't negotiate an advance for a book I know nothing about."

"Ah, but you can. The next book Henry James submits, I want you to pay him a handsome sum—somewhere in between five and ten thousand dollars, but closer to ten, and I shall ask him, so don't think to stint."

"It will be hard to persuade Scribner's to part with such a sum, given the poor sales of the *New York Edition*," he said quietly.

"Scribner's will not be parting with such a sum—I will. You will pay Mr. James with this year's royalties from my books."

He stared at her, feeling this must be an evil trick. He would divert the royalties, and she would pounce, screaming about Scribner's thievery and neglect.

Intuiting his fears, she said, "It's not a trick. We'll put it in writing if you like."

"This is extraordinarily generous."

"Yes."

"May I ask why?"

"Because the world is wicked. And the marketplace vague. And readers are faithless and fickle, their taste growing coarser by the day." She thought of David Graham Phillips's rant about readers who only wanted confections about wealthy people racing about in automobiles and falling in love in foreign countries. Soon, *Susan Lenox* would be unleashed upon the world, and someone could rant about that. And he would not be here to rant back, she thought sadly.

To Brownell, she said, "Who else do writers have but other writers? Who else can we rely upon but one another? When one of us has more success, more . . . resources, it seems only right to share. Never let Mr. James know, of course. He's still furious with me over my last intervention."

Brownell smiled, lowered his voice. "One day, we shall get him the Nobel."

Hesitant to break the mood with controversial topics, he said, "I am looking forward to *The Custom of the Country*."

A story of New York, she thought. And a woman who wanted things.

She said, "And I look forward to your guidance on it. But you may get a different story first."

She watched as he considered arguing. Was pleased to see him smile.

"Any story by Edith Wharton is worth having. But allow me to ask, what is it that so intrigues you about rural New England?"

Taking in the bustling, buzzing crowd of the tearoom, the hum of people talking about themselves, talking about others, she said, "It is lonely. And your choices are few."

She thought of a young Carolyn Frevert, tricked and abandoned, then married and taken, not in a battered wagon, but not at all where she wished to go.

"You are trapped and your hope of rescue fades as the years pass. There is no electricity, no motors to speed you away. It is a darkness, alleviated only by fire and perhaps one other person who depends on you to sustain them. You see your duty. But you feel drained. Then, just when you've become resigned to this shadow existence—you see a chance of happiness. But your happiness means the destruction of that other person's life. What choice do you make?"

He hesitated. "The honorable choice, surely? If someone depends on you . . . ?"

"The honorable choice does not always lead to happy outcomes. The heart denied begins to feel nothing. It grows cold. Even cruel. That, too, is dangerous."

She looked at him over her teacup. "Well—have I persuaded you, Mr. Brownell?"

"I am intrigued as always."

As they made their way out of the tearoom, he said, "Jewett tells me you have read *Susan Lenox*. What did you think?"

"There was a great deal I admired. Like its author, it had tremendous vitality. Like its author, it was also tedious."

No, she thought, that was ungenerous. The man deserved a better epitaph from her.

"He was wrong, but not wholly wrong and not in all things."

They were at the point in the lobby where he would depart and she go to the elevator. He asked, "Does this mean I am forgiven for introducing you?"

Her first instinct was to say no; she liked to keep the advantage. But then she thought of this odd stay in New York without the mystery of David Graham Phillips. She would have rarely left the hotel. Would not have spoken to people with whom she violently disagreed—but whose views were perhaps enlightening. She would never have visited Appleton. Never made the acquaintance of Mr. Jewett.

Then she realized, *Oh, dear. Poor Brownell.*

Taking his hand, she squeezed it. "Of course. How could I not?"

"I'm relieved."

He turned to go. Then, as if reminded by the ring of china and silver coming from the tearoom, he turned back to ask, "But what of your dinner? Your . . . matter of life and death?"

She smiled. "Oh, I chose life, of course, Mr. Brownell."

The hotel managed the trunks; she managed Choumai. Arriving at the docks, she directed the purser in the proper handling of her things, then took Choumai to do his business. Poor thing. He had been seasick on the voyage over. She hoped this would be a calmer passage.

It was an off time for travel. No one she knew was in the first-class lounge. Choumai, worn out with the morning's activity, lay down at her feet and fell asleep. Gazing down at his trusting peaceful presence, she remembered David Graham Phillips's note to himself on his writing desk: "Work is the only permanently interesting thing in life."

Well, and dogs, Mr. Phillips. And gardens and friends and a good roast chicken . . .

Still—she disliked sitting and doing nothing in such unappealing circumstances. Taking out her notebook, she considered doing a quick sketch of the walrus gentleman opposite her. He might serve as a two-line character. There was an opera scene in *Custom*, and she needed faces and voices. But as she tried to conjure the bustle of a night at the opera, Undine's machinations working her way from one man to the next, it seemed altogether too busy for her mood. Instead, her mind went to loneliness. Thwarted hopes. Darkness, cramped rooms and crushed feeling. *Only love gives you the power to say farewell to your old existence and to take flight toward a new one.*

Or crash, she thought. *That is also possible. Still, one can crash and limp away. Even recover.*

She set pen to paper and without hesitation, wrote:

*I had the story, bit by bit, from various people, and,
as generally happens in such cases, each time,
it was a different story.*

She read it over.

And was satisfied.

AUTHOR'S NOTE

A great book, full of almost all the qualities I most admire in a novelist. . . . [T]here is far too much unnecessary moralizing and lecturing. But the tremendous vitality of the book survives even this drawback, and it remains, on the whole, the most remarkable novel I have read in a long time.

—EDITH WHARTON to Rutger Bleecker Jewett on *Susan Lenox*

In his shockingly stupid essay in *The New Yorker*, Jonathan Franzen asserts that it is hard to feel sympathy with Edith Wharton because she was rich. Not nobly so like Tolstoy, but conservative, appalled by socialism, and fully at ease with the bigotries of her caste. She had one "potentially redeeming disadvantage: she wasn't pretty." He seems to suggest that the only valid reason to read her is, well, one ought to read the occasional woman.

To me, what Franzen fails to do is what Wharton herself does so well: take deep pleasure in human nature, especially when it is flawed. As a writer, she is warmly sympathetic and endlessly curious. Who else could have created Mrs. Manstey, a New Yorker who burns down a house that threatens to block her view and dies joyfully gazing upon its charred ruins?

Like most people, my introduction to Wharton occurred in high school when I read *The House of Mirth,* as well as *The Portrait of a Lady.* The ambitious, compromised Lily Bart felt more real to me than the tediously ideal Isabel Archer. At that time, my vision of Wharton was the female artist as invalid, a woman held captive by society who took to her bed and lived in the mind. That vision was later displaced by something closer to Franzen's: a harridan draped in furs and tiny dogs. But neither of those images matched the mind and spirit behind *The House of Mirth.*

It wasn't until my research for one of the Jane Prescott novels brought me to Wharton's letters that I finally heard Mrs. Wharton speak for herself. Bestowing a parrot on a child for his birthday, she writes: "As you know, parrots talk, and I have asked this one to give you my love and wish you many happy returns of the day. If . . . he is noisy and vulgar, as I am told parrots sometimes are, you had better have him cooked and give him to Beguin to eat."

She battled with her editor, advocated for friends, adored and despaired of her caddish lover, and critiqued her own work. Privileged, yes, but intensely engaged, witty, determined to venture beyond what was deemed suitable for a woman. Here was the author of *Mrs. Manstey's View,* a chronicler who dared to depict morally imperfect, even unlikable, women.

So when I proposed a novel about the 1911 murder of David Graham Phillips—a writer who would have loved Franzen's essay—and my editor asked if a woman could anchor the story, I knew exactly who that woman should be.

When Edith Wharton solves a murder, the reader is on notice

that we are not in the realm of strict fact. *The Wharton Plot* combines two historical events, both of which are true. The first is Phillip's murder by a mentally ill man named Fitzhugh Coyle Goldsborough. Phillips was shot on the twenty-third of January, dying the next day, on Wharton's birthday.

The second event is the famous dinner that occurred when Wharton was stranded at the Belmont Hotel. She met with Henry James, Walter Berry, and Morton Fullerton, seeking their advice on the state of her marriage. As Wharton fans know, that meeting occurred on October 17, 1910, three months shy of the murder. But the temptation to put Wharton and Phillips in conversation was too strong to worry about a few months. The murder—a writer shot by a stranger outraged by his novel—feels disturbingly modern, while the setting of Gramercy Park is classic Gilded Age. Wharton, as she contemplates the shocking step of divorce, seems perfectly poised between the past and the future. She and Phillips were strong personalities, each writing about women and the transactional aspect of love and marriage.

Goldsborough believed Phillips had satirized him and his family, an act of "literary vampirism." He took rooms in the building opposite Phillips's; both buildings still stand today. Goldsborough sent Phillips many notes, including the one that said, "This is your last day," signing it David Graham Phillips. (In my book it reads "Tomorrow is your last day" to avoid confusion in the timeline.)

In reality, Goldsborough shot himself immediately after killing Phillips. He did not work at Appleton. But a whodunnit demands fair play—not to mention a living murderer. The diary excerpts are accurate, although dates have been changed. One of the notes Edith receives is based on Goldsborough's epigrams: "A man in this world who does just about what he wishes." Phillips reported the harassment to the police.

His pronouncement that he could die tomorrow and be ahead of the game is accurate, and all the quotes of his work are genuine.

The broad facts of Wharton's life as presented here are true. She was present for the Vanderbilt events, such as the Breakers fire and Christmas at Biltmore in 1905. The depiction of her writing habits is accurate, although her process of writing *The Custom of the Country* and *Ethan Frome* is altered. I have included several of her comments, such as "Words fail to express how completely I don't like it," throughout. Her declaration to Fullerton that "Nothing else lives in me but you" are her words, and "I love you so much Dear that I want only what you want" are his. He never returned her letters; it seems he sold them. Wildly desirable in his own time, Fullerton now reads as the archetypal toxic boyfriend. His complicated relationship with his adopted sister is factual, although it's unclear what Wharton knew of it. James's advice to her to "live in the day" is genuine, as are his statements about Oscar Wilde. *Town Topics* reported Wharton's relationship with Berry, but the article quoted here did not appear until later.

Most of the people who appear in the book are real: Brownell, the Freverts, the Wallings, the Vanderbilts, and Senator Depew and his son. I have no evidence that an affair occurred between Phillips and Anna Walling. After his death, she wrote a passionate appreciation of him; some of her dialogue is drawn from that piece. William Walling's activism was more substantive than depicted here. A woman did sue him for breach of promise. The Walling marriage ended due to the husband and wife having differing views of World War I. *Fortune's Children* reports that Reggie Vanderbilt did kill three people while driving.

Another key character who is part-real, part-invention is Choumai. The Whartons were passionate dog lovers. But the experts at The Mount informed me that the dog Wharton traveled with on this trip was Nicette. She had a Pekingese named Choumai, but a 1929 photo of him shows him to be a much smaller, less hirsute dog, and it's unlikely he would have been alive in 1911.

Carolyn Frevert lived apart from her husband and inherited her brother's estate, but she had nothing to do with his murder. She died in 1930, a wealthy woman.

After the events of this book, Wharton left Scribner's for Appleton. She left Teddy in 1913, settling permanently in Paris. She went on to publish two of her greatest books, *Ethan Frome* and *The Age of Innocence*. During the First World War, she chose to remain in France. She raised funds for refugees and visited the front to report the ravages of war to apathetic Americans. France awarded her with the Chevalier of the Legion of Honor. In 1921, she was the first woman to win the Pulitzer Prize for fiction. In 1937, on a working visit to Ogden Codman, she had a heart attack. As she was lifted into the ambulance, she told Codman, "This will teach you not to ask decrepit old ladies to stay."

Wharton was a product of her class and time; her views seemed to grow narrower over the years, her prejudices stronger. As biographer Hermione Lee says, "the casual remarks and jokes . . . must form part of our sense of her." But unlike a character in my last book, she cheered the election of FDR and was clear-eyed about Hitler.

Poor Ethan Frome never escapes, nor does Newland Archer. Lily Bart is free only in death. But in her own life, Wharton refused to remain stranded. She pursued new challenges to the end with a joyous greed. As Franzen, who finally reveals himself a fan, says, Wharton depicts people "so clearly and completely that they emerge . . . as what they really are. . . . In so doing, she denies the modern reader the easy comfort of condemning an antiquated arrangement. What you get instead . . . is sympathy."

MAJOR WORKS REFERENCED FOR THIS BOOK

Edith Wharton by Hermione Lee

No Gifts from Chance by Shari Benstock

The Letters of Edith Wharton, edited by R.W.B. Lewis and Nancy Lewis

Edith Wharton: A Woman in Her Time by Louis Auchincloss

The Sexual Education of Edith Wharton by Gloria C. Erlich

A Backward Glance by Edith Wharton

Henry James: A Life by Leon Edel

The letters of Henry James and Walter Berry

The Master by Colm Tóibín

The Typewriter's Tale by Michiel Heyns

The Treason of the Senate by David Graham Phillips

Susan Lenox: Her Fall and Rise by David Graham Phillips

The Fashionable Adventures of Joshua Craig by David Graham Phillips

David Graham Phillips and His Times by Isaac Frederick Marcosson

David Graham Phillips by Abe C. Ravitz

Mysteries of Paris: The Quest for Morton Fullerton by Marion Mainwaring

Fortune's Children: The Fall of the House of Vanderbilt by Arthur T. Vanderbilt II

"The 'Bitter Taste' of Naturalism: Edith Wharton's *House of Mirth* and David Graham Phillips's *Susan Lenox*" by Donna M. Campbell (in *Twisted from the Ordinary*, edited by Mary Papke)

"Discretion and Self Censorship in Wharton's Fiction" by Jessica Levine (in *Edith Wharton Review*)

ACKNOWLEDGMENTS

First, I am thankful to Edith Wharton for the example of her art and her vigorous defense of herself as a writer who deserved to get paid. I hope she forgives me for what I assume she would regard as a hideous invasion of her privacy and the presumption to know how she thought and felt about anything.

When I sent the rough draft of this manuscript to my editor, Catherine Richards, I assured her that the bitterness against publishers in the book did not reflect my personal feelings. She wrote back, "Ha!" For her sense of humor as well as many other gifts, I thank her. My gratitude to Kayla Janas and Allison Ziegler for their unflagging efforts to make the public aware that my books exist. The beautiful cover was designed by David Rotstein. Huge thanks to copy editor Mary Beth Constant, who caught some truly embarrassing mistakes, and production editor Ginny Perrin for her thoughtful handling of the manuscript.

As always, an enormous thank-you to my agent, Victoria Skurnick, who makes the dreaded business side of things fun and comprehensible. Whether the news is good or bad, I always feel I have her support.

I am especially indebted to Patricia Pin at The Mount, who read an early draft of the manuscript, catching several mistakes and making excellent suggestions for improvement.

At the end of this book, Wharton asks, "Who else do writers have but other writers?" Writing this book put me in mind of the writers who have offered their friendship, time, and effort to support my career. They are many, but this time, in honor of Wharton, I'm going to thank the women: Anna Quindlen, Meg Cabot, Susan Elia MacNeal, Karen Odden, Carol Goodman, Joanna Schaffhausen, Sharon Short, Ellen Byron, Sujata Massey, E. R. Frank, Carolyn Mackler, Rachel Vail, Alyssa Maxwell, Elizabeth Kerri Mahon, Jean Hanff Korelitz, and many more. I am also very grateful to the Orso/Joe Allen dining companions (you know who you are) and the stalwart mystery writers of Queens (and Brooklyn).

A special thank-you to Ellen E. Mason, a book lover who always shows up to support writers!

The Wharton Plot is dedicated to my son, Griffin. It is way past time that I dedicated a book to him. At first, I wasn't sure a novel about Edith Wharton was the best choice. But there is no reason a young man about to leave home to embark on the next exhilarating stage of life can't take inspiration from a middle-aged woman who does exactly that. I hope he sees that bold new beginnings are something that happen throughout life, not just when you're eighteen.

Thank you to my husband who, despite a year full of challenges, always made time to read my work and, even more importantly, was always honest in his feedback. If you enjoy my work, thank him. He makes it possible.

Finally, I am thankful for the tight deadline that required I get writing as fast as possible; had I had more time to think about writing a novel about Edith Wharton, I would have lost my nerve.